OMEGA: RED ALERT

By

Loren and Ethel Price

Remnant Publications, Inc.
Coldwater, MI

Omega Red Alert

Cover Photo by Ethel Price
Cover Design by Penny Hall

ISBN 1-883012-12-0

Dedication

This book is dedicated to our four adult children: Beverly, Steven, Debbie, and Christine. They have been a motivating force in our lives for more than forty years, and we count them as great friends as well as family.

As with any family structure in today's world, there have been times when they likely would have traded us in for more accommodating parents, and visa versa. But, perseverance, prayer, and forgiveness, has seen us through those difficult teenage years. Now they have blessed us with grandchildren, which, for some reason, are a lot easier to deal with than our own children. We work hard at not spoiling them, but we aren't perfect.

A great blessing to us is that all of our family is within easy driving distance. This is no small thing for grandparents who not only grow lonely without contact with their children, but equally with their grandchildren. So to them all, we wish the best of life here and now, and even more so in the stupendous future we expect to share in eternity.

CONTENTS

Preface

What does the future hold? Will there be a nuclear holocaust? Will there be a one-world government? What will be the role of religious institutions, angels, and God? Questions such as these, and many more are on people's minds. This book is an effort to answer some of these questions in subtle and direct ways through the lives of a typical American family.

Is truth stranger than fiction? Many of the accounts of this book are based on actual events in the lives of the authors and others known to us, but of course, are in the past. If the future was easy to predict everyone would be doing it. In fact, many have tried and continue to do so even though their efforts fall short of respectable. But there will be a future with real people in it and real events that affect our lives. So why should we put ourselves out on a limb to be scoffed at along with the others?

First of all, we have done our homework. We actually have the inside track on what lies ahead. But the source of that information is cloaked in the story itself. So to find out how we know so much about the future, you will have to immerse yourself in the story. Then too, we have not revealed all our sources of information, but have dropped some clues as to how you can find additional answers. Follow these leads and you will not be disappointed.

Secondly, we do not claim to know every detail in everyone's future lives. But we are confident in the major tenants of the story and the outcome for the people living at the time this story portrays. How the future plays out for you, the reader, is up to you.

Finally, some may want to know when this will all play out. For us to answer this question would be speculation. We don't know and doubt there is anyone alive who does. Never the less, there are some clues about our fast moving world that give us reason to believe in a rapid culmination of world history. Look for these clues and follow them to their conclusion. We hope you are challenged by this book and will check out the clues we have planted throughout the story.

1

LOCK-DOWN

"We will rid the world of evildoers."
President George W. Bush, 2001

Seven-year-old Sara stumbled breathlessly into the front door of her school. Falling and getting up in haste she ran crying and screaming toward the only place of safety she could remember—her classroom. Flinging open the door, the bruised and bleeding child fell into her stunned teacher's arms.

"Mrs. Miller! Mrs. Miller!" Then the sobs overtook her again and she collapsed onto the floor.

With instinct born of recent school safety training, Mrs. Miller leapt for the keypad on the wall and dialed a hasty "911." At once the school emergency alert system started to shriek over the intercom, while classroom and outside doors were automatically secured. Teachers, secretaries, and janitors joined the security staff and principal in accounting for all students.

The system simultaneously dialed the nearby police station and within seconds police and emergency vehicles were arriving at the now locked-down campus.

Educated in the school of terrifying experience, the state educational system and police departments had opted for an "act first, ask questions later" approach to perceived danger. The all-too-real specter of school violence, kidnapping, and murder of children loomed large in the minds of everyone and the question flew from nearly 500 mouths—"What is happening?"

Motioning to her students to lie quietly on the floor under their desks, Mrs. Miller flicked off the light switch and gathered little Sara into her arms, scooting under her large teacher's desk.

In the quiet dark comfort, Sara began to tell her teacher a story that brought tears—and a cold fear—to the seasoned educator. Reaching for the cell phone, required to be on each teacher's person at all times, Mrs. Miller dialed the next code, which would connect her with the command center she knew was being set up both inside and outside the locked-down school.

The instant the phone rang, two buttons were pushed: one inside a bunker-like room in the school, where the principal and security head were monitoring—the other in the armored police vehicle just outside the perimeter of the grounds. Relating the story just told her by Sara, Mrs. Miller heard the reactions of both parties as police and security issued commands to their respective forces to look for a small black car with two occupants dressed in black hooded sweats—considered armed and dangerous.

With repeated proof of the effectiveness of the "Amber Alert" in Oregon and other states, a bulletin was now issued to all police and media in the state—with the highest urgency level. Even though Sara had managed to bite, fight, and kick her way to freedom against the would-be kidnapper, authorities knew the next child might not be so lucky.

Now a second system was put into operation. Part of the armored police vehicle began to separate from the rest and move rapidly toward the front door of the quiet building. Arriving at the bottom of the stairs, the body of the vehicle reared up on its wheels and proceeded to climb the stairs. Reaching the entrance, it expanded right and left until it formed a sealed cover over both doors. Heavily armored and armed militia punched numbers into an electronic keypad to one side and took a defensive position as the doors swung open.

They spread out over the whole school, advancing and securing each area. Three officers—two bearing the red emblems of medics—headed directly for Mrs. Miller's classroom. The recent innovations included a computerized map with camera feed-ins for instant information of any problem area. Reaching the room indicated on their palm pilots, the medics again disarmed the lock on the door and entered.

Mrs. Miller now brought Sara out of cover and briefed the medics on her physical injuries. Sara clung to her teacher, fearfully eyeing the two, until they took off their riot helmets revealing two women officers—one with flaming red hair the color of Sara's own. Fascinated by the gentle manner of this medic, who said her name was Arella, she let them examine her injuries, then place her on a small portable stretcher. Once she was strapped on, they covered her with a clear plastic dome to protect her head and a sheet of Kevlar to guard against any possible further attack.

Sara tried to reach for Mrs. Miller's hand, but was tucked securely into her little cocoon. Her teacher briefly reassured her, adding that her parents would probably beat her to the hospital. Now the process was reversed—don the riot helmets, disarm the lock, and enter the hallway where the third officer had remained on guard. Toting their tiny cargo, the three advanced to the entryway and into the waiting vehicle.

The stairs were descended in a moment and soon the vehicle was rejoining the command post recently left behind. A waiting ambulance backed up to the access closest to the street and Sara was transferred directly into its doors. Once she was safely inside, the EMT's carefully removed the protective covering, tucked a teddy bear in beside her, and began their triage.

Rushing through their city, sirens wailing, they glimpsed a large American flag painted on the side of a building. With a pang they remembered when it was put there—after 9-11-01. The 21st century had begun with terror. It wasn't getting any better.

2

"OH GOD, WHERE ARE YOU?"

"It were better for him that a millstone were hanged about
his neck, and that he [were] cast into the sea, than that he
should offend one of these little ones."
Luke 17:2

Monday had begun with promise for the Johnson family. School was going smoothly both for Sara, in second grade, and Mark, in seventh grade. Their mother, Karen, had finally landed steady nursing work for a private family—a job that she could work around her kid's school schedule. Bob was juggling two remodeling contracts with several more promising bids coming up.

Waving a hasty goodbye that early October morning, they had gone through the usual motions of "pecks-on-cheeks," grabbed lunches, and slammed doors. There might not have been a lot of "quality time" for the children—or a lot of love lost between two frustrated and financially strapped parents, for that matter—but everyone was in a comfortable rut.

Karen had left just before the school bus arrived so she wouldn't be late to work, trusting Bob to see the kids off. Thus, it was with shock and confusion, that she arrived at her destination, only to be met with an emergency message from Sara's principal.

Part of the emergency alert system the school had recently instituted included an automated, computer-dialed, notification sequence to the work and home phones of all parents—in case of emergency. Being the parents of an "involved" student, Bob and Karen's work and home phones had been the first to receive notification.

12

The departing nurse offered to stay if Karen needed to go somewhere. Karen mumbled her thanks absentmindedly as she dialed the school's emergency contact number. Listening to a description of what had occurred, she became aware of a live bulletin coming on the television— with pictures—to add to her chills.

The counselor assigned to interact with the parents, endeavored to calm Karen's fears. But without knowing exactly the medical condition of her daughter, Karen was on the verge of hysteria. She dropped the phone, mid-sentence, and without seeing or hearing anything else ran to her shiny black Honda. She had to be at the hospital when Sara arrived . . . she will be so frightened there all alone . . . hurt by God-knows-who . . . oh my precious baby . . . her thoughts tumbled.

Karen groped to remember what to do . . . key in lock, turn ignition, back into street . . . screech of brakes. Oh, look for cars . . . hospital-hospital-hospital-where is the hospital-oh, right . . . where was Bob . . . what happened . . . did they? Oh, God! Where are you?

Without knowing how she got there, Karen nearly drove into the ER doors. A waiting school counselor opened her door and they raced to the ambulance bay where Sara had been unloaded just moments before. Karen was glad she knew the counselor; glad to have someone to lean on and share whatever monstrous situation she was so afraid had happened.

They heard another screech of tires just as they caught sight of Sara, lying wide-eyed and still, on the hospital gurney. Glancing around, Karen saw Bob loping toward them, his long strides eating up the distance. Looking at each other, they cried out in unison "What happened?"

"I thought you saw her off on the school bus," accused Karen.

"I did," retorted Bob. "They were both on the bus before I left the house!"

"Well, how did this happen?" Karen looked up into his eyes as if trying to read the answers in the very depths of his soul.

But, before the blame-game could go further, Sara caught sight of them and started crying. Instantly, they were at her side, the picture of harmony and parental concern. Walking along beside her, they accompanied the medical staff into a triage area. The counselor, at a cue from the doctor, urged Bob and Karen to step back, so the staff could attend to Sara's injuries, assuring them they could stay in the background—for now.

Now, they held hands, frightened and silent. Squeezed hands, really. The shock was beginning to wear off and Karen felt the tears start to slip down her cheeks. As the nurse began to undress Sara, Karen felt the room grow hot and distant. Then Bob's strong arms were around her and she heard her friend directing them to a place to sit down, out of the triage room.

After that, Karen let herself slip into blessed unknowingness. When she awoke, there was a strange smell in the air. Startled, she tried to jump up, but was firmly, though gently, restrained.

"Mrs. Johnson, you fainted. Just rest a bit." The nurses breathed a sigh of relief and turned their attention back to their over-loaded schedule.

Forgetting, for a minute, where she was and why she was there, Karen noticed things she hadn't seen before. Armed officers were standing outside the door of the triage area. Several official-looking people were talking with someone at the desk and kept glancing their way. Looking at the counselor with questions in her eyes, Karen felt a strange uneasiness growing in the pit of her stomach. Before she could begin to formulate a question, the two officials—a man and a woman—started walking toward them.

Looking at Bob with a sympathetic smile, the gentleman reached out his hand and introduced himself. At the same time, the woman reached down to pat Karen's shoulder and offered her support in "this difficult time." Karen thought the smile looked a bit too practiced, but decided to give her the benefit of the doubt. Out of the corner of her eye she saw Bob being skillfully guided to another part of the waiting area and wondered why he would be leaving her side.

The counselor squeezed Karen's hand and told her she would just "pop in" for a minute to check on Sara. Reluctantly, Karen was left alone with the visitor. After a few minutes of just silence, the official began to ask questions.

"This came as a terrible surprise, didn't it?"

"What?" Karen blinked away the fog in her mind and tried to understand. "Oh, yes; I had just arrived at work, when I got a message that I was to call the school immediately—Red Alert. I couldn't fathom what could possibly be wrong."

"Did you drive your own car today, or did you and your husband exchange vehicles?"

"Huh? Exchange vehicles? Oh, no. I never drive his pickup—he needs it for work. He was just a little later leaving the house than I was, because the school bus was late, and I couldn't wait this morning. I had to be at work on time, and—oh! I'm supposed to be at work! What is happening to Sara? How is she? Do you know what happened?"

Looking around, Karen didn't see Bob anywhere. Who did that man say he was? Who is this woman? Looking closer at the visitor, Karen saw a name tag; "Ruth Lyre, Child Protective Services." Why would Child Protective Services be here?

"Mrs. Johnson, were you able to park your car properly when you arrived?" asked Ms. Lyre.

"No, I don't think so. I can't really remember," Karen responded.

"My partner, Mr. Storie, will be happy to move it for you, if you have the keys handy."

Looking up, Karen saw Bob and Mr. Storie coming in from outside. Mr. Storie reached out his hand just as Ms. Lyre finished her offer. Not knowing what else to do, Karen fished around in her purse, then dropped her keys into his hand. Hearing Bob cough, Karen noticed his face was white. Still, she didn't comprehend what was happening.

Another question from Ms. Lyre brought her up short. "Has your husband ever hit you before?"

Now, Karen felt the blood drain from her face. Her mind raced back to the days before Mark was born. She was newly pregnant and Bob hadn't taken the news well. They were deeply in debt, underemployed, and definitely not ready for a family. When she refused to get an abortion, Bob had stormed out and returned hours later—drunk. He

15

had never been so angry with her before and Karen began to be afraid. She tried to edge quietly toward her purse and the door, but Bob cut her off, stumbling in his stupor, knocking her heavily onto the floor.

He was immediately apologetic, but she was bleeding and frightened, so they called an ambulance. Everything had turned out all right with the pregnancy, but Bob had been held and questioned, eventually being sentenced to attend an anger management course and court-ordered to stay away from alcohol for two years.

Karen didn't know what to say. Did this woman know all about them? What if she lied? Would they just find out anyway, then cause more trouble? In the end, Karen knew that this time they had nothing to hide, so she determined to tell the full truth.

"He was drunk and angry just once about twelve years ago and stumbled against me and I fell. But it was an accident; I know it was. And it was just the once. He has never touched a drop of alcohol since then."

The questions only continued, "Were you fighting this morning? Was he happy about having another child when Sara was born?"

"No! I mean yes. I mean no we weren't fighting and yes he was happy about having another child when Sara was born. She was planned!" Karen almost spat out the words. Angry, confused, upset, and still uninformed about Sara's condition, Karen now stopped feeling helpless.

Standing up she pushed open the doors between the two guards, daring them with her look to try and stop her. Marching up to Sara's bedside she demanded to know—immediately—what injuries her daughter had and how she had gotten them. She took Sara's hand and stood close by her, relieved that no one had tried to stop her. She wasn't sure why that thought had popped into her mind but it began to take over her thoughts and a new fear washed over her. What if they think this was our doing and they take Sara away from us?

The doctor's soft voice brought her back to earth. "Fortunately, Sara isn't seriously hurt. The bruises will be painful for a while, but the cuts were mostly superficial. There is only one deep one on her left arm here, where she apparently caught and tore the skin trying to get out of the door of the car. We put a few stitches in there." He appeared to be trying to give her as much information as he could without seeming to say anything unusual. The CPS caseworkers had slipped into the room and were watching their every move—trying to listen to their very thoughts, it seemed.

Catching the direction of the doctor's remarks, Karen rejoiced: There would be blood on the car of whoever had tried to kidnap her baby. They wouldn't find any on either of their cars, no matter how hard they tried!

Glancing toward the caseworkers, the doctor added a bit louder "We will just keep Sara overnight to observe her and make sure there are no surprises from our brave little sweetheart." He winked at Sara and she smiled shyly back at him.

3

REAP THE WHIRLWIND

"And the times of this ignorance God winked at;
but now commandeth all men everywhere to repent."
Acts 17:30

Bob had always wanted to be his "own boss." He loved the freedom of making his own hours, setting his own pay scale, and doing quality work without someone always looking over his shoulder. His struggling new contracting business had its ups and downs, but all in all it was pretty successful and definitely more satisfying. Over the last several years he had begun to get a loyal clientele base. Repeat business meant customers were satisfied. He also liked being able to justify long hours away from home where things were a bit strained with Karen. Work had become his stress reducer.

It was only 8:30 when the cell phone rang. Pulling the phone from his tool belt he gave his usual greeting, "Hello, this is Bob."

The sequence of noises greeting his ear sent chills up his spine. It took only a few seconds for the sounds to form meaningful thoughts, and it didn't spell good news.

"OK, hit 'one,'" he muttered to himself. He had practiced this numerous times at the urging of the school when the emergency system was first implemented. But that was just practice. Suddenly, shockingly, this was the real thing. He had only a few seconds of computer noise before a school counselor came on the line. "Mr. Johnson?"

"Yes"

"Please, give your authorization code."

There were a couple of seconds before the numbers surfaced on his mental screen, "4629."

"Mr. Johnson, there has been a Level 3 Red Alert incident involving your daughter, Sara. You will find her at Portland General Hospital. Have a good day." Click.

Dropping his tool belt he motioned to one of the subs on the job. "Got an emergency involving my daughter, John. If I don't get back, will you lock up for me?"

Not waiting for a reply he turned as the younger man nodded. Making his way to the truck he was soon on his way. The 15-minute trip was like no other he had ever experienced. Level 3 meant Sara had been injured, was thought to be alive, but prognosis was not known. What could have happened? The counselor seemed calm enough, but it isn't his daughter lying injured from . . . from what? Who? If someone hurt my baby girl, I swear to God, I will kill him! Bob felt an old sickening hot fury arise in him, and he did nothing to beat it back.

Seeing his wife's car in the ER driveway, Bob pulled in behind it and stopped barely six inches from the rear bumper. He would find out now what had happened and who had hurt his baby. Seeing Karen and then glimpsing the quiet form of his little daughter just beyond her he panicked for a second and growled "What happened?" to his wife just as she asked him the same question.

The ensuing argument did little to calm his frayed nerves, but his daughter's cries brought him to his senses, and to her side in an instant. The sight of blood on her clothes, in her hair—the bruise on her soft arm was nauseating; Bob was not able to comprehend who would want to hurt a little child in this way. Now he was scared—scared that Sara was seriously hurt. He felt Karen slip her hand into his and squeeze it and he eagerly reciprocated the gesture.

When Karen started to wobble he grabbed her and began to direct her to the outside waiting area. Suddenly, she went limp in his arms, and he yelled for help. The counselor motioned two nearby nurses to assist and they laid Karen on a long bench near the wall. Placing smelling salts under her nose one nurse watched somewhat distractedly for Karen's response while the other took her pulse.

It wasn't until after Karen was fully awake that Bob noticed a man walking toward him. The man stuck out his hand, introduced himself and taking Bob's arm guided him toward the outside entrance. Bob glanced back at Karen where a woman had just sat down beside her. He started to protest, but Mr. Storie—the name he had given—reassured him that his wife would want to talk to his partner. She was just there to comfort and assist in any way she could.

Turning his attention back to Bob, Mr. Storie asked him how he was doing.

"Mad as a hornet!" Bob replied. "Does anyone know yet what happened? Did someone try to kidnap Sara?"

"Why, Bob? What have you heard?"

"Nothing more than what the counselor from school told me over the phone."

"Did he tell you there had been an attempted kidnapping?" Mr. Storie was persistent.

"No, I just thought. Well I don't know what I thought. I just was afraid something like that might have happened. There is so much of that in the news," he finished lamely.

Outside the doors now, Mr. Storie turned to Bob "What time did you leave the house this morning?"

"I left about 7:45 just after Mark and Sara boarded the school bus."

"Where did you go and what were you driving?"

"I headed for my job site a couple miles from home in my truck."

"Did you talk with anyone—see anyone around your home that didn't belong there?"

"No. There were no cars or people out when I left. I only talked to the sub at the job site just before I left."

"Bob, you know I'm a CPS caseworker trained and assigned by the police to follow up on all cases of suspected abuse. Do you want to tell me what happened to Karen when she was pregnant with Mark?"

Bob felt like he'd been snake-bit. Backing away from Mr.

Storie, he took a deep breath and dragged out the old and painful memory. How he had been struggling with finding work, how Karen was only working part time, how she had gotten pregnant when she was supposed to be on birth-control pills, his demand for her to get an abortion and her refusal. Then storming out of the house to cool down at a local bar . . . the anger, tripping and knocking Karen down . . . all of it he related to the caseworker, fearing if he left anything out it would come back to haunt him. He remembered it all as vividly as if it were yesterday. Could feel it. Smell it. Taste the fear in his mouth when he saw she was bleeding. Hear the wail of the ambulance arriving. Remember the pain and fear—of him—in her eyes. He had vowed to a God he had never learned anything about to never let anything like that happen again. And it hadn't.

"I did more than they asked me to do in the anger management class and not only did I not drink for the mandated two years, but I have never touched another drop of alcohol." Bob's voice caught as he finished the story. Clearing his throat he asked if he could go back to see his wife.

Mr. Storie asked if this was Bob's truck they were leaning against and Bob nodded. "Do you mind if I look inside?" Bob waved him on and Mr. Storie opened the passenger and driver-side doors looking carefully at the latches. Noting the sander, saws, drill, and other tools crowding the seat and floor he appeared satisfied at last and shut the doors.

"Certainly you may see your wife—you're not under arrest, you know," Mr. Storie finally responded.

Arriving back at his wife's side he recognized the interrogation that was taking place but was powerless to intervene. Having to listen to her retell the incident he had just recounted to Mr. Storie cut him to the bone. He silently cheered when she rose up in indignation and ended the interview herself.

The two caseworkers now turned their backs to him, conferred for a moment, then entered the triage area. Bob saw Karen in conversation with the doctor and knew she would get answers. Seizing the opportunity, he strode back outside, dialed his son's pager number, added an "urgent" code and waited.

Mark responded quickly. "Dad? I'm scared, Dad. What's going on? Why did the police come get me from school? I've been here at the police station and nobody would let me call you or Mom until you paged me."

"What?" Bob felt blind-sided again. "They took you from your school?"

"Yeah, and I'm hungry. They wouldn't let me take anything from my locker."

"Son, you stay right where you are. I'll be there in 10 minutes. Don't say anything more to anyone. Do you understand me?"

"Sure, Dad. But they've been asking me all kinds of weird questions. I'm scared. Hurry."

"Ten minutes, son. Count 'em."

Bob's mind began to expand to cover this new and unexpected twist. With deliberate calmness he walked back and into the room with Sara and his wife.

Leaning close to Karen he whispered "Honey, I'm going to pick up Mark. It's late and I don't want him hearing about this from some kid." He bent down and kissed his daughter.

Turning to leave, he stopped to kiss his wife on the cheek and said, in a loud voice, "I love you both."

The caseworkers pretended to be greatly interested in some paperwork they'd carried around all day. Bob ignored them and jumped in his truck. Mark was waiting.

4

BROKEN

*"All those gathered here will know that it is not by
sword or spear that the Lord saves; for the battle is the Lord's."*
1 Samuel 17:47, NIV

Bob drove carefully to the police station, not one mile over the speed limit. Walking in, he introduced himself to the guard and stepped through the metal detector. Retrieving his cell phone, keys, wallet, and change, he followed the directions of the guard.

"Sergeant, I'm Bob Johnson—here for my son Mark?" Bob's statement came out as a question.

"I'm sorry, Mr. Johnson. Mark isn't here. He's been transferred to—" he consulted his forms, "to a foster care facility. I'm not able to give you the exact information."

"But I just talked to him. He said he was here. I told him I was coming. Are you sure he isn't here?"

"Yes. He left about five minutes ago. I'm sure the caseworker will be in touch with you in the next hour or so."

"Well, what should I do? How will the caseworker know where to find me?"

"We have your cell and home numbers. You will be contacted." With that the Sergeant turned to a ringing phone and Bob was summarily dismissed.

Returning to his truck, Bob slumped over the wheel. His mind needed to rest, but there would be no rest from this living nightmare. Finally, looking around, he started the engine and slowly made his way back to the hospital. How will I tell Karen? What are we going to do? I think we had better get a lawyer.

Back at Portland General Bob discovered that Sara had left triage. He found her room number from a friendly volunteer, made his way to the elevator and poked the button for the pediatric floor. A cute lamb decorated the button. Somehow the image only made his heart feel empty. Once he had wondered how he could survive with children to support. Now he wondered how he could survive the night without his children. He never considered it could go longer than that.

"Hi, Punkin'. How are you feeling?" He managed a smile.

Sara turned sleepy eyes to her Daddy. "OK, Daddy. Are you going to stay with me? Is Mark coming?"

"You bet I'm going to stay with you. And, Mark is staying with some friends for now."

Karen turned questioning eyes to Bob, but caught the subtle shake of his head and didn't ask the question on the tip of her tongue. They held Sara's hands, one on each side, until the medications did their work and Sara fell into a sound sleep.

Slipping quietly into the hall, Bob proceeded first to caution, and then detail to Karen the latest development. He suggested they call a lawyer and try to get a meeting right away.

Not knowing where else to begin, they found a phone book, turned to the yellow pages and started dialing numbers. Bob listened to one receptionist after another stating, "I'm sorry, we no longer handle cases involving Child Protective Services." Finally a lawyer actually answered the phone.

"Hi, James Wright, attorney—how may I help you?"

"Mr. Wright, this is Bob Johnson. My daughter is in the hospital with not-too-serious physical injuries from an attempted kidnapping this morning. My son has been placed in an unknown foster facility. I seem to be under suspicion for the kidnapping attempt. Can you help us, please, or do you know someone who can?" Bob's voice was starting to show the emotional turmoil going on within.

"Have you heard from CPS yet regarding a hearing date?"

"No, they told me at the police station about 45 minutes ago that I would be getting a call in an hour or so."

"Good. I want you to come straight to my office at once. Now follow my directions exactly. Don't say a word more or less. If you get that phone call before you arrive tell them you are in traffic but will call them back as soon as you arrive at your destination in about— where are you now?"

"We are at Portland General."

"OK. It takes about 20 minutes to get here from there. Tell them you'll call in about 30 minutes—whenever it is that you get the call. Are you clear on this?"

"Yes. Certainly. And thank you, Mr. Wright. Thank you so much. You have no idea how scared we are."

"I'd like to reassure you that you have nothing to fear, but the reality is CPS has been getting more and more powerful and I can promise you a battle. But the battle belongs to the Lord. Just don't waste any time getting here."

With that Mr. Wright hung up and Bob was left speechless for a minute.

"What did he say?" Karen had only heard Bob's side of the conversation and was anxiously waiting for the details.

"He said he'd take us, to come at once and to prepare for a battle. Then he said something strange for a lawyer—he said 'The battle belongs to the Lord,' whatever that means."

Then snapping to attention Bob jumped up and strode over to the nurse's desk. "Excuse me, we are Sara Johnson's parents. We have an important appointment we must get to right away."

"Sara is asleep now," added Karen.

"If she wakes up I want you to call me on this cell number immediately." Handing his business card to the nurse, Bob got her consent and reassurance that Sara would be asleep for some time.

The drive to Attorney Wright's office proved uneventful. No phone call from CPS seemed like a blessing. Until they got to his office, that is.

After introductions Mr. Wright got down to business. "They didn't call you yet, did they?"

Puzzled Karen answered, "No. How did you know?"

"You need to expect a minimum of communication, consideration, and answers from CPS. Once they suspect someone of abuse they close around the victim—real or imagined—and will treat you as already convicted." Mr. Wright spoke bluntly.

"They can't do that! People still have rights in America! A person is innocent until proven guilty!" Bob was indignant.

"Mr. and Mrs. Johnson—Bob and Karen, if I may—we are going to know each other well before this is over. You have obviously never had contact with CPS before. That is good, and it speaks well for you. But in this system you will be guilty until you are proven one hundred percent innocent."

Stunned and shaken, Bob and Karen tried to absorb the magnitude of that statement. Scarcely able to believe him Bob wondered briefly if they had entered one of those parallel dimensions Star Trek was known to portray.

Mr. Wright continued, "I want you to fill out the information requested on these sheets. Each of you should answer independently. Karen, have you any indication that you are a suspect?"

"No. I don't think so. They asked me if Bob had ever hit me. They didn't question my actions at all."

"That's OK for now. It doesn't really mean anything, though, because domestic violence is often assumed, as well as child abuse, and perceived as a two-way street. If you are named as a suspect you will need your own lawyer."

Karen started to cry. "Except for one incident, early in our marriage, there has never been anything that could even be construed as domestic violence."

Bob stood up, paced around the office, then punched his fist into his hand. "I don't know what is happening. I don't know why it is happening. But, we will get through it. Somehow. I'm not going to let this, this, whatever this system is, beat us." He hated to see his wife cry, yet he could feel a stinging in his own eyes.

"Bob and Karen," interrupted Mr. Wright "I know this may sound strange, but I want you to know up front that I am a Christian. I have specialized in CPS cases because I have found so much injustice, heartache, and damage to families with our current system. Without God I couldn't hear the stories like yours that I hear every day and not go crazy."

The Johnsons didn't think it so strange that this business could drive a person crazy. In fact they began to feel a certain comfort by the fact that this attorney was a Christian. They weren't sure what that really meant or how it would affect them, but if he was willing to help them they'd take just about anything.

Aloud Karen said "I was raised Catholic but Bob and I really aren't anything now. I hope that doesn't matter. We do want you to take our case, if you will."

"No, it doesn't matter at all. I will take your case, but I'd also like to take it to God if I have your permission."

Bob and Karen looked at each other with a how much stranger can this day get expression and said in unison, "I guess so."

Then right before their eyes Mr. Wright bowed his head and proceeded to say a simple prayer: "Father in heaven, You see this couple before You. You have heard their story. You know the truth. Now I ask that you will give them and their children strength and a sure knowledge of Your loving arms around them, and that You will give me wisdom to help them. This I pray in Jesus' name. Amen."

After that, things proceeded about like the Johnsons had expected: Paperwork, financial arrangements, statements, questions, questions, questions.

Toward the end of their visit Bob's cell phone rang. "Hello, This is Bob Johnson."

"Mr. Johnson, this is Portland General. The police and CPS caseworkers are here and are taking custody of Sara. They have asked that you return immediately. Goodbye."

Bob wished he could faint. Just to escape this nightmare for a few minutes would be preferable. Instead he turned to his lawyer and said "Well, I think we are going to need you with us at the hospital.

They are stealing Sara right out of the hospital." Bob could no longer even try to justify the actions of Child Protective Services.

"Of course I'll go with you," Mr. Wright smiled. "And if you have any family in the area—with no police record of any kind, I might add—you'd better call them and have them meet us there at once."

5

"IT WAS DADDY"

"And it shall come to pass, that before they call, I will answer;
and while they are yet speaking, I will hear."

Isaiah 65:24

Hi, Mom, I don't have time to give you any details, but I need your help."

"Karen? Is everyone OK? Nothing has happened to the children?"

"Mom, listen carefully. Everyone is OK, sort of. I need you to come to Portland General in the next twenty minutes. You've got to come soon. Please."

"Of course, honey. But I don't understand . . . if everyone is all right why am I going to the hospital?"

"It's too complicated—but Mom say a prayer for us, 'bye."

Marie Golden sat for a moment trying to understand her daughter's phone call. Then hurrying to her bedroom she rummaged around in a drawer and found her old rosary. Grabbing her purse she headed for the door, then turned back for a second. "Wishing that you were alive, Darling, isn't going to make it so, but I think I'm going to need your strength. I don't feel good about this." Speaking into the room, empty for the last four years, had become a habit. There was no one else to listen.

Headed at last to the hospital Marie let her mind wander. *I can't remember the last time Karen said anything about God, let alone asked for prayer. This must be terrible. I'm afraid my beads are a bit rusty.*

And there, driving down the road, unable to finger her beads, Marie offered her first heartfelt prayer to God. "Oh God, I don't know if you will listen to me without a priest, but my children need help. Please help them . . . um . . . thank you."

Marie walked into the hospital, not really knowing where to go. "Are you Mrs. Golden?" The friendly stranger, with striking red hair, seemed to recognize her. Without waiting for her answer she directed her to the floor and room number of her granddaughter Sara.

Turning to thank her, Marie discovered she had already melted into the crowd so she quickly headed for Sara's room. Once there she entered and stood quietly by the door trying to listen to everything at once and get some idea of the drama being played out before her.

"Why are you going to take Sara out of the hospital?" Bob was asking. "The ER doctor said she would need to stay overnight."

"Dr. Christopher is in charge of her care on this floor, and he has determined that she no longer needs in-hospital care." The woman answering his question was not a nurse, but seemed to be in charge of events.

Karen now asked "Where will you take Sara if she can't come home with us?"

But before anyone else could say anything Marie spoke up firmly. "She can come home with me! I'm not sure what is going on here, but Sara is my granddaughter, she knows me and has stayed overnight often. She can stay with me."

All eyes turned toward the voice. Karen rushed to introduce her mother to Ruth Lyre and Mr. Storie from CPS. The two police officers stood quietly watching in the background to assist in any possible violent reaction of the parents.

"Mom, this is our attorney James Wright." Karen tried to fill up the silence so no one could say they were taking Sara now.

Mr. Wright addressed the caseworkers; "State law provides for immediate family members to assume temporary custody until the hearing."

Almost reluctantly, the caseworkers agreed to the arrangement. There were no papers to sign, no documents outlining charges, nothing. Ms. Lyre stated that it wasn't needed. "The judge believes what I tell him." There was a verbal announcement of the day and time of a hearing to determine if custody of the minor children should remain with the parents and that was that.

Mr. Wright wasn't willing to let that stand, so he pulled a blank document form out of his briefcase, filled in the information according to what the caseworkers had verbally agreed upon, and insisted that they both sign the document. Mrs. Golden also signed that she would assume temporary custody for as long as necessary. He asked to have it copied so each person would have written proof and they completed arrangements to have Sara discharged.

The next item Mr. Wright addressed was the temporary living arrangements of Mark. The caseworkers said it was too late that day to make any changes, and suggested he file for a modification to the order in the morning.

The group saw Sara safely seat-belted into her grandmother's car and dispersed. The caseworkers had given strict instructions that Sara was not to be allowed in the presence of her father without her mother and grandmother both present and that the parents were not to stay at the grandmother's home overnight.

Bob and Karen arranged to meet Marie and Sara at a local restaurant for supper. They had totally forgotten about food during this nightmarish day. They really weren't hungry now, but it gave them a little longer with Sara.

On the way to the restaurant Sara started to tell her Nana about her morning encounter. Marie assured her she didn't have to talk at all if she didn't want to, but Sara apparently needed to get it all out.

"Nana, when I got off the school bus this morning, I saw Mommy's car pull up behind the bus. I thought I had forgotten something so I started to run over to it. Then I saw Daddy stick his head out of the window and say 'Hi Punkin.' I thought Daddy had gone to work in the truck."

"It was Daddy?" Marie sounded surprised.

"No, it wasn't Daddy and it wasn't Mommy or Mommy's car. It just looked like it, 'cause it was black."

31

Sara was silent for a few minutes remembering what had happened next. "Then he grabbed me and tried to throw me into the car." She looked up at Marie with fear in her eyes. Marie pulled over to the side of the road so she could give Sara her full attention, and waited.

Taking her Nana's hand for courage, Sara continued "I screamed and he put his hand over my mouth so I bit him. I put my feet against the car, hit, and kicked. I was bad, wasn't I Nana?" And the tears began in earnest.

"Oh Baby, no, you weren't bad! That man was bad to try to take you. You did everything right to protect yourself. You were so brave. I'm so proud of you." Nana slipped out of her seatbelt and hugged Sara gently. The sight of her cuts and bruises and the story of her close call nearly overwhelmed Marie.

They sat with Sara snuggled and safe in her Grandmother's arms. Then Sara straightened up and said, "I want my Mommy."

Arriving a few minutes later at the restaurant they found Bob and Karen waiting anxiously. There had been too many unpleasant surprises in this day, and they were starting to worry again.

"Oh, there you are Mom! I was getting scared."

Marie gave her daughter a quick hug and turned Sara's hand over to her. "Your daughter wants to see you, dear." Karen noticed her Mother's tearstained face.

After everyone had ordered Sara discovered that Mark wasn't there. "Daddy, where is Mark?"

Bob cleared his throat, looked at his wife and plunged in. "Well, Punkin, you are such a big, brave girl. I think you need to know the truth. He is staying with someone, but the police and caseworkers thought it would be best if he had his own place to stay tonight. Just like you are getting to stay with Nana."

"Well, where is he staying and when can I see him?"

"I, we don't really know for sure. The nice lawyer, Mr. Wright, said tomorrow he would try to see if Mark can also stay at Nana's."

"I like Mr. Wright," Sara continued, "He brought me a beautiful dolly and asked Jesus to keep me safe. That felt nice."

All of a sudden Marie remembered the stranger in the hospital lobby. "Oh, that reminds me, the woman—the one you left in the lobby to give me directions to Sara's room—she was certainly kind."

Bob and Karen gave her a blank look "What woman, Mom?"

"In the lobby—just as I walked in and looked around not knowing where to go she walked over and said, "Mrs. Golden?" Then before I had a chance to answer she gave me directions to Sara's floor and room number. It's a good thing, too; if I'd been a few minutes later who knows where those social workers would have decided to take Sara! I turned to thank her, but she was already gone. Be sure to thank her for me. And she had such beautiful red hair."

"Mom, I'm telling you there is no one else. Mr. Wright is the only person we have found to help us in this entire day!"

"But she knew me! I thought you had given someone my description. If it wasn't someone you sent, who was it?"

They all sat mystified looking at one another.

Later when they had hugged and kissed Sara a thousand times and read her a dozen stories, Bob and Karen reluctantly set out for home. It was a painful trip, but not as painful as entering their quiet and lonely home.

6

"PERSON OF INTEREST"

"When the enemy shall come in like a flood,
the Spirit of the Lord shall lift up a standard against him."
Isaiah 59:19

Exhausted, heartbroken, and fearful, neither Bob nor Karen could find one more word to say to each other. They didn't even turn on the house lights; it would have made even starker the absence of Mark and Sara. Somehow they made it through the bedtime rituals and crawled under the covers—far apart from each other.

In the morning they were in nearly the same position. Sleep had finally, mercifully, overtaken them both, but not until the day's scenes had replayed themselves over and over in their minds.

Still in the cocoon of their own private pain, the ringing telephone startled them.

"Hello, this is Bob"

"Bob, James Wright here. I wanted to let you know the latest. I went to the juvenile court first thing and filed a written request to modify the custody of Mark to allow him to stay with Karen's mother."

"Oh good! When will that happen?"

"Well, not as soon as we would like. I was able to look over the notes transferred with him, and it doesn't look good. When the police questioned him, he made some statements that you often yelled at him and Sara—or at least that is how it was interpreted. You know how a kid can say, 'He always yells at me to clean my room,' and not really mean anything violent."

"I'm not perfect, but I don't physically or verbally assault my family. Everyone raises their voice sometimes."

"Of course they do, but our whole country has gone into a 'lockdown' mind-set. So many cases of real child abuse were neglected by CPS, for one reason or another, that now they take no chances."

"What can we do? When can we see Mark?"

"I'm working on that. Hopefully you will be able to see him for an hour before the end of the day, but it may take until the hearing to get him put in to Mrs. Golden's custody. Try to do the normal things today; I'll call you as soon as I know when you can see Mark. Remember, the battle belongs to the Lord. 'Bye."

"Normal, what's that? OK, 'bye—and thanks." Bob slumped a little when he hung up the phone.

"What now?" snapped Karen, more to the world than to Bob.

"Patience dear, you're going to need a lot of it. He says to go about our normal duties today. He'll call us when we can see Mark— for one hour—and Mark might not get to go to your Mom's until after the hearing tomorrow."

Disappointed, Karen handed Bob his lunch. "I'd better get going or I'll be late for work—if I have a job left after missing yesterday. I can't believe how quickly a person's life can be turned upside down."

"I know," echoed Bob. But neither knew just how far upside down their lives would get.

When Bob arrived at work he found the sub already there and on the job. "Good morning" he called out, swinging his tool belt around his hips. It actually felt good to be doing something where he could be in control.

The contractor looked around at Bob. "Oh, hi. Uh, did you talk to Mrs. Olsen yet?"

"Nope, just got here. Has she got another idea for this project?" He chuckled.

"Something like that."

Bob strode off to find the homeowner. "Good morning Mrs. Olsen, did you want to see me?"

Mrs. Olsen looked up unsmiling. "Sit down, Mr. Johnson. I'll just be a minute."

Bob sat down and pondered the situation. Mr. Johnson? I've been here three weeks and have been "Bob" the whole time. This can't be good news.

"Now, I'm sure you understand," Mrs. Olsen began, "but I have decided to find someone else to finish my project. I've just gotten off the phone with my lawyer, and he says that where a felony is committed I no longer have to honor our contract."

"A felony? What are you talking about? No, I don't understand."

"Mr. Johnson, I watch the news just like everyone else. That lock-down of Wilson Elementary yesterday scared me to death. I watched it all day. It will take goodness knows how long for those poor children to begin to get back to a normal life. And your own daughter—how could you do such a thing?" She scolded him like a child.

"Whoa, hold everything, are you saying the news reports claimed I tried to kidnap my own daughter? Mrs. Olsen, I was here—you know that! Somebody tried to hurt Sara, but I will guarantee you it wasn't me!"

"Well, that's how I understood it from the interview the press had with those two social workers. Anyway, it's too risky for me to continue to have you here. I've been getting phone calls all morning from my friends saying I'd better let you go. I'm sorry, but there's nothing else I can do. Here's what I owe you till now." She handed over a check to him.

Bob thought there certainly was something else she could do, but knew it would be futile to argue. Going to his truck he stopped to tell his sub, John, goodbye. "I guess you will be finishing this job alone, John. If you need any advice, call me."

"Sure, Bob—and say, man, I'm sorry. I know you were here at the time your daughter was grabbed. If there is anything I can do for you, just yell."

"Yeah, thanks."

Now Bob was concerned. Losing the remainder of this job wasn't a big deal, but what if everyone felt the same way about hiring him? Work was tight enough since the economy had tanked last year, but a good carpenter always had work. He drove home to check out the news for himself. When he got there Karen's car was in the driveway.

"This doesn't look like good news," Bob began as he walked in the door. But before he could say another word Karen shushed him.

"Listen. Here is a replay of an interview with our two caseworkers from last night."

"No, the police haven't arrested anyone yet."

"Why are you holding the children? Is the father a suspect?"

"It is customary to provide protection to the children no matter who may be found at fault. The father is just a person of interest at this time."

Bob snorted, "Person of interest! Another word for 'suspect' in people's minds."

"The movie review for the weekend," Karen snapped off the TV. "Our lives are no more important than the latest movie! What a crazy world. Bob! Why are you home?"

"Karen, why are you home?"

"The family I was working for told me they had to have someone reliable and let me go. Oh, no! Not you, too?"

Trying to keep his sanity, Bob started to laugh. "This really is like a bad movie. Maybe we should have watched the reviews—we could be in the middle of our own horror show!" Then he had an idea.

"Let's go get Sara and Nana and spend the day at the Science Museum. We'll eat at the Spaghetti Factory—Sara loves it—and when Mr. Wright calls we can all go see Mark together!"

Karen caught the excitement in his voice. "That's a great idea. When was the last time we all had a day off in the middle of the week? Sara will love it!"

They looked at each other with new appreciation and a feeling of hope.

7

WHAT WILL TOMORROW HOLD?

"Call to me and I will answer you and tell you great
And unsearchable things you do not know"
Jeremiah 33:3, NIV

"Mommy! Daddy!" Sara was jumping up and down with happiness. "Let's go right away."

Marie knew the idea of taking a day off probably wasn't the whole story, but she willingly entered into the excitement of the day. Sara needed some family fun and she would walk her legs off, if necessary, to help her have it.

During the day Marie had an opportunity to talk with Bob and Karen when Sara was busy filling her shopping cart in the museum's grocery area.

"Sara had a hard time going to sleep last night. She would only sleep in my arms and every time she started to doze she would jump and gasp, looking around wildly until she saw she was with me, then relax again. It was heartbreaking. I couldn't get up to get my beads without disturbing her even more, so I did what I did yesterday in the car—I talked to God myself."

Karen looked at her Mother in obvious surprise. "Really? I've never even heard you talk about God much before. The beads were always the only way to pray. What did you say, Mom?"

"I just asked God to help Sara sleep—and you know what? Before I finished thinking my prayer she had relaxed and was sound asleep. She didn't wake up all night. I felt such comfort knowing God was helping Sara."

They all gazed at Sara, lost in thought.

At that moment Bob's cell phone sang it's usual song. Bob glanced at the face of his phone; "Hi, Mr. Wright, what's up?"

"Sounds like you are having a happier day than yesterday! I just called to make it better. You can come down to the CPS office and visit Mark in half an hour."

"Great! Karen and I sort of had time on our hands unexpectedly, so we are close by with Marie and Sara. We'll be there right away. Will you be coming? Can we take Mark home?"

"I will be there and maybe, and I stress maybe, I can put some pressure on them to let Mark go home with Marie. See you there soon, 'bye."

"All right! 'Bye."

All three of his "girls" were crowded around to hear Bob's announcement. "We get to see Mark right away—and maybe, maybe he can go home with Nana."

"Oh, goody, goody," sang Sara and hopped a circle around them.

"Mom," Karen carefully began, "do you suppose you could ask God for one more favor?"

"Well, I don't know much about all that, but I'm not going to let my grandson sit in some foster home without trying everything I can to get him home!" she stated emphatically.

Right there in the corner of the grocery store display Marie shut her eyes and said softly "God, I know You are really busy. I don't want to bother You too much, but my grandson is so important to me. Please let him be able to come home with me. Thank You."

Bob felt a bit embarrassed in case someone had heard Marie right in the middle of the museum—praying! But he found it comforting at the same time. Who knew? Maybe . . .

At the state offices they were ushered into a room where Mark waited. He looked tired. Tired, confused and angry. "Why didn't you come get me like you said, Dad? They said they had waited long enough and needed to get me settled for the night. You said you'd come!"

"Son, yesterday was a bad dream—for you and all of us. I came in ten minutes just like I said. They told me you had been transferred to a foster care facility five minutes before and wouldn't tell me where. I'm so sorry. We have been trying to get to you ever since."

Mark's attitude began to soften and unwanted tears squeezed out of tightly shut eyes. Willingly he allowed the embrace of his family, soaking up their love.

Then he saw Sara with all her bruises and bandages and gasped, "What happened to Sara?" He had neither been told nor allowed to see any news report of the kidnapping attempt of his sister. Now he sat with his arm around his little sister, looking the part of protective big brother.

"Hey Sara," Nana spoke quickly, "why don't you and I go get some pop from that machine for all of us?"

While the two of them were off on their errand, Bob and Karen told their son all the events of the day before. "You are old enough to know exactly what is going on," Karen added. "Mr. Wright, our attorney, is trying right now to see if you can stay with Nana." Karen hugged her boy tightly as if trying to take some of his burden.

"I'm really sorry, Daddy, for being so mad at you. I didn't know all this stuff."

"I know you are, Mark, and I would have probably reacted the same way. Don't worry about it. I love you." Bob was finding it easier and easier to say those three little words these days.

Just then Nana and Sara returned, and they were all sipping on the pop of their choice when Mr. Wright entered the visiting room. "Hope you weren't too bothered by the two-way mirror on that wall." He gestured to an area behind them. "They like to make sure you don't do anything illegal when you visit your children."

The Johnson family turned to look and spontaneously waved at the mirror. "Nope," said Bob, "we didn't mind it at all! We are too happy to have Mark with us to be bothered by the little things."

"I have good news for you," Mr. Wright continued. "Since there is no evidence against you, Bob, and there has been no warrant issued for your arrest, they are allowing Mark to go home with Mrs. Golden tonight." He smiled, adding, "Same rules apply to Mark about being with her at all times, just like for Sara."

The family could restrain their joy no longer. "Hurray!" shouted Mark and Sara. After a round of hugs and kisses—which included Mr. Wright—they began to head for the door.

"Don't forget, Bob and Karen, the hearing is still at 9:00 a.m. tomorrow."

"No problem, see you there! Remember, James—the battle belongs to the Lord!" Bob grinned as he beat Mr. Wright to the now familiar quote and the family headed for the Spaghetti Factory for a belated celebration dinner.

The meal was much like old times, but then came the drive home. Bob and Karen in one car: Marie with the children in another car. Time was that would have been a welcome arrangement; now it was a reminder.

"Bob, do you think we will regain custody of Mark and Sara tomorrow?" Karen's voice trembled slightly; she cleared her throat. The question hung in the air.

KIDNAPPED

"Be still, and know that I am God:
...I will be exalted in the earth."
Psalm 46:10

In the morning all the family arrived early at the Juvenile Courthouse. Going through the metal detectors and having her bags searched was new to Karen. She quickly rehearsed in her mind the contents of her purse. Remembering that she had left her pepper spray in another purse, she breathed a sigh of relief. That could be construed as a weapon and there had been enough of the unexpected.

Going into the small courtroom they quickly surmised that the right side was for the state, left side for them—the defendants. Mr. Wright quietly briefed them on proper courtroom deportment.

"Whatever the state says, do not react in any visible way. No frown on your face, not a squirm in your chair or a shake of the head. This goes for the family sitting in the seats behind you also, Bob."

"Let's get this over with." Bob was beginning to look and sound nervous. He glanced at the deputy sitting in the back row, watching everything.

"One more thing folks," Mr. Wright added, putting his arm out to guide them outside the doors of the courtroom.

Leading them to a quiet room across the hall, he asked everyone to bow their heads for a moment. "Lord, may Your presence be in these proceedings today. May truth and justice prevail, and Your name be honored. Amen."

Looking around at the somber group, the attorney assumed his professional air and gave the marching orders: "The battle belongs to the Lord! Let's get the children home."

Seated in the tiny courtroom again, they awaited the entrance of the judge. "Hear ye, hear ye, hear ye! All stand for the honorable Judge Steven Pierce," the bailiff's monotone sounded.

Everyone on both sides of the aisle obediently arose, then sat down again. Momentarily, the District Attorney stood up to read the opening statement. Calling the caseworkers and police interviewers, he proceeded in trying to build a case for keeping the children away from the parents.

Then it was Mr. Wright's turn. "Your Honor, it was not possible for Mr. Johnson to have attempted his daughter's kidnapping. He was at work more than ten miles away and his wife, driving her own car, arrived at her job just two minutes after the alleged attempted kidnapping occurred. I have witnesses that place them both at or near their respective scenes of work at the exact time of the incident." He gestured toward the rear of the room where a man and a woman had quietly slipped in and were now standing.

Bob and Karen both looked surprised. They had been so busy they forgot their attorney had been equally busy.

After both attorneys had their say, the judge spoke. "That won't be necessary, Mr. Wright. I see no facts in evidence of any guilt on the part of Mr. Johnson. The case is dismissed with prejudice. Mark and Sara Johnson are remanded to the custody of their parents immediately."

With that he arose and left the courtroom. Everyone hastily stood up then and began to mill around.

"Hallelujah!" exclaimed Mr. Wright. "I never expected an immediate decision. Usually the judge takes a week to write his opinion. We will still get a written opinion from him, but this settles it right now! Hallelujah!"

The caseworkers looked grim and unhappy. But they had no recourse. Their job was over. There would be no bonuses earned for this case.

"What does 'with prejudice' mean?" Marie questioned.

"It means CPS cannot follow up with you in any way for this case. It is gone. Praise the Lord!" Mr. Wright could not contain himself. "I have never seen a case handled so rapidly. Truly, the Lord battled for you."

"You mean it's all over—we can go home? Mark and Sara can go home with us?" Karen was feeling nearly as confused as she had been at the hospital. She sat down and hugged Sara and Mark tightly.

"It's all over, my love, and we are going to celebrate, then we're all going home." Bob was radiant with joy. He turned to the two potential witnesses in the rear of the room. "Please, come with us. Better yet, let's go to our place and celebrate—would you come, too, James?"

"Well, this ended several hours before I expected, so I can spare some time to come help you celebrate. Sure, why not?" Mr. Wright now led the procession from the courtroom, thanking the two witnesses in the process.

It was a cheerful group that exited the courthouse. Standing out front, the air seemed fresher, the sun brighter. Bob stuck out his hand. "Isn't it a great day, John? I can't thank you enough for being willing to come testify for me. I'd like you to meet my family. This is my wife Karen, my son Mark, and daughter Sara."

Turning to his wife he said, "Karen, John works with me often as a carpentry sub."

"So kind of you to come, John," Karen offered.

"It's very nice to meet you folks," John returned. "I can see why Bob is always in a good mood at work! You have a great family, Bob."

Karen now went up to the other witness. "Lori, it was so thoughtful of you to come down for us today. I hope it hasn't inconvenienced your work."

"Bob, this is the nurse that worked an extra shift for me yesterday." Karen explained.

"Lori, this is Mark, Sara, and my mother, Marie Golden."

Lori shook hands around the group.

"It is so nice to meet you all and to see justice done so swiftly. Praise the Lord for His goodness to you today. I'm happy to be able to help, and very happy for your family."

"Well everyone, if you have an hour please come help us welcome our children home. We want a big party, and you are our new best friends!" Karen echoed her husband's invitation.

On the trip home everyone chattered and tried to fill each other in on all the details of the last 48 hours. It hardly seemed possible that so much had happened in such a short time. They all agreed that life would never be the same again.

At a lull in the conversation, Karen quietly said to Bob, "There is still the matter of who tried to take Sara. And what are we going to do for money?"

Bob sighed as he answered, "I can only hope the police find those guys before they succeed in taking a child. This is such a crazy world—what is happening?" Then squeezing her hand he added, "Don't worry, love, I will get work again."

The neighborhood seemed unusually quiet when they arrived home. The usual gaggle of preschoolers playing in one another's fenced yards was absent. Probably gone shopping or having hot chocolate indoors, thought Karen absentmindedly.

Presently the others arrived, and everyone trooped triumphantly indoors. "Welcome to our humble home, Lori, James and John."

Turning to his children, Bob sang out, "Ta da—welcome home Mark and Sara!" He bowed with a flourish.

Everyone laughed and clapped. Karen felt a warmth and friendship that she found surprising. It seemed they had known each other forever. I guess going through adversity together bonds you more quickly, she thought.

Clearing her throat, Karen held up her hand. "I'd like to say a few words, if I can get past this lump in my throat. Then I'm going to get us some refreshments! These last two days have been the worst of my life. If it hadn't been for you, James, we couldn't have made it through that first horrible day—and we wouldn't have our children back I'm sure.

"Mother, if it wasn't for you, I shudder to think where our Sara and Mark would be right now."

"Lori and John, you went beyond the call of duty to help us. Thank you. Thank you all. Bob and I will never forget your compassion. You are now an honorary part of our family forever. Children say hello to your new Aunt Lori, Uncle James and Uncle John."

"Yep," Bob agreed, "you are definitely heroes to us. Thank you."

The next hour flew quickly as the little group got better acquainted. Sara seldom left her mother's lap and Mark wandered from his father's hugs to his mother's embrace. They all had acquired a new appreciation for the really important things in life.

They found out that Lori was a Christian, also. She and James seemed to have a lot in common to talk about. They were both single and happy with it that way.

John confessed that he and his wife were estranged. They had no children, and it had become too bitter of a pill for his wife to swallow. He had given a lot of thought to families over the last two days, though, and was ready to talk to his wife to see if they could patch things up.

Presently, James looked at his watch. "Oh! I'd better get going; I have another client coming to the office in about 45 minutes."

Karen was reluctant for the festivities to end. "This has been so nice. Would you all consider coming over next Saturday afternoon for a barbeque?"

"Would you mind if I brought my wife—if she will?" asked John.

"That would be great," Bob responded. "How about you two?"

"I can make it around 4:00," responded Lori.

"That's fine with me, too. Could I bring a few extra things to barbeque?" asked James.

"We'll have plenty, but go ahead if you wish." Karen was ever the gracious hostess.

"See you on Saturday, then . . . bye all." "Uncle" James tousled the children's hair on his way to the door. Opening the door, he nearly ran headlong into a neighbor just ready to ring the doorbell.

"Are Bob and Karen home?" The woman looked like she had been crying and was tightly holding the hand of a small girl.

"Just a minute, Ma'am."

James called over his shoulder, "Karen, you have company at the door."

"Is everything all right?" James turned again to the visitor, sensing trouble.

The woman ignored James and spoke over his shoulder, "Oh, there you two are. I was so afraid when I heard the news that they had finally succeeded in taking Sara . . ." her words trailed off, and she brushed the tears away again. "I'm sorry, can Tina come in and play upstairs with your children for a few minutes?"

"Of course, they would like that." Karen gestured for Sara to take Tina to the playroom. "Come in, Sharon, and tell us what has you so upset."

"I'm sorry to bother you, I can see you are busy with company—it's just so awful!" At this point, the neighbor broke down in earnest.

Immediately, Karen and her mother put their arms around her, guiding her to the sofa. The guys stood awkwardly around, shuffling from one foot to the other. James was the first to speak. "What do you mean by the news?"

Sharon looked up at James then to Karen, questioningly. "Excuse me, Sharon," Karen interrupted, "this is our attorney James Wright."

Sharon composed herself and replied, "Those men, in the black car, that tried to take Sara, have taken two girls just this morning—one off NE 160th and one off SE 180th. I was so afraid . . . They have an 'Amber Alert' out again. I knew it couldn't have been you, Bob—or Sara, either. Where were you this morning? Didn't you hear?"

"No, we hadn't heard. We had to go to court to regain custody of Mark and Sara. We just got back about an hour ago." Bob replied.

Sharon continued, "The police have told all parents to keep their children inside, or with them at all times, until they find these kidnappers. It's just awful. Oh, I hope they find those poor children soon."

They stood in silence, Sharon still sobbing, Bob and Karen holding hands. James walked over and sat down beside Sharon. "Sharon, I know you don't know me, but I'm a Christian. We have just had an amazing answer to prayer for the Johnson's children. Would you—would you all mind," he glanced around at the group, "if we prayed for these children?"

"That would be wonderful," Marie entered the conversation. "I would very much like to have you pray." Everyone nodded in agreement.

Bowing his head James began "Our Father in Heaven, we are so grateful to You for the miraculous way You have brought Mark and Sara home. We ask you to be with this family in a special way. Bless and heal their hurts and their hearts and lead them closer to you, I pray. Now, Lord, two more little ones have been viciously taken from their homes. Please watch over them, keep them safe, and if it is in Your will, please send someone to help them. You know how it is to have a child away from home. Thank You in the name of Your Son, Jesus. Amen."

James stood up, and shook hands around. "Now, I really must leave. I will look forward to seeing all you folk on Saturday afternoon." He quickly took his leave, asking them to tell the children goodbye for him.

The rest of the group continued to discuss this latest kidnapping, and decided to watch the live events unfolding on the news. Karen would think how thankful she was to have Sara safe at home, then her imagination would run away and she would see herself in the position of those poor, weeping mothers. How her heart ached for them. She found James' prayer echoing around and around in her mind—Jesus, please send someone to help them—it became a part of her, almost like breathing.

9

OUT OF CONFUSION

Deliver me, O my God, out of the hand of the wicked,
out of the hand of the unrighteous and cruel man."
Psalm 71:4

Lori, John, and the neighbors left shortly after James. Marie stayed a bit longer to read some stories to Sara and provide reassurance of her safety. At last the Johnson's were alone. The remainder of the day was spent in mundane chores of laundry and other housework. Bob and Karen decided it would be best to keep the television news off, while trying to regain some sense of normal life.

Karen dressed Sara's injuries as she had been instructed, then rocked her and talked with her until she fell asleep for an afternoon nap. Bob and Mark worked on a model airplane Mark had wanted help with for a long time.

By early evening Sara was beginning to worry about the kidnapped children and wanted to know what was happening. Reluctantly Karen flipped on the news. Reporters on both local and national news had preliminary information about the kidnappers. There had been a nine-year-old brother walking with one of the girls who was taken and he was able to give a fair description of one of the men. When Sara saw the police drawing she stiffened and started to scream, "That's him! That's him!" Then she sobbed uncontrollably.

Bob hurried to sweep her into his arms and into the other room. "Don't worry, Punkin," he soothed her. "The police are going to catch him. Lots of people are looking all over for them. I am not going anywhere until he and his helper are put in jail. They won't hurt you again, ever."

Karen hated for Sara to have to even think about it, but realized she would be dealing with it for some time to come. She continued watching the news, hoping there were some solid leads in the case. The FBI had just begun to put together a profile.

Local police had roadblocks set up at every exit from the Portland area. Everyone along the I-5 and I-84 corridors was asked to look for the small black car. Volunteer turnout had exceeded one thousand—and was growing—straining the staging capacity of officials. It seemed everyone was fed up with crimes against children and they were not going to tolerate one more vile act. There was a vigilante attitude among many of those volunteering.

Karen flicked off the set with one thought in mind: Jesus, please send someone to help the children. Walking throughout the house she checked all the windows to be sure they were locked. She turned on lights in the back and front yards. The doors were double locked and then she checked all the locks again. Finally she was satisfied their home was secure.

Bob decided to call the police and let them know that Sara, too, had positively identified the man in the drawing as her kidnapper. The police thanked Bob and said they would need to talk with her, but hopefully they were going to have the perpetrators in custody first. Bob smiled ruefully as he hung up the phone. "It sure is nice to be appreciated instead of suspected," he told Karen.

At bedtime Sara and Mark insisted on sleeping with their parents. Everyone was a little nervous so they decided to have a pajama party. Karen made hot chocolate and they roasted marshmallows in the fireplace. Marie called to check on the children and they invited her over to share their party. Willingly she accepted, feeling a little nervous herself with all the people and police cruising her neighborhood.

When Marie arrived she brought a CD someone had given her a long time ago. The music started to play a soft, soothing melody and the words began "What a friend we have in Jesus, all our sins and griefs to bear . . ."

"Mom, what a beautiful song!" Karen was astonished at the appropriateness of the message. "When did you get this?"

"When your father was still alive someone came to the door selling books. We bought one about the life of Christ and this CD, by The Heralds Quartet, was a free gift. I've never played it before. It is very nice, isn't it?"

They all spread sleeping bags on the living room floor and sofas, turned off the lights and prepared for the night. The fireplace still flickered and crackled. Soft music floated around them. Everything seemed better than it had for a long, long time. Karen wondered about that. How could everything be better when they had gone through so much? What did that song say? "In His arms He'll take and shield thee, thou shalt find a solace there." Maybe I am finding solace in God's arms. Wow, what a thought . . . Jesus, please send someone to help the children. She drifted off to sleep with thoughts of family, God and comfort.

The events of the week and of this day filled her mind and somewhere in the night she began to dream. Across the screen of her mind there were violent images of children of all ages being snatched from their own warm beds . . . lightning and thunder . . . sirens. The jumble of images began to organize and she somehow knew the thunder and lightning were God telling her something. Then she saw James Wright. In one hand he held an open book; with the other he was pointing to something in the Bible. It seemed very important to her to know what he was trying to tell her, but she couldn't find her way through the darkness surrounding her. She started to climb some steps—lots of steps up a steep hill. She crossed roads and passed huge trees in the darkness that seemed to reach out for her. She climbed on and on. Just when she despaired of ever reaching James, there he was beside her. They seemed to be on the small mountain's top. She wearily sat down on a park bench. Now he was pointing to something else. She could barely make out something reflecting in the dim lamplight by the winding road. It was the outline of a small, dark car. She could hear cries. Below, in the city, she could hear sirens all around. But all she could hear up on the mountain were cries. Then the faces of the

51

two kidnapped girls flashed before her, and she awoke with a scream.

Leaping out of bed she raced for the telephone. Bob and Marie had been awakened by her cry, but the children slept on. Not stopping to answer their questions she dialed "911."

"911, what is your emergency?" she heard the voice say.

"Please, I have just had a dream and God showed me where the two kidnapped girls are. Please listen! I'm not crazy and I don't even know God. But I know where the girls are, sort of." She raced on breathlessly, afraid the 911 operator would think it a crank call and hang up on her. "In my dream I was standing on a mountain top. I had climbed many steps up the hill, across roads and through tall trees. When I got to the top I sat on a park bench and I could see the outline of a small dark car in the light of a streetlamp by the road.

Then, the faces of the two kidnapped girls flashed before my eyes. Oh, please send someone . . . they aren't looking there, the sirens are all below, please hurry."

The seasoned 911 operator was speechless for a moment. "You had a dream? This is your emergency?"

"Please, I've never called 911 before in my life. Please at least try. Send someone to look on a mountaintop. It's dark, no houses, just the car, and a streetlamp, and a park bench under the trees."

"OK, ma'am, calm down. I'm giving this information to the police because they have asked to have any and all tips, no matter how crazy they sound, referred to them. They will have to decide what to do with it. Thank you for calling."

"Oh, thank you, thank you." Karen gently put the receiver in its cradle and turned to her husband and mother. "You won't believe the dream I just had!"

"We heard dear," her mother spoke. "What an incredible dream. Do you really think God was talking to you?"

"Mom, there's more . . . James Wright was in the dream. At first it was all a jumble of things, but once it started to clear, there he was. He was holding an open book and pointing to something in it. It seemed very important—like life and death—for me to know what he was trying to tell me. Then he was beside me and we were on a small mountain, he was pointing to the car. Well, you heard the rest."

"A week ago I would have laughed, but today I think anything is possible," Bob joined the discussion. "If you believe God spoke to you, well anything is possible."

"I have to call James first thing in the morning. I have to know what he was trying to tell me in the dream." Karen would have preferred to call him at that very hour. "What time is it, anyway?"

"It's just after midnight. I looked at the clock on the mantel when you jumped out of bed," Bob told her. "It said 12:00 o'clock straight up."

All three were wide-awake now and went quietly to the kitchen for a hot drink. "Let's turn on the little TV under the counter and see if there is any news on the kidnapping." Karen was sure they would have caught the two soon after her phone call.

"We interrupt this broadcast for a live report. Channel 7 news has this exclusive view from the top of Mt. Tabor. Police, acting on an anonymous tip have just taken into custody the two kidnappers . . . just a moment . . . Here they come from behind the city reservoir. There—oh look, they have the girls—they're alive! They're alive!"

Here the reporter's voice cracked and there was silence with the live feed. He cleared his throat. "I'm sorry, this is live and, well, lots of us have little girls at home. I'm not a religious man, but I thank God for finding these two girls so quickly." Then he summoned up his professional demeanor and continued the broadcast, but they had heard enough.

The three adults in the Johnson home sat in silence. Knowing it was possible that God had spoken to Karen, and knowing He had spoken to her were two different things. Karen was almost afraid. She felt different, yet unable to identify the new feeling. Strange. Elated. Stunned.

The minutes stretched out; five, ten, twenty. Bob turned to his wife. "Karen, how . . . why . . ." He couldn't even phrase a coherent sentence.

"I don't know, I don't know, I'm a little scared. I don't know what to do. I have to call James Wright. He'll know what to do."

"Now? Do you think that's a good idea? It's very late." Marie objected, but not very strongly.

"When they took Sara from the hospital he said to call him if anything else came up, if they arrested Bob or anything, even if it was the middle of the night. Maybe he won't mind about this." As no one else objected she picked up the phone.

"Hello, James Wright, attorney," came the sleepy voice.

"James, this is Karen Johnson, I'm sorry to call you so late."

"Karen, is everything OK? Is Sara all right?" James was now fully awake.

"Yes, it's just that, well, I don't know what to say. I'm scared. I had a dream that you and God showed me where the two kidnapped girls were. I woke up and called 911 and told them my dream. Just now we watched a live news report. They found the girls and the two men and the black car—just where you and God showed me."

Now it was James' turn to be silent. "Wow. Wow. Sorry, I'm at a loss for words. Nothing like that has ever happened to me before, either. God must be leading you to something very special; what a blessing. They found the girls? Were they alive?"

"Yes, they are alive. Something else in the dream has me puzzled. Before you showed me where the girls were found, you were a long way off. In one hand you were holding a book, with the other you were pointing to something in it. The thunder and lightning, which seemed to be God's voice, made me understand that it was very important for me to know something. It seemed a life and death matter, but I couldn't get to you. Then suddenly there you were beside me. Do you know what that would mean?"

Karen could hear James thumbing through a book, or something. "Praise God! Karen," his voice sounded almost reverent. "In Romans 10:14, in the Bible, it says 'How then shall they call on Him in whom they have not believed? And how shall they believe in Him of whom they have not heard? And how shall they hear without a preacher?' I think God sent you a message. He wants you to know Him, to believe in Him. I'm not a preacher, but if God told you I have truth, then I will be happy to share it with you. Truth certainly is a matter of life and death, as you have learned this week."

"You are right there. I think we all would like to hear what you have to say. Can you bring your Bible with you on Saturday?"

"I will be more than happy to. Are you feeling better now?" James could hear courage in her voice now instead of the fear.

"Yes and thank you for letting me wake you up. Goodnight." Karen still felt a little awkward about bothering someone in the middle of the night.

"I'm very glad you did wake me up—there is lots of good news and much to be thankful for tonight. Goodnight now, and may God give you rest."

Karen tried to quote the Bible text to Bob and her Mother, "James said God wants us to know and believe in him. He read it from the Bible. What do you think of that?" Suddenly she felt very sleepy. "This has been enough for one night. I think I'm going back to bed—how about you guys?"

"Way more than enough," Bob agreed. "I'm right behind you."

Marie said she would be along shortly; there was something she needed to do.

10

THE DEAD OF NIGHT

"The test of a religion or philosophy is the number
of things it can explain."
Ralph Waldo Emerson, 1836 A.D.

Thursday and Friday were "sick" days for Mark and Sara. They had been too traumatized by the events of the first half of the week to want to jump back into the school routine. Bob and Karen didn't want to let them out of their sight, either. The two kidnappings in one week had caused a great upheaval in the city of Portland. No one felt safe. Many parents kept their children home from school even after the perpetrators had been caught.

Saturday morning dawned overcast and gloomy. The old saying in Portland, "If you don't like the weather, wait a minute," wasn't true that day. The Johnson family was disappointed—the backyard barbeque might have to be postponed. All day they worked and prepared, watching the sky, hoping the sun might peek out in the afternoon.

One by one the invited guests arrived, cheerful and rosy-cheeked from the crisp air. Then just as they were deciding whether to brave the cold to cook outdoors, rain began to fall in great sheets.

"Well, I guess that decides that question!" Bob laughed. "I vote for staying inside and grilling on the stove."

Everyone heartily agreed and trooped into the kitchen to help with preparations. James produced his contribution: vegetarian hot dogs and hamburgers with all the fixings. "Thought you might like to compare these and see if you like eating the grass better than eating the cow that ate the grass." He chuckled at his own joke.

"I've never seen anything like this," Karen said. "Well, thanks. I'll sure give it a try. Grass. Hmm."

The topic of conversation was Karen's dream that led to the kidnapped girls being found. John and his wife, Denise, appeared shaken. "We were so upset about those girls we went out looking for them in our car," John confessed. "After talking, we had agreed to get back together. So this just seemed like an important thing for us to do. I was mad enough to ram their car with mine if I found it; but of course I never saw it. It's hard to believe you are the one who helped find them, Karen!"

Lori was standing at the patio doors watching the rain. Out of the corner of her eye she caught an unfamiliar movement. "Oh!" She cried out, "There's a tornado."

Racing to the doors and windows everyone gasped at the rare sight. Then as suddenly as it had appeared it dissipated and was gone. The rain still drummed on the roof and the wind howled.

"You know, this might be a good time to talk about the rest of your dream, Karen." James reached for the Bible he had brought along and sat down at the table in the kitchen.

All eyes turned questioningly to Karen. "What is he talking about?" asked Lori.

As Karen briefly related the dream she was once again drawn into the confusion and terror she had felt. "I'm afraid, James." She drew her sweater closer. "If that is God talking to me, He scares me."

"That is very natural, Karen. You have experienced something unfamiliar. Before we go on, let's have a word of prayer." James bowed his head and they all followed his lead. "God, our Father, please help us to understand Your words to us as we read about You in the Bible. Amen."

"If you will indulge me," James began, "I would like to start from the beginning. It starts with the creation of our whole world." With that he opened his Bible and read from Genesis 1, verses 27 and 31. "'So God created man in His own image, in the image of God He created him; male and female He created them. God saw all that He had made, and it was very good. And there was evening, and there was morning—the sixth day.'

"If I were in a court of law today, I would at this time bring in my evidence to support the reality of what this scripture states, namely that God created a man and a woman from the dust of the earth. But in the interest of time I'll defer that evidence to another study. OK?"

Looking around, James saw heads nodding, and he proceeded. "God not only created man, but he provided a most wonderful environment for the first couple to live in. He called it Eden. Scripture is unclear as to how long Adam and Eve lived harmoniously there, but eventually they made a big mistake. Has anybody here made a mistake?" Intent faces broke out in wry smiles, as everyone could relate.

"So I take it you all know what I'm talking about," he smiled. "When children disobey their parents, the results are not fun. When people go against the will of the Creator of the world, it isn't fun either. That's what happened here. Adam and Eve sinned, which means they disobeyed God.

"They were not the first to do so. God had created another order of beings called angels, and one of those beings originated sin prior to man's creation. Because of his great love, God allowed this angel, Lucifer, to live. Not only did Lucifer sin, but he also caused a third of the angels in heaven to sin and Revelation 12:4 tells us they were all cast out of heaven. In fact, they were given the freedom to tempt Adam and Eve to test their loyalty to God. Oh, how different our world would be, had Adam and Eve not disobeyed God.

"Here is the account of what happened when Satan tempted them to eat of the tree that God had forbidden." James began to read from Genesis 3. "'You will not surely die,' the serpent said to the woman. When the woman saw that the fruit of the tree was good for food and pleasing to the eye, and also desirable for gaining wisdom, she took some and ate it. She also gave some to her husband, who was with her, and he ate it (Genesis 3:4, 6, NIV)."

James sighed, "Here began all of the evil that has grown to fill our world, and includes the kidnapping of the little girls in Portland this week. Here is the first rebellion against law and the first lie. God said Adam and Eve could eat from every tree but one. Eve, and then Adam, believed the serpent—Satan—who told them God was keeping the truth from them. Then Satan told them they wouldn't die. But God had told them they would—and they did. Humans were created to live forever, not die. Yet to this day, we keep on dying as a result of disobedience."

"That's what I believe, also," Lori exclaimed. "I believe we live forever, too! If you choose God's side you live forever in heaven; if you choose Satan's side, you live forever in hell."

"OK, I can see how that seems to say we live forever. Remember, it was the first lie that we won't die. Let's look at that another time, though, if you don't mind." James tried to bring everyone back to the topic.

Here Bob raised his hand. "Guess I feel like I'm in school," he chuckled. "Anyway, I want to know what happened to Adam and Eve. What did God do when they disobeyed?"

James smiled. "Good news, guys! God promised them right then and there that He would send a Savior who would free them from Satan's rule. You can study all about it right here in this book." Here he waved the Bible triumphantly.

"But what about the dream I had? Why would God talk to me?" Karen was still perplexed.

"Karen, you are a sign that God's promise is real! Joel 2:28 and 29 says, in part, 'your sons and daughters will prophesy, your old men will dream dreams, both men and women.' This prophet was talking about events to happen just before the end of the world, as we know it. God did send a Savior, His own Son, Jesus Christ. He lived a perfect life, was killed by those who hated him, rose from the dead, and returned to heaven. Now it is time for Him to come back to earth and take all those who love Him back to heaven to live forever!

"Your dream is proof that Jesus is going to come very soon. He wants you to know about Him and His great sacrifice for you. He wants you to love Him. He talked to you in a dream to get your attention." James paused, then added, "He would miss you forever if you weren't with Him in heaven. He just had to tell you."

Karen looked around at the faces of her family and friends. Tears were forming in her eyes. "I can't believe God would talk to me. Why would He love me? I want to know more about Him."

"Me, too," Bob agreed, clearing his throat. "It's kind of confusing to me, but I can't deny that Karen had a real dream that led to those girls being found. Maybe there is a God that I should learn about."

One by one the whole group made brief statements of interest and commitment. Marie spoke last. "I know about creation and Jesus. I was raised to believe in angels and supernatural events. In fact I talked to my dear husband all about this dream of Karen's—right after she told me about it—and he agreed it was from God."

"Oh, will your husband be joining us?" James asked.

"Mom! What are you talking about?" Karen was perplexed. "Dad has been dead for years."

Friends and family, old and new, looked on in amazement as Marie smilingly spoke, "Dad has come back. I am no longer alone. He visits every night with me; just sits on the edge of the bed and holds my hand. It is so wonderful!"

"Ahh." James reached for Marie's hand. "Will you do something for me, Marie, the next time your husband visits? Will you ask Jesus—aloud—to come be with you?"

"I guess so. Yes, I am sure my darling would like that." Marie nodded with enthusiasm. "I'm sure he would like that."

"Now, friends, the time has come for me to leave." James stood up and began to shake hands around the circle. "Hope you enjoyed my 'high-tech' meat."

"Yes!" Karen bubbled, "It was really good. I was surprised; and it didn't taste at all like grass."

They all had a good laugh and the party broke up.

11

DUST TO DUST

"Death is not an event in life; we do not experience death."
Ludwig Wittgenstein, 1922 A.D.

Over the next few weeks the Johnson household gradually returned to a semblance of order. The children went back to school and the flurry of concern that met them was soon over-shadowed by holiday programs and parties. Bob and Karen had been vindicated in the eyes of their former employers and having work again made the whole family very thankful at Thanksgiving time.

Somewhere in the routine of things, the events of October began to take on the hue of a passing nightmare. The new group of friends hadn't had time to get together again since that first weekend. Even Marie had been noticeably absent from their home. Then, just after Thanksgiving, she called and asked Karen to come visit her.

When Karen arrived she saw that her Mother had been crying.

"Why, Mom! What's wrong? Are you ill?" Karen rushed to Marie's side.

"Oh, Karen, no I'm not ill. It's just, well, I can't believe he's really gone." With that there was a fresh outburst of tears.

"You can't believe who is gone? Do you mean Dad?" Karen asked.

"Yes. And I don't mean just from four years ago—I mean from now. He had been coming to visit me every night. Then after your attorney friend suggested I ask Jesus to come, he left. He just left. As soon as I said Jesus name he got this terrible, evil look on his face and just vanished. He hasn't come back since. I've waited every night and even tried talking to him again, but nothing has worked."

Karen just sat with her mouth open. "What are you saying? I don't understand."

"I don't understand, either. First Dad dies, then a few weeks ago, he comes back. He said he was in Heaven and happy. Then when I mention Jesus to him—he leaves. It doesn't make any sense to me." Marie suddenly brightened. "Let's call James Wright and see if he can help me. Maybe I said it wrong or something and he will know how to get Dad back. Will you call him?"

Karen looked doubtful, but reached for the telephone to dial her attorney's number. "Hello, James? This is Karen Johnson. How have you been? We are all fine, thanks. Say, I'm at my Mom's and she tells me her visits from Dad have suddenly ended when she talked to him about Jesus. She is very upset and wondered if maybe you could be of some help."

Marie watched Karen's face eagerly for any sign of encouragement. The conversation seemed to be a bit one-sided with James doing most of the talking. "What's he saying, Karen?" She could wait no longer.

"Wait, Mom, just a minute." And then into the phone, "OK. Thanks, James. Why don't you come over this next Sunday afternoon about four o'clock? See you then. Bye."

Turning to Marie, Karen repeated what James had just told her. "He said not to worry, that he will show you from the Bible everything you want to know about Dad. He's coming over Sunday afternoon to show us all. I think I'll see if the others would like to come, too."

Marie visibly relaxed. "Oh, how wonderful. I can't wait. Thank you, dear, for all your help. I'll be fine now. Please go along home and don't worry about me a bit."

"Come on over for dinner tonight, Mom. The kids are missing you and so am I." Karen gave her Mom a hug and kiss, then rose to leave.

"I'll do that, Karen, thanks. Let's play that CD about Jesus being our Friend, too. It is a comfort to me."

Sunday afternoon finally arrived, and with it the familiar group of new friends. James knocked on the door first, and had barely entered when John and Denise drove up. Lori was right behind them. Marie had stayed overnight Saturday so she would be sure to be there on time. There were warm hugs and handshakes around. Then Marie called the meeting to order.

"Everyone, I'm so glad you could come, but would it be rude if I asked you to visit later and we could study the Bible first?" She had her Bible in hand along with pen and paper.

"Marie, you are prepared!" John teased. "This looks serious. It's OK with me if we start now. What was the topic again?"

"The topic," retorted Marie, "is where has my husband gone?"

There were some uneasy smiles around the group, but James spoke up in her defense. "Marie has a very valid point, folks. Where do we go when we die? Are we aware of what goes on here on earth, or maybe in heaven or hell?"

Karen led the way to the dining table. "Have a seat around the table, if you like. I've put a stack of paper and pencils in the middle if anyone wants to take notes. James thought that would be a good idea. There is also a pitcher of juice and some cookies if you're hungry." Karen smiled as she handed each of her children a cookie.

Bob opened the discussion with a question. "James, I appreciate all you've been telling us and showing us from the Bible. But, do you really think it's reliable? I had a teacher who said it was just a collection of fables and poetry—good reading for English class, but nothing more than that."

"Yes, I've been wondering about that, too," John confessed.

James turned to Marie. "If you don't mind, Marie, I will answer both your question and Bob's. Be patient with me and you will find what you want to know, even though it may not seem like it at first."

"That's fine, James, you know best." Marie settled back in her chair and picked up her pen. "Let's get started."

Lori volunteered to pray and ask God to direct their study. Then opening her Bible, she waited.

"There are a number of ways to validate the writings of scripture," James began. "Today we will look at just one of the methods, namely prophecy. And to make it simple and quick we will only focus on one prophecy. But first I want to ask if any of you here has ever tried your hand at predicting multiple events years ahead of their actual fulfillment?" No one moved.

"The probability of that happening without error seems so remote that it would be ridiculous to even try," Bob ventured.

"Well then," James smiled, "I think you will appreciate the story we are about to read. It is found in the book of Daniel, chapter two." At that he opened his Bible and began to read verses one through three. "In the second year of his reign, Nebuchadnezzar had dreams; his mind was troubled and he could not sleep. So the king summoned the magicians, enchanters, sorcerers and astrologers to tell him what he had dreamed. When they came in and stood before the king, he said to them, 'I have had a dream that troubles me and I want to know what it means.'"

Looking up James smiled, "So what we have here is a king who had a dream but couldn't remember it, and he wanted the experts to tell him what the dream was and then interpret it for him. Now that is a tough assignment, right?" There was unanimous agreement all around.

"You probably would agree, also, that if someone could do what the king wanted it would require help beyond what most humans have available to them. None of the king's advisers could provide what he wanted. He was ready to kill them all. When Daniel heard about the king's problem he wanted a shot at this seemingly impossible assignment. It happened that Daniel was a follower of God, the same God who had created the world some 2,000 years earlier. He figured God had the answer to the king's dilemma and he prayed that God would reveal it to him. So we read in verse 19: 'During the night the mystery was revealed to Daniel in a vision. Then Daniel praised the God of heaven.'

"Once Daniel let it be known he could provide answers to the king's questions he was ushered into the king's court where he told the king about his dream. There was a great image with a head of gold, a breast and arms of silver, hips and thighs of brass, legs of iron, and finally feet and toes of iron mixed with clay. He went on to interpret the image as a series of kingdoms.

"The first, represented by the head of gold was Babylon. The second, was an inferior kingdom represented by the breast and arms of silver. We learn in Daniel 5:30, that kingdom was Medo-Persia. The bronze kingdom that would rule the whole earth next was Greece. Following Greece, Rome ruled with an iron hand—well represented by the legs of iron. Finally, the feet and toes part of iron and part of clay represent the divided world as we know it; some countries strong, some weak, never able to fully unite into a world power.

"The king was so overwhelmed, verses 46-48 tell us, that he 'fell prostrate before Daniel and paid him honor . . . Surely your God is the God of gods and the Lord of kings . . . He made him ruler over the entire province of Babylon.' This historical figure made one of God's prophets a ruler over the mighty kingdom of Babylon.

"Those countries certainly ruled the world in that order." John had been listening intently. "I'm a history buff and that surely happened. I never knew it was in the Bible, too."

"OK, let's assume that much is true. How can we know the rest of the Bible is true?" Bob was visibly struggling to understand.

"Let me turn to a verse in the New Testament, written after Jesus lived on earth. Second Timothy 3:16 says 'all Scripture is God-breathed and is useful for teaching, rebuking, correcting and training in righteousness.' The same God who created us and predicted kingdoms thousands of years in advance assured us He gave us the scriptures. It is not some collection of fables or meaningless poetry, but useful information to help us learn about Him."

Lori spoke up here. "Ultimately, Bob, it comes down to a matter of faith. You see something like this that you can read in history books and you gain faith to believe in the things that can't be proved by history. They do get proven though, by the changes they make in our lives."

"You're right on, Lori." James nodded in agreement. "The Bible tells us to test it, try it, and see if it's true. In fact, Marie's dilemma about seeing something that looked and sounded like her husband is exactly what testing the Bible is all about. Let's take a break and then spend a few more minutes answering her question."

Getting up and stretching, Bob looked out the window. "Wow! Look at the storm that's blown in; the trees are bending almost in half. It seems unusually dark—well look at that! There are no streetlights on and I don't see any house lights anywhere around us. That's odd. How can our lights still be on? I'd better grab the candles and flashlights just in case ours go out, too."

Everyone followed Bob's lead and checked out the weather and lights. There were exclamations of amazement and concern. All were wondering just how they would be able to get to their homes if all the traffic lights were out. Soon Bob had the pile of flashlights, candles, and matches on the table.

"Let's get started with the answer to Mom's question," Bob suggested, "before we do lose our lights."

Settling down in their chairs with only a few worried glances towards the window, they began again to search for answers. Marie leaned forward eagerly to hear every word.

"First of all I need to remind you about the problem our first parents, Adam and Eve, had in the Garden of Eden. Remember how Satan disguised as a serpent told Eve that God was wrong—that she would not die if she disobeyed Him?"

Heads nodded around the circle. "I don't think anyone here doubts that people die," Lori asserted. "It's what happens after they die that is Marie's concern. Am I right, Marie?"

"Yes," agreed Marie. "Just where is my dear husband?"

"I know that none of us have been dead, so what we know of death we must learn from a reliable source. There is only one source that I know of where someone can see into the future with 100% accuracy and that is the Bible. Let's turn now to Genesis 3:19. After Adam and Eve disobeyed God, things changed. God told them everything would be much more difficult for them because of their sin. They would work hard all their lives then 'return to the ground, since from it you were taken; for dust you are and to dust you will return.' They were banned from their garden home and angels with flaming swords guarded the way to the tree of life. (Look there in verse 24). This tells us that our bodies, when buried after death, return to the basic elements from which we were made. The tree of life was the only way to keep on living and they no longer had access to it. Is everyone in agreement on this point?"

Again heads nodded and murmurs of "That's clear to me" were heard from several. Bob looked out the window again and noted theirs was seemingly still the only house around with electricity.

"Now let's turn to Ecclesiastes 9:5 and 6," James began. "Here, Marie, let me help you find that verse." The few Bibles in the group were shared from one to another as each text was found. Everyone, even Mark and Sara, were taking notes so they could remember what they were learning. "Marie, will you read that verse?"

"For the living know that they will die, but the dead know nothing; they have no further reward, and even the memory of them is forgotten. Their love, their hate and their jealousy have long since vanished; never again will they have a part in anything that happens under the sun." Marie paused, then looked up thoughtfully. "That couldn't have been my husband visiting, could it? Who was it?"

"No, Marie, it wasn't your husband. You're very wise in your understanding of this verse. Do you remember how I suggested that you invite Jesus to join you? What happened then?" James was gently encouraging her.

"Yes, surely. As soon as I said Jesus' name he vanished. I don't understand that at all."

"Let's turn to the New Testament, the book of Luke chapter 10 verse 17. Prior to this Jesus had sent out seventy-two people to witness, heal, and teach others about Him. They came back joyful and said, 'Lord, even the demons submit to us in your name.' Satan talked to Eve disguised as a serpent in a tree. He talked to you, Marie, disguised as your husband. But—just like in the days of these disciples—Jesus has power over Satan and his angels—sometimes called demons. When we ask Him for help He gives us power over them, too. That's why the being pretending to be your husband had to leave when you spoke Jesus' name."

"Just one other thought," James continued just as Lori was about to say something. "The description of Jesus' death, burial and resurrection given in the book of John, chapters 19 and 20, shows that Jesus was definitely dead. He was buried in a tomb over Friday, Sabbath, and into Sunday. And as John 20:10-18 says, He definitely had not gone anywhere—to heaven or to some place called hell—during that time. By the way, most of the Greek words translated as 'hell' literally mean the grave. None of the words mean a place of punishment for sinners that burns forever and ever."

This time Lori was quicker to respond. "I have always been taught that people were immortal, either going to heaven to live forever when they die, or going to hell to burn forever when they die. This makes a lot more sense to me. I want to study this more. Is there somewhere I can go to get help on the Internet? I spend a lot of time online and it would be easier for me to do on my own schedule."

"There are several good resources online. One is the Discover Bible study you can access by going to www.biblestudies.com. You can also get them through the mail, and it's all totally free. Another great series is Panorama of Prophecy, an interactive CD from Amazing Facts that you can get at www.bibleuniverse.com. I would be happy to help anytime you like, also," James offered.

The study abruptly ended as the house lights went dark and their attention was drawn to the shrieking storm outside. "The neighbors' lights are still out and it appears the whole city is dark." Bob made a sweeping gesture. Then a knock sent him from his window perch to the front door.

"Hello." The stranger at the door was struggling to keep his balance. "I saw the lights on at your house until a minute ago. My car just stalled outside and I was hoping to get some help."

Bob turned his light toward the street where it reflected from a car stopped virtually in the middle of the street. At that very moment, a tree in the neighbors' yard blew over with a thunderous crash right in front of the stranger's car. Debris rained down all around them. "Quick, come in before you get hurt!" Bob pulled the man inside and shut the door. Looking toward the dining area where candles now flickered, he motioned for the man to make himself comfortable and bolted the door behind them.

12

BEGINNING OF THE END

"Nation will rise against nation, and kingdom against kingdom.
There will be famines and earthquakes in various places. All
these are the beginning of birth pains."
Matthew 24:7, 8, NIV

This seems like a repeat of the Columbus Day storm of 1962," Bob stated. "Were any of you living here then? Did you know there was an earthquake just a couple weeks after that? It was a big one, too, 5.6 or something like that."

A chorus of "No's" came from the others in the group. Only Marie and her family had lived in the area that long ago. She was nervous seeing the strength of the storm at hand. "I didn't like it then and I don't like it now!" she stated emphatically.

Karen began to put some of her nursing and disaster training to work and urged the others away from windows. "Falling trees or blowing debris might break them and injure someone." She barked orders like a sergeant. "Bob, you and John move the sofa clear to this end of the living room. It will be safer away from the windows and under this beam structure."

"You're right, dear, and while we're at it, let's bring the refrigerator over to the edge of the kitchen where it can shield us from the large dining room windows. James, would you and our new friend give a hand for that?"

"Be happy to," they both chorused. "By the way," the stranger added, "I'm Steven Pierce, judge for the Juvenile Court here."

There was a collective gasp, and several flashlights turned onto his face at once. "Oh! I'm sorry, I didn't mean to startle you." Judge Pierce was momentarily at a loss for words at the reaction of his benefactors.

James was the first to speak. "I don't know how I could have missed recognizing you, sir. I am attorney James Wright, and these are my good friends Bob and Karen Johnson, their children Mark and Sara, and Karen's mother, Marie."

Now it was the Judge's turn to be surprised. "I remember your family. Just a month or two ago you were in my courtroom."

"Yes sir," Bob began, "and we can't thank you enough for the courageous stand you took for our family. You are a good . . ." but the sentence was never finished. The crashing of glass brought everyone's attention back to the tasks at hand. There was a scramble to move furniture and prepare as safe a place as possible for the little group.

"Over there, Bob." Karen shone her light toward the kitchen door where the wind was now whipping rain through the curtains. "Can you find something to cover it? We'll start to get really cold in here with that open."

"Yeah, I think I can make it into the garage around the mess. I have some plywood in there. And, I'd better nail some on a few other windows on that side, too."

"We'll give you a hand," John gestured to the other men to follow.

The children had been looking on the activities as a big adventure until the window broke. Sara now began to whimper. Although she had been quiet all evening, Denise quickly went into action. "Come Sara, sit beside me and let me tell you a story." She then proceeded to draw first one, then another of the children and adults into the tale she was telling. Using only her voice she wrapped them in word pictures that buffered them from the raging storm outside.

John had returned and was sitting on the arm of the sofa next to his wife. "Denise, I never saw this side of you before. You have a real way with children. I can see why you have wanted children of your own so badly. I hope that we can have a child soon."

"That's good dear," Denise replied, "because I have an announcement I've been waiting all evening to make. I'm pregnant!"

Bedlam ensued, close to the magnitude of the storm outside. Even Judge Pierce, now introduced to group, offered his sincere congratulations.

John was ecstatic. "This is the best storm ever!" he declared laughing.

"This calls for a celebration," Karen added. "Let's build a fire in the fireplace to keep warm and I'll get some food from the frig to roast over it. It's getting late and I'm sure we will all make it through this night better if we aren't hungry. Kids, will you get the marshmallow sticks from the closet by the fireplace?"

Bob added, "I think we're all going to be here tonight. I hope no one needs to go home, because I've checked out that tree in the street and it has us all barricaded in. We have lots of blankets and pillows, so make yourselves comfortable."

The next hours were spent eating a makeshift dinner, trying to get comfortable, and discussing all the events of the day. The Johnsons were pleased to learn that Judge Pierce was also a Christian. He had a presence that made them all feel safer and was truly their hero.

One by one the refugees drifted off to sleep and the fire died away. Toward morning they were once more taken by surprise as the house began to shake violently. Now they dove for the cover of the large, sturdy old dining table still covered with Bibles and carefully scripted notes.

After a minute or two the shaking stopped. Fearfully they peeked out from under their shelter. Sara, crying, had her head buried in her mother's shoulder. They could see some damage to pictures and dishes that had fallen but it didn't look too bad.

There were a few mild aftershocks over the next few minutes, then, just as a beautiful sunrise was forming, things finally quieted. One by one they edged away from the makeshift shelter and began assessing the damage. There were some small cracks in the walls and fireplace. The kitchen was in worse shape with lots of things shaken from shelves onto the floor.

Bob methodically examined the physical structure of their home and the fireplace.

"Everything still looks fairly intact," he stated. "I'm glad we decided not to go with natural gas on our street a few years ago. Turning to his wife he nodded. "Karen, I'll go upstairs to check things out and get some clean clothes for the kids. I want to make sure everything is safe."

The other men had gone outside as the day was getting lighter and found quite a few of the neighbors milling aimlessly around. They looked a bit shell-shocked. One of them came up to James and asked if he had been in "this house" last night, pointing toward Bob's home.

"Yes, we were all stuck there during the storm," James replied.

"Well, I can't figure how your electricity was on and all the rest of the city was blacked out." He seemed rather upset at them. "Do you have a generator or something there?"

"No, there's no generator or anything different. I didn't realize we were the only ones with electricity. We were so engrossed in a Bible study we hardly noticed the storm." James tried to appease the irate man.

At this point Judge Pierce stepped up. "Good morning, sir, I'm Judge Steven Pierce; I hope there isn't a problem here." His voice was calm, but there was a commanding presence about him that seemed to cause the neighbor to shrink back.

"No, no, not a problem, Judge. Just wondering. Got to get back and check on things. He raised his arm in a gesture that seemed half a wave and half protecting himself.

"Let's go back inside," John suggested. "I don't feel very comfortable all of a sudden."

Once back in the house they all gathered around the table. Karen was scrambling eggs on the portable camping stove Bob had unearthed in the garage and things were starting to smell good. "I want the children to have some breakfast and you are all welcome to share with us before you have to face this mess." She sighed as she looked around. "I'd better see if I can reach the family I was supposed to work for today. I hope they are OK. The grandfather I care for is rather frail."

"What did that guy mean—Bob's house was the only one with electricity?" John was still unnerved by the man's attitude. "It's not like we did anything special."

James recounted the incident for everyone and they discussed for quite some time how they had light the whole time the Bible study was going. Then how it went out just as they finished. It did seem a bit supernatural.

After breakfast and a heartfelt prayer for the safety of all, the guests thanked Bob and Karen once again and began to make their way toward home. The whine of several chainsaws told them the fallen tree would soon be one less obstacle to their path. The whole family trooped out to help move the chunks of wood as they were cut. Now the neighbors seemed genial and were especially happy to see Karen come out bearing cinnamon rolls and thermoses of hot coffee.

Judge Pierce was able to turn his car around, and waved as he crept down the street trying to avoid branches, abandoned cars, and barking dogs. James decided to hitch a ride with Lori as it would be quite a while before his car was freed. John and Denise were just able to edge their vehicle around the roots of the tree that had nearly landed on top of it.

"What a night!" Karen exclaimed. "I'm just thankful none of us were injured. I wonder how the rest of the city is faring? Do you still have that battery powered TV somewhere, Bob?"

"I'll check on it. Perhaps I'll get my hand truck from the garage, too. This wood is getting heavy." He grunted as he stacked another large slice of tree trunk off to the side of the street. "It looks like we'll be cleaning up the neighborhood for quite a few days."

The news was wall-to-wall with the night's weather. First the storm, which had winds gusting up to 100 miles per hour, would be the topic of endless analysis. Then the earthquake would take precedence as more reports were coming in from seismic reporting stations around the world. It seemed the earthquake had been an unusual one with first one plate shifting, then the next in an almost domino effect

BEGINNING OF THE END

around the earth. It had varied from between a 4.6 and 7.5 on the Richter scale. Some populous cities were hard-hit with much damage. Others, on the lower end of the scale, had more minor effects. In all, millions of people had died and been injured in the quakes worldwide. Billions of dollars of damage had been sustained.

There were only a few TV stations able to broadcast. Damage to several local studios and some of the national networks resulted in "technical difficulties" from time to time. Commentators and experts were offering opinions and data trying to explain what had just occurred.

Then, just before noon, the Pope came onto the airwaves and read a message that began with "God is angry with the residents of this earth because of their blatant disregard of His righteous Law."

"Bob, quick, come listen to this—hurry!" Karen called out the front door to her husband. "You missed the first part. He said God is angry with the earth and sent these judgments to get our attention." She filled Bob in as he sat down close to the set.

13

SILENT NIGHT, HOLY NIGHT

"For God so loved the world that He gave His one and only Son, that whoever believes in Him shall not perish but have eternal life."
John 3:16, NIV

The message of the Pope was well received by the news media. They interviewed the "man on the street" to get opinions and many were in agreement with him. There had been too much violence and crime. Evidence now revealed the beginning of a groundswell of reform never before seen. One after another, church leaders added their voices to the Pope's in calling for an end to wickedness. A number of Christian churches began holding joint services, and thousands of saints and sinners flocked eagerly to their doors, anxious to find peace.

During the Christmas season the story of the birth of Jesus Christ was told and re-told from pulpit and street corner. About a week before Christmas, Karen saw an ad in the newspaper for a TV special on Christ that would air from the town of His birth, Bethlehem, and would cover His entire earthly journey. It was going to be on Sunday morning, a two-hour special of a program called "It Is Written."

"Mom, look at this." Mark and Sara were in front of the TV. "It looks like something from the Bible."

Karen walked into the family room. "What is it? Oh! That's what I was just reading about in the paper. Would you kids like to watch this? It's supposed to be all about Jesus life from the time He was a baby."

Mark, sounding grown-up answered, "Yes, I want to see for myself what this Bible stuff is all about."

"Me, too!" Sara asserted.

Karen looked closely at her children. Perhaps the adult discussions and questions were making an impression on them. "Why, certainly you may see for yourself. Do you think we should invite James and the others over for it, too?"

"I think that's a good plan, Mom. I like to hear about God being so smart and knowing what's going to happen and everything. Can we invite Judge Steven? Do you think he'd come?" Mark had developed quite an interest in the Judge since their stormy night together. "He showed me the shortest text in the Bible: It's 'Jesus wept.'" Mark beamed at being able to show his Mom something she didn't know.

"Well, you surely are learning. What will you be teaching me next?" Karen clapped her hands joyfully. "I'll ask James if it's OK to ask the Judge and hopefully all the others will be able to come, too."

By evening Karen had phoned all their friends and they agreed to come—if she would let them bring some snacks. Judge Pierce politely declined, saying he had other obligations.

The doorbell began ringing bright and early the next Sunday morning. One by one the guests arrived and were made comfortable in the Johnson home. Judge Pierce surprised them all when he showed up. He swept in with a flourish and presented a large beautifully wrapped gift to Karen. "Just a token of appreciation for your kind hospitality." His gracious words and gift caught Karen off guard.

"Why, thank you!" Karen stammered. "You certainly didn't have to get me anything. We are just so happy to see you."

Judge Pierce looked around and cleared his throat, "I can't stay—court rules keep me from socializing with lawyers who may appear before me, but I wanted to thank the Johnson family for saving my life during the storm." He looked at Karen. "Please, open the gift."

Karen carefully removed the lovely paper and ribbon, and peeked inside. Nestled there in the tissue was a beautifully framed picture of Jesus holding children on His lap.

"It's so beautiful!" She looked up at the Judge with wonder in her eyes. "He is looking at those children with so much love on His face. I don't know how to thank you—I've never had a picture of Jesus before." Turning to her family she exclaimed "Won't this be beautiful over the fireplace?" They all agreed and it immediately took the place of honor where an art print had hung for many years.

Judge Pierce looked pleased that his gift had brought so much obvious pleasure. "I became a judge in the Juvenile Court system because I love children." He explained. "Jesus has always been a part of my life and I wanted to help children like He did when He was here on earth."

At that moment the opening credits of the "It Is Written" Christmas special began to sound on the TV. The group bid a fond farewell to Judge Pierce, then found comfortable seats in front of the set. Pastor Mark Finley began the introduction in his kind yet authoritative voice. "Friends, we are so happy you have joined our "It Is Written" family for this special broadcast."

The story of Jesus began with Old Testament texts that foretold His birth. Broadcasting from the city of Bethlehem, the pastor skillfully moved from the angel visiting Mary to the shepherds coming to worship the newborn King, to texts of Jesus' ministry and life. Interspersed between actual pictures of surrounding humble homes, shepherds, and sheep, were dramatizations of Jesus' birth, life, ministry, death, resurrection, and ascension to heaven.

There were no intermissions and everyone sat spellbound throughout the entire two-hour presentation. When Pastor Finley prayed at the end asking God to bless the viewers and come into their hearts, the little group knelt in one accord. As the sweet strains of "Silent Night" closed out the program there were tears shining in many eyes.

Sara was the first one to speak as they rose from their knees: "Mommy, I never knew Jesus had to die on a cross. The pastor said Jesus died for me. Is that true?"

Karen hesitated then found an assurance she had never known before. "Yes, Sara, that is true. I have never understood this before either, but I can see from the Bible that it is true. God loves you. He loves me. Jesus came to die for you, for me, for all of us. She gazed at the new picture of Jesus and the children over the fireplace. The soft lights upon it seemed to make it glow. Karen hugged her daughter, "Yes, Sara, Jesus loves you."

14

THE DIVIDING LINE

"Then you will know the truth,
And the truth will set you free."
John 8:32, NIV

Hello, this is Bob."

"Are you the contractor?" The man's voice sounded unsure over the cell phone.

"Yes, I am. How can I help you?" Bob brightly responded.

"I'm looking for someone to repair the damage done by the storm to my house. Do you do that kind of work?"

"Yes I do," Bob was quick to reply. Then he added, "Would this be an insurance job?"

"It is covered by insurance, but the adjuster said there were so many claims turned in that I would need to find my own contractor. I was given your number as a reliable person. Could you come over and have a look at my place?"

"Sure. In fact I could be there this afternoon if that's all right with you."

After getting details of the caller's address and making notes of the damage, Bob went on with his regular work of repairing another house damaged by the big storm. On his way home he swung by the caller's residence. Sure enough, there was considerable damage requiring attention. While visiting with the owner and his significant other in their home, he noticed some things that were new to him— things that gave him a strange and rather exciting feeling. There were pictures, books, music, and the scent of something new and exotic in the air. He rapidly completed his business with the couple and made his way to his truck. Driving home Bob wondered about what he had just experienced. After supper he mentioned this to Karen and asked her opinion.

"It's probably New Age. Lots of people are into that you know."

Bob thought a moment, "Yeah, I'll bet you're right. Maybe that is something we should look into. It could benefit us. There was something really inviting in that house." With that he went to the computer room to look up "New Age" on the Internet.

After an hour of reading about "New Age" Bob was visibly excited and shared with Karen what he had learned. "So, I'm thinking this is what we should be involved in. Maybe this is how God is leading us to a more enriched life."

"Yes, uh, maybe so. Then again, how do we really know?" Karen's brow was wrinkled. There was a long period of silence while both appeared to look into space at nothing in particular. Then a smile spread across Karen's face and she spoke with assurance, "Let's ask James what he knows about New Age."

It was Sunday evening when James stopped by with the information Karen had requested. "I'm sorry it took me so long to get back to you about this," he confessed. "As I told you on the phone, I don't have any personal experience with New Age. But I did buy this book some time ago called *Deceived by The New Age*." James held up a paperback. "The man who wrote the book was a New Age zealot at one time. I'm hoping you two will read it and give me some feedback on whether it's interesting enough to give out as gifts this year."

"Sure," Bob agreed. "I'm really interested in this subject right now. You can count on me to give this a careful review."

When James left, Bob sat down with the book and began reading. At eleven o'clock he was still engrossed when Karen tapped him on the shoulder. "Are you ready to go to bed?"

"Not yet," he looked up. "This is really good. The guy has been into New Age for many years and knows all about it. I can't sleep until I finish the book."

Karen kissed him on the cheek. "OK. Don't wake me when you come to bed."

It was two o'clock when Bob finished reading. Strangely, he wasn't yet sleepy. There was a momentary debate in his mind before he went into action. Quickly he arose from the chair, turned out the reading light and strode to the bedroom. Turning on his bedside lamp Bob looked at his sleeping wife. He had to tell her. "Karen." She slept peacefully. "Karen, wake up. I want to tell you something."

"Huh? What is it? Didn't I ask you not to wake me?"

"I know, but this can't wait."

"Is there something wrong with the kids?" She was suddenly very much awake.

"No, no. Listen to me. I finished the book and you won't believe what New Age is all about. Can I read this to you? It's not very long."

"Sure." Karen nodded.

"OK, listen to this. 'At its core, New Age is primarily based on Hindu philosophy suitably adapted for the Western culture. Satan has cleverly repackaged Hinduism into a form devoid of the fearful, repulsive deities who are endlessly placated in the traditional Hindu rituals. Instead of advocating a plethora of grotesque gods, the New Age focus on a single, pantheistic god, who is presented as being the same god as the Father Most High of the Judeo-Christian tradition.

"'In the New Age religion, the Hindu teachings are combined with ancient paganism, contemporary occultism, spiritualism, and Christianity to produce a multifaceted hodgepodge of deceit.'"

"That's all I need to know." Karen spoke with confidence.

"Me too," Bob was equally emphatic. "I can't wait to tell James what a great book this is. And to think that I was interested in a religion that is actually run by Satan."

"I'm proud of you, dear." Karen reached for her husband. "You have really taken an interest in religion. In fact, I've noticed you have taken a real interest in the children and me recently. It almost feels like we're newlyweds again. I'm enjoying our new closeness." She whispered the last words as Bob snuggled down beside her.

15

SET IN STONE

"This is love for God: to obey His commands.
And His commands are not burdensome."
I John 5:3, NIV

"D id you know that the law was done away with?" Karen spoke
as she played with the food on her plate. Bob glanced at his
wife with a puzzled look. This statement came out of the blue at an
unusually serene dinner table. But without a clue as to what she was
talking about, he kept still. Mark and Sara looked at their mother for
an instant, then focused on their meal once again. There was silence
at the table.

"I was listening to a preacher on the radio today." Karen clearly
had something on her mind. "He said that God gave Moses the Ten
Commandments for the Children of Israel to live by, but after Jesus
came the law was replaced by grace." Once again all eyes were focused on Karen.

"What're the Ten Commandments?" Mark asked.

Karen wrinkled her brow. "Well, it was the law that the people
lived by back in Bible times.

"And it is said that it was written on a tablet of stone by God
himself," Bob chimed in.

"Cool", Mark grinned. "How did God write on stone?"

"I don't know, do you, dear?" Bob looked at his wife.

"I'm sorry, but I don't know nearly enough about this whole
subject," she shrugged. "But I know where I can find out more. There
is a set of Voice of Prophecy Discover Bible studies that came in the

mail months ago. If I can just remember where I put them." With that she left the table and the dining room.

Shortly, she returned with a smile on her face and some papers in her hand. "Would anyone like to learn about the law of God?"

All agreed that would be fun to study, so they cleared the table and brought out some Bibles. Karen started the study. Then she abruptly stopped reading. "One thing I have learned from James is that when we read from the Bible we should ask God to open our minds so that we can properly understand what He wants us to know." With that she closed her eyes and said a short prayer.

Mark and Sara looked at their mother with amazement. They had never heard their mother pray before. Bob smiled. This was definitely plowing new ground for his family.

Well into the study, Sara read from Exodus 31:18, "When the Lord finished speaking to Moses on Mount Sinai, he gave him the two tablets of the Testimony, the tablets of stone inscribed by the finger of God."

"Sounds like that might be important information," Bob spoke while still looking at the statement in his Bible. "OK. dear, where does it tell us what was on those tablets?"

Karen glanced at her study guide. "It says here to look up Exodus 20:1-17." Quickly, all Bibles were opened to the appropriate page and the family members took turns reading the verses. After the last verse was read she read from the study guide again. "The first four commandments detail our responsibilities to God. The last six speak to our responsibilities to other people." There was silence for a minute while all re-read the information to themselves.

"That is true. Now I can see how it is organized," Bob spoke almost to himself. "How come I've never read this before?"

"This is fun, learning this stuff," Mark said.

"And we aren't done with the lesson yet. So let's keep going," Karen said, beaming.

Text after text was read and appropriate comments were noted in the study guide. Before they were done it became clear to the family the difference between the Law of God and what was commonly called the Law of Moses. Whereas the Law of God is the guiding principle of God's creation, the large body of the Law of Moses was rules given to the Israelites for maintaining a safe, well-ordered society. By keeping these rules they would enjoy good health, be respectful of others, as well as understand and adhere to the plan of salvation God had set in motion when sin entered the world.

"So when the preacher on the radio said the law was done away with which law was he talking about?" Bob looked at his wife.

Karen shrugged, "I thought he meant God's law. But now that we have studied about it, I'm not so sure." She was silent for a moment. "No, he's wrong! I remember now that he was talking about the Law of God. That's really bad. I guess you can't believe everything you hear until you prove it for yourself."

"Mama, what does it mean to remember the Sabbath day to keep it holy?" Sara spoke with a puzzled look on her face.

"Good question, honey. The fourth commandment does say that doesn't it?" Karen noted. "Bob, do you know what that means?"

"Well, people do go to church on Sunday, so I think that is what it refers to." Bob smiled.

"But Daddy," Mark pointed out, "Sunday is the first day of the week."

"Uh, yeah, so it is. Can anyone help me out here?" Bob was without an answer this time. "OK. I'm going to find out about this and I'll let you all know the answer."

But, work and family activities put Sabbath research on the back burner. Another Thanksgiving, Christmas and New Year came and went. January brought snow to the city, lots of it. Driving was slow and risky but with all the jobs Bob had lined up he continued to work—which meant lots of driving. Then one day late in the month, Bob was driving home, exhausted and barely awake on the dark slick street near home when he was startled to see a car skidding out of control in front of him. There was no time for contemplation. Without thinking he hit the brake and immediately he, too, spun out of control. Once, twice, he saw the same scenery. Suddenly, as if the car had been on dry pavement it veered off the street and into a church parking lot where it came to a stop. Bob was as amazed as he was shocked. He sat there for a minute regaining his bearings. Noticing an illuminated reader board sign in front of the church, he read: Which Day is the Sabbath?

"Wow, I forgot all about that. I promised my family I would get the answer to that question," he whispered to himself. Continuing to view the sign he read the next line. Pastor Ralph Smith will answer this question Saturday, 7 p.m. at this church. In an instant Bob knew he would be there to hear this lecture.

After supper Saturday night, he excused himself. "I have some business to deal with, Karen. Be back about nine." But at the church parking lot Bob's courage dipped. It had been years since he had been in a church and he reasoned, "This could be a far-out cult or something like that." Then he remembered the unusual and perhaps even miraculous events that had led him to this place. "I'm going in!" He spat out the words.

Once inside he found friendly people who welcomed him and showed him to a comfortable seat. After some preliminary music, announcements, and prayer, Pastor Smith began his lecture. Bob noticed the informal style and the ease with which the topic was discussed. It became obvious to Bob that this man knew his Bible, a fact that made him very believable. Carefully, the history of God's people who have kept the Sabbath was discussed, including the Apostle Paul. Then the pastor showed how the need for the Law of Moses was fulfilled when Jesus died on a cross, thus meeting the requirement of death to sinners. The pastor quoted from Colossians 2 where Paul said that the Jewish sacred days pointing forward to the cross of Jesus were a part of the Law of Moses; hence those holy days were no longer a requirement for Christians to keep. But the seventh day Sabbath which God blessed for man's use at creation remains an institution for man's benefit. It also serves to identify the people of God who will ultimately be loyal to Him.

At the end of the lecture, Bob walked to his car with a written summary of the lecture—and a headache. This information was too revolutionary, too revealing, too costly. How could he tell his family the truth about the Sabbath and go about his life as usual? He had a problem and needed time to sort it out.

16

THE OPENING DOOR

"Our scientific power has outrun our spiritual power.
We have guided missiles and misguided men."
Martin Luther King Jr., 1963 A.D.

A re you watching the news?" John's voice sounded excited over the cell phone.

"No. What's up?" Bob was curious.

"Turn on your TV and you'll find out."

Walking into the family room, Bob picked up a remote and poked the "on" button. Immediately, Bob was aware of what his friend was talking about. A news reporter was seen speaking into a microphone. "Here is what we have learned so far near the site of the devastation. A relatively small bomb, by nuclear standards, has exploded about ten miles east of the small town of Hampton, Oregon. The explosion was felt in several towns in the central Oregon area about four p.m. So far little is known of the extent of damage done to the impact area or if any lives were lost. Also at this time, we do not know where the nuclear device came from and why it was detonated here."

"Andrea, this is Brian back at the studio. The network, has alerted us of new information just in. We are going to join them now."

"Here is the latest from the bombing in Oregon this evening. According to a spokesman at the Homeland Security Department, a message was left on the department voice-mail claiming responsibility for launching the nuclear warhead, aimed at Portland, Oregon. Since a nuclear explosion has occurred in a remote area of central Oregon, we are assuming the rocket never made it to its intended target. Now we are going to take you over to the pentagon where General Rollins is answering questions from reporters."

"General, what do we know about the group who claims they launched the bomb?"

"Not much. These groups seem to be springing up every week. Save the forest. Protect the wildlife. Free the prisoners. You name it. This group calls themselves STOP. We don't know what it means yet, or if they are based here in America or offshore. But working together with Homeland Security I'm sure we will find them and bring them to justice."

"Where did the nuclear device originate?"

"It is too early to know that at this time. But we can say that all our known military nuclear warheads are accounted for. Even as we speak, the White House is in communication with Russia and other nations as to whether they are missing any of theirs."

"General, had this bomb detonated in Portland, what might have been the result?"

"Good question. So far we do not know the exact type and size of the device. But in general these smaller warheads are capable of considerable damage. I could envision a couple hundred thousand deaths had it detonated near downtown."

"What is being done to determine the damage?"

"It is my understanding that there are only a few roads in the area where the bomb was detonated. State and local police have blocked off those roads. Army personnel and bomb squads are en route to the site for the purpose of determining the nuclear hazards that may exist. There is a probability that the area will need to be quarantined to protect the public from radiation."

Hearing a noise at the door Bob muted the TV. Karen was struggling in with bags of groceries. The look on her face told him she had been hearing the news on the car radio. There was a moment when their eyes met in disbelief. When the bags were safely on the kitchen deck she spoke first. "Can you believe what just happened? We could have all been killed today by a bomb!"

"Yes we could have. Guess we are kind of lucky—or something." Bob's forehead wrinkled. "You know, I have noticed lately that there is more and more serious violence in the news. In fact, people we know are being affected by crime and violence. But so far our family has not been touched. Why?"

The next day at work Bob and John discussed the bomb story and listened to the news on the radio as they worked together restoring a house. "So what do you think about all the crime and violence in the world these days, John?" Bob casually asked.

John stood still for a moment as if meditating on something. Then he turned to Bob. "As you know, I have been pretty much an independent kind of person. I make my own decisions based on what seems good for me. I have always believed that God is a crutch for the weak. But now I am beginning to think differently." John laid down his drill and unbuckled his tool belt. "A couple of weeks ago I was channel surfing when I came upon 3ABN. Ever heard of it?"

"No, can't say I have." Bob too laid aside his tool belt.

"Well, this guy on a show called 'Amazing Facts' was saying some things that really made sense to me. And since then, that is all I have been watching on TV. So far I have learned more about Bible prophecy than I ever thought possible. According to the speaker all the things we are hearing on the news are signs that Jesus is about to come." John hesitated.

"What do you mean, 'Jesus is about to come?'" Bob was clearly interested.

"The man read out of the Book of Matthew, Second Peter, Second Timothy, and other places that these things are going to happen just before Jesus comes back to take his people to heaven. This will be the end of the world, as we know it. Bob, I'm convinced it is true." He scanned Bob's face for some reassurance.

"OK, you have really given me something to think about. I mean, I can't say you are wrong. Whoa! Life is getting real complicated. But I'll tell you this much—I'm going to study this out for myself. And John, I want you to know how much I appreciate your input."

When Bob arrived at home in the evening he mentioned to

Karen about his conversation with John. The two of them agreed to check out the 3ABN channel that very evening. Just in case it was some "wacko" station they decided to do it after the kids had gone to bed. The moment they found the right channel they settled into their chairs to listen. And just as John had indicated the speaker taught with authority. Everything he said was backed up by verses of scripture. The reality of what was said gave Bob the chills. He reached for a blanket and draped it over his shoulders.

Karen picked up the phone and dialed. "Mother I think you should have a look at this 3ABN station. Watch it for a while and give me a call. OK?"

An hour later the phone rang. It was Marie. "Where did that station come from, dear?" She asked. "I've never seen it before."

"We haven't either, Mom. I think it used to be available only on satellite—Sky Angel, or something. But what did you think of this last show—Quiet Hour, I think it's called?" Karen pressed her mother.

"It was very interesting. I like what he had to say about prayer. And now that I think about it maybe it was time I was going back to church on a regular basis."

"Well, Mother, that is quite a step for you. What church would you go to?" Karen raised her eyebrow.

"Probably the same one I used to attend—Catholic. I went there for years, you know." Marie seemed in no mood to experiment with anything new.

"Well, maybe we will go to church, also." It was almost as if Karen was thinking out loud. "Anyway, we'll talk about it."

Before going to bed Karen brought up the subject to Bob. "So if you were to attend a church, which one would it be?"

Bob grimaced. "Oh, I forgot all about that."

"What did you forget?"

"Do you remember when we had that discussion about the commandments and the Sabbath?"

"Yes."

"Well, I forgot to tell you what I learned about the Sabbath," Bob began. As he started to recall the night when he had spun out on the street and ended up in the church parking lot, more and more details came out. "So," he concluded, "If I were to choose a church to attend I would want to give that one a try."

Karen was thoughtful but not convinced. "You sure seem convinced about the Sabbath, dear. And I admit it does seem like a miracle that instead of having a wreck you ended up in a church parking lot. But . . ." she hesitated, "would you really go to church on Saturdays? That seems rather strange to me."

"You're right. It does seem strange." Bob admitted. "But it all kind of makes sense to me. If there is a God—and I'm beginning to believe He exists—then it makes a lot of sense to me that He wouldn't arbitrarily change the day of worship. What I'm saying is that I am going to attend there at least once, this Saturday. That way I'll find out for myself if there is anything to the Sabbath."

"All right then," Karen agreed. "What do you say we include the whole family in this expedition?"

Three days later was "D-day." Bob loaded up the family and made the short trip to the church. It was eleven o'clock when they pulled into the parking lot. "OK, gang, as we agreed, it is time to hit the ground, and remember, keep your eyes and ears open for anything unusual or suspicious."

Upon entering the building, the family was greeted with warm handshakes and smiles. The people didn't appear to be cult members. Next they were shown to a seat near the back where they could not only observe the speaker but also observe the people in the pews. Very soon Bob found himself engaged in the music and other parts of the service before the speaker began. This isn't bad, he thought to himself. When he looked to the right he noticed Karen smiling and the kids were obviously enjoying the music. As the speaker approached the lectern Bob wrote a note that said, "This is the man I heard speak about the Sabbath," and handed it to his wife. Karen nodded slightly.

Pastor Ralph Smith spoke about the gospel and how far God was willing to go in order to save sinners. He pointed out that all have sinned. All have disobeyed their Heavenly Father. Yet God was not willing to give up on His created beings. He was willing to allow His

Son to come to planet earth, live a sinless life, and die at the hands of sinful men to bring forgiveness to all people who would accept it. But Jesus was not to be contained in the tomb. He arose and ascended into heaven where he makes intercession for sinners today.

"Someday soon," Pastor Ralph said, "Jesus will come back to earth and take God's people to heaven, where we will never die."

It was a different family who left the church that day and made their way home. Gone were the suspicions. Gone were the awkwardness and the fear. The Johnson family liked the pastor's style and respected his seemingly endless knowledge of the Bible. They had found a church home.

17

WHERE CAN WE GO?

"And if anyone takes words away from this book of prophecy,
God will take away from him his share in the tree of life and in the
holy city, which are described in this book."
Revelation 22:18, NIV

In the nation's capital today the Presidential Five Star Guidance Council met for the first time since being approved by Congress. This group of scholars, Catholic and Protestant church leaders, scientists, and leaders in the financial world are preparing to offer creative new ways to solve some of the nation's most pressing problems. The group chose Cardinal Martin as chairman. He is said to be well qualified for this work, and well respected by both government officials and business leaders. The first two problems the council will address are the economy, and the alarming national crime rate.

"At an impromptu news conference after today's session Cardinal Martin had this to say, 'We want to thank the President for the confidence he has placed in this Five Star Guidance Council. You can be sure we will take our responsibility seriously. By putting to use the talents of group members, and with the help of God, I am confident great strides will be made toward a safer, more secure, and more God-fearing country."

"In other news today army nuclear experts, who have been analyzing the aftermath of an errant bomb which detonated in remote central Oregon, have determined the device was not made in this country. Their best guess at this time is that it was stolen from bunkers either in Russia or Pakistan. Officials in both countries say they are not missing any warheads. Meanwhile, the Homeland Security Department is working on a list of possible terrorists who may be responsible for the bombing."

Karen touched the mute button on the remote. "Can I ask you something?" She looked at Bob sitting next to her.

"Sure," he grinned.

"I don't know what we can do about it but I don't feel safe any more. There is so much crime around here now. Then there was that bomb which missed us. Do you think we could move somewhere else?"

Bob saw something in her eyes that told him she was serious. She really was afraid. Never before in their married life had he seen this kind of fear written on her face. "It disturbs me, too," he admitted, "but what can we do? The housing market is bad, so we probably couldn't sell our place. And where would we go where crime isn't so bad? Besides, at least here I have work on a regular basis. Moving would be like starting all over again."

"I know. I know. It was a crazy idea. I just was hoping . . ." She looked away and wiped her eyes.

The conversation kept repeating in Bob's head for a week and a half. It was Friday evening. Bob came home from work early, put some tools away and cleaned up. "Do you want to go to church tomorrow?" he casually asked at the supper table.

"Yes, yes," the kids responded. Karen smiled.

Bob cleared his throat. "I've been thinking. Maybe the answer to your question about our security has something to do with God. Right now I'm beginning to think that God would like us to start worshiping Him instead of just learning about Him."

"Wow, that is quite a statement." Karen spoke slowly and looked at her husband. "This sounds like a big change in our lives. Are you suggesting that God actually is in charge of people's security?"

Bob thought for a moment before answering. "I'm not at all sure how that might work. But I do know this; it is time we started spending time with God. And when that happens, I think He will do what is right for us."

The next four weeks found the Johnson family in church on Saturday mornings. In that short time the kids became acquainted with other kids who attended there. Bob and Karen also began to make friends and started to become comfortable talking about the Bible and spiritual things. Pastor Smith was friendly and helpful in answering questions, yet he never pressed the new family to endorse a theology they didn't understand or agree with. On the fourth consecutive week that they attended church, the Johnson family was invited to eat lunch with Pastor Ralph and his wife Barbara.

Once they had arrived at the pastor's home and the small talk was done, Bob started asking questions. "What does the Bible say about God's involvement in our daily lives? How can we really know what God wants from us? What happens to people when they die? What difference does it make which day we go to church?" The pastor and his Bible worker wife were kept busy looking up Bible texts. After a while Barbara took the children into another room and put on a video about the life of Jesus from the Book of Matthew. She stayed with them and helped explain some things when the children had questions. By four o'clock Bob and Karen noticed the time and apologized for staying so long.

"Don't worry about the time. What we are doing here is just as much for me as it is for you folks," Pastor Ralph explained. "In fact, I was just thinking that perhaps we could study together like this once a week. My calendar has an opening on Tuesday evenings. Would that work for you?"

"Yes. It sure would," Bob agreed. "Sometimes I work a little late, but I won't do that on Tuesdays if we are going to study together."

At that moment Sara and Mark came into the room followed by Barbara. There were big smiles on their faces. Sara couldn't contain herself. "We saw the neatest video about Jesus. And there are more videos about Him that we haven't seen yet."

The Johnsons were supercharged with new information and great respect for their pastoral family. "I think we have stumbled onto something really important here," Karen said to her husband after Mark and Sara had gone to bed.

"I couldn't agree more." Bob answered. "I'm really excited that we get the chance to study with such God-fearing people who prove everything from the Bible."

Switching on the TV to catch the late news Bob was stunned by the leading story. "After just six weeks of work the Presidential Five Star Guidance Council has submitted its first report to the President. In a briefing to the media this afternoon reporters were told there are three recommendations in the first manuscript. Because the committee was hand picked by the President, White House insiders believe all these recommendations will be implemented.

"Here are the three recommendations: (1) Implement a sizable tax credit to all companies who increase employment numbers by at least five percent this calendar year. (2) Place an immediate moratorium on issuing new work visas. (3) Immediately institute Sunday as a National Day of Worship throughout the nation, giving all employees the day off except for police, hospital workers, security workers, transportation workers, and other necessary occupations. 'Due to the seriousness of current affairs in the nation,' it was noted by Cardinal Martin, 'we must reach out to God for Divine help.' Number three is the council's plan to accomplish that end."

Bob's mouth was open as he turned toward his wife, "A National Day of Worship on Sundays? But that's not right! The prevailing church changed the day of worship over 400 years after Jesus without any authority from God. What right have they to make Sunday a national worship day?"

By Tuesday evening when the Johnsons arrived at the suburban home of Pastor Ralph and Barbara, they had heard way too much about the new proposal given to the President. How might this impact their lives? This was what Bob and Karen were anxious to know and it was the first question they proposed as the Bible study began. Even Mark and Sara expressed concern about this latest development.

Barbara first explained that her husband was called to the hospital to have prayer for a critically ill church member. Then she fielded the question. "Like everyone else we have discussed this issue since we heard about it on the news. Normally we like to start

Bible studies with people right at the beginning, where God created the earth and move on through all the important doctrines of our Lord through the second coming of Jesus. But we thought you would want to know more about the Sabbath/Sunday issue since that is what has everyone's interest at this time."

"Good," Bob reassured her.

"Let's look at Revelation 13, shall we?" the seasoned Bible worker began after a short prayer. After reading the chapter she stopped and asked the question, "What do the two beasts spoken of in these verses represent?" Bob shrugged. Karen raised an eyebrow. "OK, here is some help." Barbara was quick to come to their rescue. "Beasts in prophecy represent nations or organizations. The sea represents an area where there is already a population of people. The earth represents an area where there is little or no population. The dragon in prophecy is Satan. So let's see if we can decipher this riddle.

"Here we have a worldclass force entering the scene of human history. From the seventh chapter of Daniel we can see a description of three beasts which look like a lion, a bear, and a leopard. In that chapter these beasts are identified as the nations of Babylon, Medo-Persia, and Greece. So, here in Revelation 13 where we see these three beast characters combined into one beast we are getting a picture of the next world power to come on the scene. From your knowledge of history, what world power do you think that would be?"

Karen brightened. "That would be the Roman Empire."

"You're right on target, Karen." Barbara smiled. "Now follow the progression of history from that time. It was the Roman Empire that was in power when Jesus was born and lived on earth. It was the Roman Empire that was in power when the early Christian church was formed. In fact, it was the Roman Emperor, Constantine, who was responsible for bringing Christians and pagans together in a way that created a super church now known as Roman Catholic. As the Roman Empire declined, Constantine moved the capitol from Rome to Constantinople, a city he had built for this purpose.

"When this occurred what became of the city of Rome? In the Vatican today one can view a huge painting 75 feet long. It shows Pope

Sylvester, the First, receiving a figurine of a warrior from Constantine as the Emperor was preparing to leave Rome for his new capitol. Under the picture are the words: Donation of Rome from Constantine to the Pope. This occurred in the year 538 A.D. From that time on, the Pope assumed authority as a spokesman for God. He and the priests under him claim power to forgive the sins of mankind. The Bible says that only God can forgive sins. You see, sin is a very serious thing. In fact the only reason that God can forgive sins is that He died on the cross two thousand years ago. The song puts it this way: 'Jesus paid it all. All to him I owe. Sin had left a crimson stain. He washed it white as snow.'"

"Now back to Revelation 13," Barbara picked up her Bible. "Who do you think is represented by the ten horned and seven headed beast?"

Bob looked down at the Bible, then back up again. "It looks to me like it is the ancient Roman Catholic Church."

"Very good. I can see that you two are beginning to see how world history and Bible prophecy come together." Barbara turned toward the children. "Mark and Sara, I know that this may be a little advanced for you but this is so important I thought you should get in on it rather than watch the video today. Do you mind?"

"No. This is fun," Mark said, grinning.

"I like learning about Bible things," Sara agreed.

"OK, it's time to do the math." Barbara handed a blank piece of paper and pencil to each family member. "The Roman Catholic Church was the dominating religious and political force in the world from 538 to 1798 when Napoleon's general, Berthier, took the Pope captive. During that period the organized church persecuted and killed millions of God-fearing Christians whom the church considered to be 'heretics.' Please calculate the period of time the Roman church was in full power."

Each of the family members wrote their numbers on the paper. Barbara looked at Mark and asked, "What do you have?"

"I have 1260 years," he answered tentatively.

"And the rest of you, what do you have?" she asked.

"1260 years." They all agreed.

"You all get an 'A' for the day," Barbara beamed. "Now for the significance of that number. In deciphering real time in Bible prophecy it is necessary to apply the formula: one day equals one year. Now, let me re-read verse five. 'The beast was given a mouth to utter proud words and blasphemies and to exercise his authority for forty-two months.' When you multiply forty-two by 30 days you come up with 1260 days. Go ahead and do the calculations."

One by one family members looked up from their papers with a smile. Barbara went on. "As we now know, a day in prophecy equals a year. According to this prophecy the Roman Catholic Church would rule for 1260 years—which is exactly what happened. You can see here that when God predicts the future, you can be sure that history will validate the prediction."

"Wow," Bob exclaimed, "How come I've never learned this before?"

"I can't answer that question, Bob." Barbara looked serious, "But the real significance of this chapter is yet to be discovered. Shall we go on?"

"Yes," came the unanimous decision.

"Take a look at verse seven which talks more about the beast we now know is the church. 'He was given power to make war against the saints and to conquer them. And he was given authority over every tribe, people, language and nation. All inhabitants of the earth will worship the beast—all whose names are not written in the book of life belonging to the Lamb that was slain from the creation of the world.'

"This is a strong indictment of the Roman Catholic Church in the future. Verse three indicates that the church will once again become a persecuting church. This is the last big struggle just preceding the second coming of Jesus. Now, of all the false ideas about salvation, the nature of God, the state of those who die, and other Bible topics, one of the most successful and significant lies the church has taught is that it has the authority to change the day of worship from the seventh day of the week to the first day of the week. You recognize the fact that all Catholics and most Protestants worship on Sundays." Barbara reached for a book and held it up. "This is The Convert's Catechism of Catholic Doctrine (1957 edition). I am going to read straight from the book. 'Question: Which is the Sabbath day? Answer: Saturday is the Sabbath day. Question: Why do we observe Sunday instead of Sabbath? Answer: We observe Sunday instead of Saturday because the Catholic Church transferred the solemnity from Saturday to Sunday.'

"God established His sacred day during creation week. He reaffirmed it to the Children of Israel. Jesus honored it and kept it during His ministry on earth. The Apostles kept the seventh day Sabbath and taught their followers to do the same. Yet the Catholic Church believes it has the authority to change the day of sacredness from Saturday to Sunday.

"Now, watch what happens next. Verse eleven introduces another player in the great drama of the ages. It is the beast that comes up out of the earth, not the 'sea' of peoples and nations. A wilderness, a sparsely settled area is depicted here. This beast is springing up at the time the leopard-like beast is going into captivity, which occurred in 1798 (exactly 1260 years after 538 A.D.). The only nation or world power rising at that time to prominence was the United States of America! This beast is said to have horns like a lamb, a fitting symbol of the docile, peaceful tendencies of our great nation all through its 200-year history, fighting only to maintain its freedoms when threatened. Yet, it says that it will someday speak 'as a dragon.' This denotes a marked change of policy.

"This beast makes the earth and its inhabitants worship the first beast. This is done by well meaning Protestants in the U.S. forcing Sunday observance. We see this starting to happen in our country now. Finally, this beast has great power to cause all who refuse to honor the first beast to be killed."

Looking around the circle, Barbara saw sober faces as the reality of this logic struck home. Karen spoke first. "Now that I think about it, there was a talk given on 3ABN television that referred to this happening here in our country some time in the future. What is happening with the Presidential Five Star Guidance Council means we are there doesn't it?"

Barbara nodded. "I must admit it does look that way to me also. But it is still early. In the months ahead we will see the real workings of Satan and the workings of God. In the meantime, go to God often in prayer that His will might be accomplished.

"Oh, yes, there is one other thing I want to be clear about right here. Even though we have seen how Satan has worked through the Roman Church in the past and is still doing so today, God still does love Catholics as individuals. And He wants to save those individuals just as much as any other church group or unsaved individuals. God has children in many churches and some haven't had a chance to learn these things."

18

I PLEDGE ALLEGIANCE

"If you want to get along, go along."
Sam Rayburn, 1961 A.D.

"Blessed are those who hunger and thirst for
righteousness, for they will be filled."
Matthew 5:6, NIV

We begin our coverage tonight with news from our nation's capital. In an unprecedented move today, the House of Representatives voted to accept the entire recommendation of the Presidential Five Star Guidance Council by a margin of three votes."

Bob listened to the reporter with interest. "The bill was in the hands of the House for only three weeks prior to today's vote. Two parts of that bill were no problem for representatives. But the third part, relating to the setting aside of Sunday as a day of rest for all people, raised many issues—not the least of which is freedom of religion. In an unusual alliance, Muslims, Jews, Sabbath keeping Christians, and others testified as to how this measure denies the freedom of religion guaranteed in our nation's constitution.

"In the end, most representatives were of the opinion that desperate times justify desperate measures. Many were also of the opinion that a properly written provision would pass the scrutiny of the Supreme Court. The measure will now go to on to the Senate where it is also expected to pass by a narrow majority."

"That is just incredible." Bob turned to his wife. "It doesn't seem possible to me that this is really happening just like we have been learning in our Bible studies."

"You are right. This is like we are living our life in someone's novel," Karen agreed. "Just think about the things that have happened to us in the last two years."

"And think of all the things we have learned about the Bible and prophecy in the last two years," Bob added.

It was Thursday evening. After the news report Bob and Karen were busy planning work schedules and doing bookkeeping. Mark and Sara were busy with homework. The routine of work and school had a numbing effect. Then at church on Saturday, that changed.

Jimmy Dexter, the twelve-year-old son of church members was scheduled to have special music. Jimmy was a good singer and everyone looked forward to listening to some fine music. Tammy, Jimmy's mother, played the introduction on the piano. At the appropriate time, Jimmy failed to come in. Tammy looked over to where her son stood in front of the microphone. Jimmy glanced back. Thinking that he had just missed the cue she played the introduction again with the same results. What happened next caught everyone off guard and changed the lives of everyone present.

"I am seeing a most unusual sight," Jimmy began. "It is night, but there's a glowing light in the sky with beautiful colors all around. I sense something awesome is about to happen. There are some people with me. I recognize some of you standing there with me."

Tammy stood up from the piano bench but she saw Pastor Ralph shake his head. Not knowing what was happening or what to do she sat back down. Pastor Ralph faced the congregation and spoke into his portable microphone. "Church, what we have here is a young man having a vision from God. Let's pay attention to what he has to say." The church was as silent as if it was midnight with no one there.

Jimmy went on. "There's been a change. A cloud is coming toward earth from far out in space. In the center of the cloud is a bright light. I feel so excited I can hardly contain myself. What is happening here? Oh, can it really be? Can this be the second coming of Jesus? Yes it is! I can see Him now. This is such a sight! I can't even begin to describe what it." There was a moment when Jimmy stood still and gazed upward with a smile on his face. Then his face assumed a more sober appearance and he spoke again. "I have been told by someone of authority to get ready. Get ready now. The great day of God is nearer than you think." Having said that, Jimmy descended the steps from the rostrum and sat down beside his father. Tammy left her place at the piano and joined her son and husband. The congregation sat stunned.

Pastor Ralph lifted his hands upward as he spoke, "Praise the Lord! Our God has delivered a far more important message to this church than what I had prepared for you today. Listen to me, Church," he went on, "What you have just witnessed is a fulfillment of the prophecy of Joel 2." Leafing through his Bible he stopped, then began to quote, "And afterward, I will pour out my spirit on all people. Your sons and daughters will prophecy, your old men will dream dreams, your young men will see visions. Even on my servants, both men and women, I will pour out my Spirit in those days (Joel 2:28,29)."

Bob and Karen looked at each other with big eyes as if looking for reassurance they were not asleep and dreaming.

Pastor Ralph went on. "For several months now my wife and I have been hearing and reading about this very manifestation of the Spirit of God in the church in various parts of the world, as well as here in our country. This is evidence that God is making a final push to bring people into a saving relationship with Him before probation closes. If there are some here today who have not committed their lives to Jesus and who have not been baptized," the pastor hesitated just a moment as he looked over the congregation, "then listen to God's voice today calling you to this glorious privilege. The Bible says it this way in second Corinthians six verse two, 'I tell you, now is the time of God's favor, now is the day of salvation.'

"I believe God is leading me to make a call right now for anyone who would like to make this commitment to God, to come up to the front of the sanctuary. If God is speaking to your heart and you want to respond by being baptized, just move out of the pew where you are and come forward right now."

Without hesitation, Bob rose to his feet and froze there for a moment. Then he felt a touch and turned to see his wife also standing. He clasped her hand and stepped toward the aisle when he saw Mark and Sara also stand. It was a united family who walked down the aisle indicating their desire to pledge their allegiance to God. Several others joined them at the altar where Pastor Ralph and his wife Barbara waited to shake their hands.

After the service was over the pastoral couple sat with the group who had come forward and set up a series of Bible studies on an accelerated basis. It was decided for all the people desiring baptism to schedule the happy event in four weeks. There was lots of work ahead to complete all the Bible studies prior to that date. As Pastor Ralph put it, "We want you to know exactly what you are committing to and why you subscribed to the principles of Christianity and of this church."

The next four weeks were indeed busy, not just with Bible studies and work. Economic woes began to threaten the Johnson family's financial and medical security. Problems large and small seemed to unfold almost on top of each other. While lifting some lumber at work, Bob strained his back seriously enough that he had to see a doctor. This resulted in a week off work along with prescribed medication and physical therapy. Mark came down with pneumonia and spent two days in a hospital. Karen was involved in an automobile accident. Although shaken she was not seriously injured, even though the other driver who failed to stop for a red light totaled her car. By this time money was in short supply. Yet the family continued to study Bible truths in preparation for their baptism. Then the big day came.

The church the Johnson family attended was equipped with a heated tank where the baptisms were conducted during the church service. One by one each of the participants was lowered into the water in the same manner as John the Baptist had baptized Jesus. There were hugs and tears of joy as Karen, Bob, Mark and Sara stood together after the last one had been lowered and raised to newness of life. Karen's mother, Marie, attended the service and was fascinated by the whole process. Even before the church service was over she began to ask questions.

"Why don't these people baptize by sprinkling like other churches?" Marie asked her daughter after the service was done.

"Well Mom, in the Bible the only kind of baptism ever performed was by immersion, just like you saw today. Jesus was baptized by immersion and the Apostles used this method for all their baptisms. In fact, the Roman Catholic church baptized by immersion for hundreds of years before they changed over to the sprinkling method." Karen reached for her mother's hand. "Besides all the history, Mom, baptism is symbolic of burying the old sinful self and rising up sinless and clean as a newborn baby. Sprinkling wouldn't do that would it?"

Marie nodded. "That's a good point, honey. Good point."

Life went on as usual for the Johnsons after the baptism with no thought of what was coming. The Senate passed and the President signed into law the new bill making Sunday a "Day of Rest for all people." All residents of the United States—citizens and registered visitors alike—were required to sign a pledge declaring their intent to abide by the law. This could be done on the Internet or at any county courthouse or city hall. There was a flurry of activity for six weeks as millions complied, then it dropped off to nearly nothing. Government officials calculated there were still about ten million people who had not signed.

Church leaders began to agitate for stronger enforcement of the new measure. They claimed recent increases in crime were the result of a loss of respect for God evidenced by poor church attendance. But on Saturdays when the "Sabbath keepers" met for worship they had a different explanation. They saw the new law to be a forerunner of the "Mark of the Beast" of Revelation 13. The overwhelming conclusion among them was, "Stand up for the seventh day Sabbath." Meaning: "Don't ignore God's commandment in order to conform…whatever the cost."

In the nation's capital the President's office and Congress were busy trying to solve an increasing array of problems in addition to the economy. Crime, terrorism, war, and national disasters were on the increase. Wars or near wars were occurring on all continents and the United States was involved in most of them. The United Nations was frantic to find solutions to these skirmishes, both large and small. But with a seemingly never-ending supply of despot leaders in the world who blatantly ignored UN edicts, the peace process moved slowly.

Over the period of a half-year the U.S. went through a severe drought in the American heartland. This made a huge impact on the grain supply, which of course, resulted in sharply increased prices at the grocery stores. Also, during this same period major floods occurred in California, Texas, and Florida. All combined, thousands of lives were lost, thousands of dwellings were destroyed, and once again crops were decimated. By this time the Federal Emergency Management Agency (FEMA) was appealing for additional funding to complete their mandated work. Thinking people everywhere were asking, "Why are we having all this trouble and what can we do about it?" The Five Star Presidential Panel was about to come up with what they thought was the only answer.

19

FORCE IMPLIED

"How long will you waver between two opinions? If the Lord is God, follow Him; but if Baal is God, follow him."
I Kings 18:21, NIV

It was another day of work for Bob. He was the contractor on building a large new duplex for a previous customer. The framing was going nicely with John's help and the assistance of a couple of temporary workers. When his cell phone rang, Bob answered it as he continued to work. It was Karen with some big news.

"I was on the Internet when an announcement showed up on the news. The President has just invoked an emergency order to compel people to sign the Sunday law already in force. Failure to do so will result in severe fines. What are we going to do?"

Bob dropped what he was doing and stood frozen. "Are you sure about this?" he asked. "I didn't know he had the authority to do that."

"Just a minute," Karen responded. "I'm listening to the news. OK, it's on the radio also. It really is happening."

Bob's mind was searching for some solution when an idea came to him. "You know what? I'm going to call our attorney, James." Quickly he dialed the office number and heard someone pick it up. "James Wright, please."

It took awhile, but eventually he heard a familiar voice. "This is James."

"Hi James, this is Bob Johnson, and we're up against a problem again." Bob thought he detected a good deal of stress in his own voice.

"Long time, no hear, my friend. Does that mean you've had no problems for awhile?" James talked more like a friend than an attorney.

"Not too bad, really. Some good. Some bad. You know how that goes." Bob began to relax.

"We should get together sometime for supper and share what has been happening in our lives, don't you think?" James asked.

"Sounds good," Bob agreed, "but right now we are trying to figure out what we are going to do about this Sunday law thing. The President is invoking an emergency order to force everyone to sign up for Sunday worship service."

"Yes, I had heard that." James seemed happier than Bob thought he should. "Here is what we could do. Meet me at that new Country Restaurant on Stark near Mall 205, say about six o'clock this evening and we'll talk, OK?"

Bob nodded. "We'll be there."

Bob and Karen left the kids with Marie and headed for the restaurant. They arrived right at six o'clock and found James already seated. There was lots of catching up since James had been out of town with a family crisis for several months. Then James asked the key question, "Tell me where your spiritual journey has taken you since we last talked."

Karen and Bob looked at each other and she asked, "You or me?"

Thinking that Karen was anxious to tell the story he smiled and said, "Go ahead."

Once started, she talked nonstop until they were nearly done with their meal. When she told about their baptism, Karen's eyes misted and she hesitated to go on. James began to shake his head. "This is wonderful! It's too good. I have been praying for your family ever since the last time we were together. God has answered my prayers, and I didn't even know it. This is incredible!"

The people at the table nearest them looked over at James. He noticed their look and acknowledged them. "My friends here just told me they have been baptized, isn't that great?" The people at the other table smiled, then looked at each other and became involved in their own conversation.

Looking back at Bob and Karen, James changed the subject. "Now about the Sunday legislation and the President's emergency measure." He lowered his voice. "No one, not even the president, will ever make me violate my conscience. I have studied this for many years and have known it would come sooner or later. This looks like the real thing to me."

Bob jumped in. "What do you mean by the real thing?"

"Oh, I'm sorry. What I mean is this looks like the first stages of the Mark of the Beast spoken of in Revelation 13. I expect this law to progress to tougher measures that will cause people to have the Mark of the Beast. God's people, on the other hand will have the Mark of God by being true to the Sabbath."

"I believe you're right," Karen agreed.

"Here is how much I believe it," James added. "I have sold my law practice and will be leaving the office at the end of this month. I can no longer practice law and live by my conscience."

"What will you do?" Bob wanted to know.

"My only plan is to tell everyone I know about the soon coming of Jesus. I don't know how that will be accomplished but whatever God wants me to do, I'll do it." James seemed content and happy. "Oh, something else." He lowered his voice again. "I have sold my home and will be moving into the country. That is where God wants me and there will be less problems with my Sabbath keeping."

"What a good idea," Bob agreed. "I wish we could pull that off."

James looked at his watch and began to get up from the table. "You can, with the help of God. I'll be praying for you."

As the three of them left the table, the couple that had heard some of their conversation looked for eye contact with James. When James glanced at them the man arose and spoke. "Sir, I hope you don't think me rude, but we heard enough of your conversation to be very interested. Would it be too bold of me to ask for some of your time to ask you some Bible questions?"

"Not at all," James returned. "In fact I would count it a privilege to share what I know with you." Quickly he wrote his name and home phone down on a piece of paper, handed it to the man and asked, "What did you say your names are?"

"Larry. Larry Jenkins. And this is my wife, Eva." They shook hands and James started to leave when the man spoke again. "I'll call you later this evening."

"Good." James smiled back as he left the restaurant with Bob and Karen.

At work the next day, Bob was still wrestling with how to handle the Presidential Executive Order requiring Sunday registration. Knowing that his friend and co-worker, John, was also a Christian, Bob asked him for his opinion.

"Well, Most Christians do go to church on Sundays," John began. "So if they are requiring people to register for the purpose of keeping the day holy, I guess that is alright."

"So what do you do with the fact that God established the seventh day as His holy day?" Bob wanted to know.

"I know He did," John agreed. "But that is not practical in the world we live in. And when the law requires it we must give Caesar his due. That is what Jesus said," John concluded.

"I'm not so sure. I'm not so sure." Bob shook his head.

By the end of the week the details of the executive order were made known to the nation. People had six more weeks to register. Naturally this was a huge issue for Sabbath keepers. And to further complicate matters, lawsuits were filed to allow Sabbath keepers such as Jews and Sabbath keeping Christians to be exempt from this law. This brought hope to many, that maybe they would be spared having to make a difficult decision.

As the days passed rapidly, Bob and Karen began to notice something unusual happening. People who before never expressed any interest in religious things were now very interested. Others, who were firmly established in church life, began to question whether they had chosen the wrong Christian pathway. Neighbors that Bob and Karen didn't even know knocked on their door and asked questions about what day was the right day to worship. Others loudly decried the "infidels" that were "ruining the country." In the end, people were taking sides for or against Sunday worship.

But when it came down to registering or not registering, the Johnson's were not sure.

There were seven days left to decide when a letter came from the Construction Contractors Board advising Bob that if he failed to comply with the federal mandate to register as a Sunday worshiper, his license would be revoked. After the kids went to bed Bob showed the letter to Karen. After reading it she looked up and smiled. "Guess we are going to make our decision soon, huh?"

"I don't know why I've been avoiding this decision. Maybe in the back of my mind I was hoping to be rescued by a court decision or some other external thing. But I know now that ultimately I am the one who must decide what is right for me." Bob stared off into space. "So, I am going to decide for myself tonight." Then he looked into Karen's eyes. "What about you? Are you ready to decide tonight?"

"Yes," she said. "I'll decide tonight. But I would like to talk it through with you if you don't mind."

They began the discussion right where they were the most insecure. "As we have just learned, if I don't sign I will lose my license to work as a contractor. That means no more work for me, no more income for us. I can't imagine us surviving more than a couple of months without an income, can you?" Bob's face was beginning to show the stress.

"In the past, I probably would have agreed with you," Karen shrugged. "But now, now I can see some possibilities."

"What possibilities?"

"Maybe we could sell our house and move out of town. You know, into the country like James is doing. You are smart and a good worker, so something might open up for you there. Maybe we could barter or something."

"Hmmm. Never thought of that. Could make sense. But selling our house might not be that easy. Still, hmmm."

"Are you ready to hear my concern?" Karen asked.

"Go ahead, hit me with it." Bob's attitude was more positive.

"I worry about the children. It could come down to a place where our children would be taken away from us because we refuse to go along with the system. That really scares me."

"Do you know what? They tried that once and God prevented it. So now we know that with Jesus on our side we can overcome anything." Bob shook his head. "Who said that? I can't believe this is Bob Johnson talking!"

Karen wiped her eyes. "You're right. You are probably more right than you even know. But I am so programmed to solve my own problems. Trusting God to solve my problems is still very new to me."

"Me too," Bob agreed. "But now that I think about it, why shouldn't we just do it God's way? He hasn't failed us yet. Are you with me to trust God completely with our lives?"

In an instant she was in his arms. "I'm with you," she whispered.

The next day the Johnson's house went on the market. Then Bob spoke to John about his plans to leave the construction business at the end of the next week. "It was the only option that made sense to me," he told his friend.

"I really admire you, Bob. It takes guts to do a thing like that. And you have such great faith. Wow! I wish . . . it doesn't matter." John turned away.

20

SHUT DOWN

"Ask and it will be given to you; seek and you will find;
knock and the door will be opened to you."
Matthew 7:7, NIV

L ook at all the people here. There's hardly an empty seat in church," Bob whispered to Karen.

"Who are all the new people?" she mouthed back.

Just then Pastor Ralph's wife Barbara stepped to the podium and welcomed visitors and members to the Sabbath services. Without skipping a beat she went on. "As a way of explanation, I want to inform our members as to why we have such an unusually large number of visitors here today." For a moment she allowed her eyes to pan over the audience, then she went on. "In recent weeks there has been an explosion of interest in our beliefs. Whereas we used to receive a few phone calls expressing interest in our church, in recent weeks those calls have been upwards of a hundred per week. In the past Pastor Ralph and I have conducted from two Bible studies per week up to eight per week. Now we are studying privately with thirty people along with one group of twelve each week. Already sixteen people have expressed interest in accepting God's love and being baptized."

"Amen, hallelujah," was heard all over the church. Members and guests alike were smiling. Many were raising their hands to heaven and praising the Lord. Old and new members were uniting in their expressions of praise to God.

Barbara continued, "This is reminiscent of what happened just after Jesus left the disciples for heaven. Within a short period of time the Holy Spirit caused thousands to be converted and baptized. Now we are approaching the day when Jesus will return to gather the faithful for the trip of a lifetime to heaven. We don't want anyone here to miss this trip. Your ticket has been bought by the blood of Jesus. Your heavenly mansion is awaiting your entrance. I personally want to greet you by the tree of life. Don't miss it."

After a rousing song Pastor Ralph stood up and spoke. "This week I worked on a sermon for today's service." Holding up some papers he said, "Here are my notes. But today this sermon will remain silent. The Holy Spirit has prompted me to speak from my heart and that is exactly what I will do.

"As a child I heard my parents speak of the soon coming of Jesus. My parents are now awaiting that blessed event in their graves. While in college I had professors prove to me that time here on earth could not possibly exceed ten years. Those professors have also been laid to rest, but Jesus has not come. In my years as a pastor I have heard and read many predictions of when this earth will end. All of those predictions have failed to produce the second coming of Jesus. But now it is my turn."

Pastor Ralph sobered as he looked out over the full church. "Friends, we live in a unique period of time. The events of these past two months are a fulfillment of Bible prophecy. These events will lead to some very troublous times where God's people will be severely tested. The faith of everyone here today will be at risk. Already there are some missing from our fellowship today who have decided to disregard God's clear leading because they couldn't trust Him to care for their physical needs. But those who pass the test will live to see the ultimate reward—the second coming of the King of Kings. The probation of this world of sinners is about to expire. It will do so regardless of whether or not we are ready. Today God is calling each of us here with the challenge found in the last chapter of the Bible. 'And, behold, I come quickly; and my reward is with me, to give every man according as his work shall be. I am Alpha and Omega, the beginning and the end, the first and the last. Blessed are they that do his commandments, that they may have right to the tree of life, and may enter in through the gates into the city.' (Rev 22:12-14)."

The pastor continued, "God has done His part. Jesus died that we might live. The prophets have spoken that we might know what is coming on the earth. The forces of evil are even now carrying out their plans to decimate this planet. God's Spirit is working with individuals all over the world and more specifically with each person here today. There may not be another opportunity like this one to fully commit yourself to Jesus. So if God is speaking to you right now, stand on your feet and tell him the desire of your heart."

It was a sight such as never witnessed before in the church. Church members stood. Visitors stood. Children stood. Many looked heavenward and raised their arms. People were hugging with tears falling from their eyes. After the solemn, yet jubilant, period of time, Pastor Ralph spoke again into the PA system. "Before we leave here today I want to announce two very important things. First, because of the large attendance in our church, starting next week we will have two services. The early church will take place at 8:30 and the late service will be at 11 o'clock. Everyone is welcome to attend the service that best suits your schedule. And the second announcement is: there will be a baptism held for all whom the Lord has called out of the world into a life of commitment to Him. Please let me know this week if you would like to be included in this baptismal service."

After the church service people stood around and talked for a long time. Everyone appeared to savor the moment. When the Johnsons finally walked to their car, Bob noticed a note stuck under the windshield wiper blade. Unfolding the note he read, "Beware, Sabbath legalist! By next week it will be the law that all citizens are to pledge allegiance to Sunday worship. Your license number has been recorded for possible future legal action should it be found that you are not in compliance with the presidential executive order."

"Who would have put that on our car?" Karen wondered.

116

Bob shrugged, "I don't know, but it looks like every car here must have gotten the same note. I don't know about anyone else but it will take more than that to intimidate me."

"Me too, Daddy." The young voice of Sara added emphasis to her father's determination.

On Tuesday a man and a woman were shown through the Johnson's home as possible buyers. Two hours later the listing realtor showed up at the door with the couple's offer to purchase. The offer included a fair price and, though rather small, the down payment was in cash, with the promise of the balance at closing. In almost no time at all, Bob and Karen signed the agreement. As soon as the realtor left, the celebration began. Karen started making calls to everyone she could think of. Bob started making lists of things to accomplish. Mark and Sara ran to their rooms to begin packing.

The next day Bob turned over his business to his friend John. At this point, Bob was now unemployed and would soon be homeless. Nevertheless, he was full of optimism and faith. That, too, was about to be tested.

Looking for property with a house in the country at a price they could afford soon appeared to be nearly impossible. With only two more weeks to vacate their house, stress began to make its appearance. Together in their bedroom Bob and Karen reviewed their options—which were few. Karen suddenly threw up her hands. "I know! Let's pray about it."

"Good plan. Why didn't I think of that?" Bob countered with a grin. Then they held hands and made their request to God. They found themselves talking to Him just as if talking to one of their friends. When they were done, Bob had a thought to go down to the Clackamas County Courthouse. Perhaps, he reasoned, there might be a country property-foreclosing list posted there. As he opened the door to the courthouse, there coming toward him was James Wright. After a warm handshake, the two took a seat in the hallway just outside the secure section.

"What brought you here?" James asked.

"We sold our house, but can't find a place in the country to live.

So I thought maybe I could find a foreclosing list here in the court-house." Bob's face was showing the stress.

"What's your work situation?" James inquired.

"CCB shut me down over Sunday registration. I turned my business over to my helper. So at this time, I guess you could say I'm trusting the Lord."

"Well then," James moved closer to Bob and lowered his voice. "As you know, I have some property in the country—quite remote. There is an old house on the property. In applying for a remodeling permit, I have hit a brick wall over—guess what?"

Bob thought a moment, and then suggested, "Sunday registration?"

"Exactly! All permits now require a Sunday Registration number to get approval. Naturally, I believe this to be a violation of consti-tutional rights. But there is no use fighting it. So, here is my proposal. Bring your family out to the property. Live there. Help me build a place hidden in the forest. I think we would be good for each other." James was thinking and talking fast.

"Really? You are inviting us to live at your place?" Bob found this quite unusual.

"Of course. We all have the same goals and serve the same God. I trust you and hope you can trust me. Tell you what. Bring the fam-ily out to the property tomorrow about noon. Then you decide what is best for you and I'll be good with it." Pulling out a piece of paper from his shirt pocket, he handed it to Bob. "Here is a map showing how to find the property."

The significance of what had just happened rattled around in Bob's brain all the way home. He kept questioning himself to be sure this wasn't a dream. At home he recalled the chance meeting with James and his proposal. Then, cautiously he asked, "What do you think?"

Karen looked contented and her head began to nod. "I like it. I see the hand of God working here. Your meeting James at the court-house was no coincidence. You know that don't you?"

The next day the family piled into the Dodge minivan and

headed out into the country. Paying close attention to natural markers shown on the map James had supplied, they were able to find their way to the remote property. They pulled up beside the Chevy Suburban that James had driven. Stepping out, they were struck by the beauty of the place as well as the sense of remoteness.

"Welcome, travelers. As you can see, I have traded my suit for these work pants." James emerged from the trees where he had been working.

"Well, whatever you're doing must be the right thing," Bob said, "because you sure look fit."

"Thanks. Actually all the work I have been doing around here, cutting trees and bushes, has been good for me—but enough about me. What do you say we take the tour?" With that he motioned and took off on a fast pace with the Johnson family at his heels.

As they walked the perimeter of the 40-acre property they dodged around trees, climbed over boulders, and walked a log over a stream. At one point they stood for a minute looking over a vista of the valley below.

"This is absolutely beautiful," Karen spoke reverently. "How did you find this place?"

"I handled a big case for a large lumber and mining company a few years ago. We won a sizable award and the company offered to turn over the deed to this place as payment for my services. I agreed without even looking at the property. Later, I wondered if maybe I acted too quickly. Then I came up here, and saw what God had given me, and I knew it was the right thing." James spoke with conviction.

"So here's the deal," James changed the subject. "I've just bought some supplies and will be moving out here next week. Since you folks need a place to live, and because I consider you good friends, I am giving you an invitation to move here and make this property your home."

"We are really blown away by your generosity, James," Bob replied.

"Before you get too smitten with my random act of kindness," James laughed, "consider this fact. I don't know the first thing about remodeling and adding on to the old dwelling that I hope someday will become a lodge. On the other hand, you," pointing to Bob, "you are a builder. Eventually we all will want to live in a permanent dwelling, especially when winter comes. So the way I see it, we all need each other. And, since this property is really a gift from God, it belongs to all His people anyway, even though my name is on the deed. So what do you say? Will you join me?"

Bob and Karen looked at each other and at their two growing young people they loved so dearly. Both of them started to nod and Karen broke the silence, "You have a deal."

The rest of the afternoon was taken up with planning on the lodge and exploring the topography. Before the informal meeting ended, a general drawing on paper had been established for the old house facing the Cascade Mountains to the east. As they walked together toward their vehicles James spoke. "By the way, we are too far away from the nearest power line, so be on the lookout for a good generator that will meet our needs."

Bob always did like a challenge. While driving home, he was already mentally calculating the size of generator needed to accommodate a modern four-bedroom dwelling.

Upon arriving home, Mark looked down the street to where a For Sale sign was visible on a small travel trailer. "Look, Dad, the Bensons are selling their trailer."

Bob shaded his eyes from the setting sun. "I believe you're right, son," he said. Then an idea came to him and he spoke to the whole family. "What do you say we all walk down there and have a look at the travel trailer?" Agreement was universal.

It didn't take long for the family to fall in love with the unit. It just seemed right. Mr. Benson was bent on showing all the details and how they worked. When Karen asked the selling price, he made a point of the fact that he was retiring and wanted to purchase a true motor home so the two of them could travel. Therefore, he said they were going to let it go for a mere $5,000. Bob excused himself and motioned to the family to follow him. Once they were standing out on the lawn, they all expressed their interest, even the children. "Let's take a vote," he said. "Raise your hand if you think we should buy it for $5,000." No one raised a hand. "How many think we should buy it for $4,500?" All four family members raised a hand. "Well, let's see what happens." As a show of unity he held out his hand. One by one, other hands were laid on the pile of hands just like a sports team might do.

"Well, Mr. Benson, the family council has determined that this travel trailer is worth $4,500 to us at this time. We are willing to pay cash for it today if we can agree on that price." Bob appeared friendly but firm. Then another thought struck him, and he added, "However, if you would agree to read a very important book which I will give you, we will pay another one hundred dollars."

Mr. Benson looked at Bob and began to smile. "You know I was about to turn down your offer. Then you mentioned the book. For some reason which I can't explain, that made a difference." Sticking out his hand he announced, "Congratulations on a fine purchase."

Walking back to their house, the family found it hard to keep their feet on the sidewalk. Out of the Benson's earshot, Karen asked, "What book is it you want them to read, dear?"

Bob broke out into a big grin. "Truth is I didn't know at the time I said that, but it hit me that we should do something to bring the real truth about God to our neighbor. Now I feel impressed to give them that little booklet we like so well on the Mark of the Beast. What do you all think?"

The booklet Bob referred to—The Mark of the Beast by Charles T. Everson—thoroughly documented the history of Sabbath and Sunday worship. It made a strong case for forced Sunday worship as being the Mark of the Beast. Upon arriving at home everyone pitched in preparing the driveway for the new RV. Bob found the booklet he was giving away and they all jumped into the work pickup. Shortly, there was a flurry of activity of signing, and exchanging the keys and money. At that point, Mr. Benson asked, "Where's my book?"Hoping to make a point, Bob asked, "What book?" But by the look on his face it was obvious to the family that Bob was having some fun.

"You didn't forget . . . ohhh. I get it." Mr. Benson broke into a grin.

Bob pulled the book out of his pocket. "Here it is Mr. Benson. Hope you enjoy it half as much as I did. And I hope you will let me know what you think after you read it."

"I will, Bob. I will." Mr. Benson looked down and began reading.

21

EVIL APPROACHES

"If I rise on the wings of the dawn, if I settle on the far
side of the sea, even there your hand will guide me, your
right hand will hold me fast."
Psalm 139:9, 10, NIV

Bob and Karen worked hard at packing for the move. They held several big yard sales and voted to give the money they earned to a little publishing company they had discovered on the Internet— RemnantPublications.com. They had been buying lots of their books about Jesus and handing them out to friends and neighbors. After a couple of days, they made provision for some temporary workers to help them load the rest into a rental truck and move to the country. They purchased some tarps to cover their belongings until the old house was fixed up.

"I think it is time to take the kids out of school," Karen said to her husband as they completed the day's activities.

"Oh, I hadn't even thought about that," Bob admitted. "How are we going to get them to school when we are living so far out in the country?"

"Don't worry," Karen advised. "I have that all planned. We are going to home school them."

A smile came over Bob's face as he responded. "You have thought this out. And it is a brilliant plan." Then he sobered and asked, "Where are we going to get all the books and other learning materials?"

"Very simple really. I have done some research and have already ordered the supplies. And by the way," she assured him, "the kids are really looking forward to this.

"Good." Bob was satisfied that this solution was a good one. Switching on the radio, he sat down on his recliner.

"I'm worried about my Mom, though. She isn't at all interested in moving away from the city and hasn't made a decision to follow God even with all the knowledge God has given her about the Sabbath and other Bible truths."

Bob turned down the volume on the radio as soon as Karen started talking. "We will have to get the kids together with us to pray for her every day."

Bob's concern touched Karen and she basked in his newfound spiritual confidence.

"Thank you, Bob," was all she could say.

Bob turned up the volume just in time to hear a reporter speak from an African country. "Things here are rapidly coming to a head. The president of this small country is struggling to hold on to power. But radicals have been on a killing spree all day and claim they will keep it up until the president resigns."

"Now we go to Jack Robertson at the State Department."

"Thank you, Barry. At the State Department, officials are scurrying to find a solution to this, yet another international crisis. Already American military personnel are involved in fighting or peace keeping in some fifteen countries. The practicality of one more such effort seems improbable."

"Coming up after the break, we will bring you further evidence of the nation's deteriorating financial outlook. Experts will tell us just how low the Dow could go before a recovery begins."

Bob switched off the radio. "It gets harder and harder to listen to the news," he complained. "Although, now that I have been reminded about the economy, I am wondering what we should do with that IRA we have in the credit union. The last report I received showed it had shrunk considerably.

Karen nodded. "Yes that has crossed my mind lately, too. Let's put that on our prayer list."

The next morning Karen spoke to Mark and Sara at the breakfast table. "We were talking last night about officially withdrawing you both from school. Since we will be moving today it makes sense to do it first thing this morning. What do you think?"

They both looked at their mother and then at each other. Mark spoke first. "I'm good with that," he said. "I just want to say good bye to my friends. Although, they are fewer and fewer since we haven't signed the pledge. The kids are really getting mean. I'd be happy to leave."

"Me too," Sara echoed.

By ten o'clock Karen and the kids arrived back at the house after saying goodbye and checking out of school. Bob arrived soon after with two temp workers and a small rental truck. Marie showed up at noon with armloads of "comfort food" and to help her children and grandchildren in any way she could. With everyone pitching in, the truck was soon loaded with furniture, clothing, pots and pans, and the few personal items each was taking along. They were definitely downsizing with this move. In addition, the pickup was loaded with tools and building materials. Looking at what remained behind, Bob made a mental note that there would be about one more pickup load before the moving job was done. Marie stood at the empty doorway waving a tearful goodbye. The extra hour they would be from her home would mean less time with her grandchildren.

At the country property, the moving team set up some boards to keep things off the ground, moved the personal property onto them, and tied down the tarps. Then the men went back to the house and reloaded the pickup. It was getting late so Bob took the temps to their office and returned the rental truck. After hooking onto the travel trailer he headed once again to the country property. This time James was there to meet him. Together they leveled the trailer and made sure everything was working. Finally, the Johnsons were ready to turn in for the night and start a new life.

Country life had its good points including hard work and sound sleep. The spirit of cooperation and harmonious relationships exceeded anything known to them in the past. On the negative side was the small size of the travel trailer. A novelty at first, the small space soon became an ever-present agitation. But for the short run, everyone seemed willing to make it work.

A week passed. Everything left at the house was eventually moved and the house keys were turned over to the new owners. They gave Bob an additional $5,000, and showed him the paperwork on the house they were also in the process of selling. The couple assured them all was in order and the expected close on their house would be in just one more week. They would pay the balance then.

Bob reminisced as he drove away from the house where so much of his family's life had taken place. So much had happened. He thought about the fights he and Karen used to have. Those were gone. He remembered the crude jokes of his co-workers and the worthless movies that had disgusted him even at the time. He was glad he wasn't caught up in all that anymore. Glancing in his rearview mirror he took one last look at their home. Just beyond it he saw someone is his yard and his attention was brought back to the present. Mr. Benson was picking up his mail.

Bob had been really curious to know whether Mr. Benson was reading the booklet he had left with him. Finding the phone number on a piece of paper on the dash, Bob dialed him up on the cell phone.

"Hello Mr. Benson. This is Bob Johnson."

"Bob, I've been wanting to talk with you. How's the trailer working for you?"

"Very well really. Everything works like it is supposed to."

"Good. That's what I wanted to hear. But what I really wanted to talk with you about is that book."

"Oh?" Bob sounded apprehensive.

"Yes. Why haven't I ever heard about this before? This makes a whole lot more sense than all the popular theories going around for the last twenty years. I've got to tell you, Ilene and I are very interested in learning more about the Sabbath."

Bob was slow to process this information. "Mr. Benson, how much have you read in the book?"

"The whole thing, twice. And by the way, just call me Tom. That's what all my friends call me."

"You got it, Tom." Bob was beginning to see God working and he didn't want to be left behind. "Maybe we could get together this week and study, if you have the time."

"If I have time, ha, ha, ha. That's good. I'm retired! What do you say about tomorrow?"

"All right, Tom. I'll be over at one o'clock and we'll study this thing together."

After hanging up, Bob was hyper. Never had anything like this happened to him. Then slowly it dawned on him that he was not prepared to give a Bible study to another person. When he arrived home he began a rapid search through the trailer for a set of studies but found nothing. There was a moment of panic, then Karen suggested they have prayer. A glimmer of hope made its way to Bob's mind. The family formed a circle and Karen prayed asking God to make a way for Bob to be able to help the Bensons learn more about His love and will for their lives. After prayer, Bob looked up as though viewing a high screen. "I know where it is in the tent. I remember now where I put it," he half yelled on his way out the door.

Returning with a smile and a box of books, study guides, and Bibles, Bob set about to master the topic of the Sabbath. Long after the family had turned in for the night, Bob studied on. Finally, exhaustion forced him to find rest along side his wife. Although tired and sleepy, he sensed a feeling of well-being. Gently he put his hand on Karen's hand and fell asleep.

In the morning, Bob awoke before the others. The tiny sleeping area he and Karen shared often put cramps in his legs. He jumped up and gingerly stretched his tired muscles. Stepping out of the "home away from home" he headed over to the cabin where James was staying. Hoping he was up by that time he tapped on the door. "Come in," James' voice could be heard.

Opening the door Bob spoke quietly, "Hope I'm not too early."

"Not at all. I'm preparing for some Bible studies I'll be presenting today to those people we met in the restaurant. Remember?"

"Of course I do. That's great."

James was shaking his head. "It is incredible how these people are consuming the word of God. We study twice a week for two hours and they never want to quit. I think they have even started sharing them with their family in California."

"Well, this looks like something I may have on my schedule in the future, too. Remember, I told you about giving the book to the neighbor who sold us the trailer?" James nodded. The man told me yesterday he wants to study with me, and the sooner the better. So today at one o'clock is my maiden voyage."

"Great! I know God will be with you and give you guidance in how to proceed. Just do your part and He will do the rest."

Back at the trailer, Bob and Karen worked out the details for the Bible study. The two of them would go together to the Bensons, leaving Mark and Sara home to complete their school assignments. The kids were old enough now to be on their own for periods of time. Then, too, the remote location of the property where they now lived meant very little chance of unwanted intruders causing trouble.

On the way to the Bensons, Bob stopped and picked up a newspaper. Without electricity in their temporary residence the family didn't keep up with the news. Looking at the front page of the paper was a grim reminder that all was not well in America—or in the world for that matter. Unemployment had risen for the sixth straight month. Crime was rampant, especially in cities. Wars were jumping from continent to continent. State governments were crying for more money. Karen exclaimed, "It sure is a blessing that we don't watch the nightly news anymore."

The Bensons welcomed Bob and Karen with open arms. After a few minutes of discussing the latest world events, Tom directed the conversation to the business at hand. Being the first Bible study Bob had ever conducted, he was a little tentative and kept to the script. When they had completed the first lesson, Bob endeavored to bring it to a close. But Tom wasn't ready to quit. "Can't we study more?" he inquired. Bob hadn't anticipated this, but couldn't think of a compelling reason why they shouldn't continue. So they launched into the next lesson.

It was past three when they concluded. Bob held out a packet; "Here are the rest of the studies in this series. I would like to suggest the two of you do two of the lessons each week."

"You know, we are going to be gone for the rest of the summer starting four weeks from today. Could we rev this up a bit so we can complete them before we leave?" Ilene asked.

"Sure." Bob smiled. "We could set aside Monday and Thursday at this time to go over the studies together if you like."

Tom stuck out his hand. "Sounds good. I really appreciate you folks doing this for us."

This kind of event became common for members of the Sabbath congregation where the Johnsons attended. It seemed that the Sunday registration requirement had awakened a lot of interest in basic Bible concepts. But despite the good feelings and apparent blessings from the Lord, problems continued to touch the lives of people from all walks of life all around the world. One of those problems was right in the church. The enthusiasm of some members actually seemed to anger others. There was even a campaign by some to join with the area churches in a common coalition to spread what seemed to Bob and Karen to be a watered-down version of salvation that lacked Biblical foundation. Eventually many couldn't see how they could get out of the city or they couldn't support their family without signing the registration. They would always believe the Sabbath was important, but they just couldn't agree God meant them to sacrifice their whole lives for it.

One Thursday, just at dusk, Bob and Karen were leaving the Bensons after their Bible study. As they were walking out the door, Bob thought he noticed someone sitting in their van. Figuring it must be a friend, he walked closer and bent down to get a better look. At that moment a shot rang out breaking the passenger side window. Bob immediately grabbed his leg and noticed blood. Instantly he dropped to the ground. Karen momentarily froze for a few seconds then started toward Bob. "Go back to the house. Run!" he commanded.

Karen spun around and headed for the house where the Bensons stood in the doorway. Another shot was heard—this time from the stocking-capped assailant as he was running away from the van. Ilene Benson called 911, giving all the details she could. Once the shooter was out of sight, Karen went back out to check on her husband. Though Bob was in pain and losing blood, he assured Karen everything would be OK. A distant siren told them help was on the way.

Once in the emergency room of Portland General Hospital, the ER doctor cleaned the wound in his left thigh and sewed it up. Since the bullet had not damaged the bone, Bob was allowed to go home with his wife. On the way out of the hospital, two police officers approached them.

"Bob Johnson?" the taller one asked.

"Yes, I'm Bob," he responded.

"We're here to take your statement concerning a gunshot wound you received."

There were a number of questions. Since neither Bob nor Karen recognized the shooter, they could not be of much help except to give a general description as seen from the back. At that point the interview was over and Bob was free to go.

When they arrived at home Mark and Sara, who had been informed of the incident, were anxious to hear the details. Karen filled them in while Bob rested in his bed. There he considered the significance of what had happened to him. "I could have been killed but I wasn't. Why?" he wondered in a whisper. "Why me? Was I being tested? Maybe it was just the luck of the draw. Maybe this is God's way of toughening me up." The thoughts and questions kept coming until he nodded off to sleep.

22

GO QUICKLY

*"This day I call heaven and earth as witnesses against
you that I have set before you life and death, blessings and
curses. Now choose life, so that you and your children
may live and that you may love the Lord your God...."*
Deuteronomy 30:19, 20, NIV

The country property began to take on the feeling of home. Little
by little the old dwelling was repaired enough to make it livable
and the roughed-in addition completed. By the end of summer the
generator initially purchased to power the constructions tools was
permanently installed at the "lodge." The fireplace added a peaceful,
cozy touch—and was the only heat source. Bob's healing leg didn't
slow him down too much, and he was able to accomplish a lot with
the help of James and Mark. All this work, of course, was being done
without a building permit. James and Bob talked often about this.
They knew the risk but felt the chances of being found out and red-
tagged were extremely small due to the remoteness of the property.
Then too, they reasoned, being required to have a Sunday registration
number surely was unconstitutional. Further, God had made this place
available to them, so the Higher Power directive held sway.

Mail was not delivered on the road leading to the country property. James and the Johnsons were content to use the nearest post office to receive their mail. They also figured the extra autonomy of not
having a street address might be a good thing. There was no electricity
connection or phone connection to give the location away, just cell
phones, with the P.O. box address.

It did make it more difficult to keep in touch with the couple that had purchased their home. There had been one excuse after another about why they couldn't pay. "Just one more week" had stretched into many more weeks and even months. They knew they would never see another dime from them. The Johnsons had little money left after the purchase of the trailer, school supplies and a bit of food. The government had seized their IRA savings for non-compliance with the Sunday law before they could get through the red tape to withdraw it. Now they would have to depend even more fully upon God. Was their relationship with Him strong enough? Could they trust Him?

As the cool days of fall began to color the leaves, a sense of urgency gripped them—and many Sabbath keepers—that had nothing to do with money. Some went to their friends and relatives begging them to consider accepting God's love. All too often the invitation was turned down. Those who made the decision to cast their lot with God stepped out in simple faith. Sometimes they left parents, husbands, and even children to stand for truth. Sadly, as time went on, fewer people made this commitment. Whereas for a while many new faces were seen at church, now most of the people there were baptized members.

These concerns were foremost in the minds of Bob and Karen as they approached winter.

Lingering at the table one evening Bob reflected, "I think it is time to ask our friends some difficult questions."

"Yes. I agree." Karen didn't look up. "Let's start with Tom and Ilene, OK?"

"Sure. We can do that." Bob looked at his wife and thought he saw her wipe her eyes. "You're worried about your mother, aren't you?" he added.

Karen continued to look down at her plate. Tears were beginning to fall faster now. "Oh, I just don't understand why she is being so stubborn. We have studied with her for so long. Why doesn't she turn her life over to God and trust him completely?"

Bob reached over and put his hand on her shoulder before he spoke. "Turn it over to God, my dear. She is close to making the right decision. Maybe now the time is right."

The next day was Tuesday. Bob and Karen decided to make the rounds to their friends and bring their plea in person. As agreed, they started with Tom and Ilene. Sitting on the couch in the Benson's living room, Bob tried to find a way to cleverly work the conversation toward spiritual matters. He tried to listen as Tom talked on and on about their summer trip in the new motor home.

How can I break into this conversation with such a different subject? he kept asking himself. Then suddenly there was a pause in the conversation. Bob seized the moment. "What a great adventure the two of you had. Now we want to ask you to embark upon another great adventure."

Ilene straightened up in her chair. "What are you talking about, Bob?" she asked.

"Ilene, Tom, we believe Jesus' coming is near." Bob looked at each of them and hesitated before going on. "We have gone through the studies with you and at the time each of you seemed to see the importance of what we learned together. Now we are asking you to make your move for God. In other words, make a commitment. Join us in following God and finding His plan for your life." In the silence that followed Bob felt his heart pounding. Time stopped while he began to question his reason for being there.

Slowly, Tom looked over at his wife and asked, "Shall we tell them?" Ilene nodded. A smile appeared on his face as he looked back to Bob and Karen. "Just this morning we were talking, and we came to the conclusion that it was time we got off the fence. So your timing couldn't have been better. We have accepted Jesus as our Savior. We want to be baptized to show our commitment to Him. Do you think your pastor would do that for us?"

Bob and Karen jumped to their feet with arms open, and hugged their friends. All tension was gone. To them, all the time and effort they had put into the studies were more than compensated. They were on a high rarely experienced before. Then, after making arrangements for the Bensons to meet with Pastor Ralph, they made their way to the location where Bob's long time contractor friend John was working.

Seeing Bob and Karen walking toward the job site, John laid

down his carpenter belt and walked to meet them. Bob naturally was interested in the new construction, so he made a quick tour with his friend to see how things were developing. But in his mind, the mission he was on loomed large before him. Finally he could hold back no longer and came to the point.

"John, you and I have talked a lot about God. We share much of the same theology. We have read the same books and magazines. So here is my question. What are you going to do with this information?"

John looked down at his boots. "I don't know," he said. "I believe most of that stuff, you know. But I can't really leave my work. I have a family to support . . . mortgage and car payment. This doesn't seem like the time for me to be doing something radical."

"Radical, John? Jesus died for you. That's radical. All he asks from us is to live for Him." Bob stood his ground.

"You probably are right, Bob. But the timing just isn't right for me." He hesitated for a moment and then stuck out his hand and added, "But thanks for coming by. It was good to see you."

Back in the car, Bob and Karen talked about what they had just experienced. Disappointed, Bob questioned himself. "Maybe I could have said things in a better way."

Karen shook her head. "Honey, you were doing exactly what the Holy Spirit inspired you to do. John cannot be sweet-talked or forced to make this decision in the way we think is best. What do you say we leave it with God?"

"You are right, my dear wife. What would I do without you?" He squeezed her hand. Then he asked the question Karen was hoping to avoid, "Are you ready to talk with your mother?"

"Yes," she said without hesitation. "I'm ready and at the same time I'm not ready. But like you I believe the time is right for Mom to make her decision. Let's take her out to supper. Then I'll ask her."

Bob was happy to go along with his wife on this one. She would be carrying the load this time and he would be the back-up support. After the meal Bob could sense the tension mount as Karen began to approach the issue that had brought them to the restaurant.

"Mom, I want to ask you a very important question."

"OK, dear. Ask me."

Karen looked at her mother and was flooded with thoughts of the times they had shared together. Mother and daughter had shared moments of joy and sadness, highs and lows, moments of splendor and of defeat. In a split second she knew that she had to bring this woman, who was so much a part of her life, to a decision. So she began. "Mom, you know how convinced we are that the second coming of Jesus is about to take place. Well, we are very concerned for you."

"Why is that, dear?"

"Well, Mom. We are worried that you have not taken a stand. You haven't indicated that you are on God's side in the struggle taking place between God and Satan."

"What makes you think that?" Marie was puzzled.

"For starters, Mom, you haven't seen the need for following God's clear counsel in the Bible, such as baptism, nor indicated your commitment to keep the Sabbath.

"I guess that is right," Marie pondered. "It is getting a lot harder for me to make decisions lately. When I go to the grocery store, I have the hardest time making selections.

"Mom, are you feeling well?" Bob interjected.

"Oh yes, I feel fine. It's just this decision thing that is hard for me."

"Maybe you need to see a doctor," Karen's concern had changed directions. "How about I help you get in for a check-up?"

Marie brightened. "I think that's a good idea. And why don't I come to church with you this week?"

At home, later, Karen related the day's events to her children. Mark and Sara were elated that Grandma would be joining them at church. Confronting so many people they loved in one day left Bob and Karen exhausted. When they lay down for the night their sleep was quick and satisfying.

The following day Karen called her mother's doctor's office to arrange a check-up. A previous caller had just canceled her three o'clock appointment for that day so Karen was able to get Marie penciled in. As usual Karen accompanied Marie for the examination, helping to fill in some of the details of her symptoms for the doctor. Thankfully, when they offered cash in payment, no one asked for their registration card. After spending an unusually long time with his examination, the doctor concluded that Marie was experiencing some mild depression and wrote out a prescription for an antidepressant. She immediately had the prescription filled and began taking them as prescribed. Within a few weeks she reported to Karen that she was sleeping better and not having so much trouble with decisions. Then it happened.

23

OH, MOMMY!

*"Wickedness is always easier than virtue: for it
takes the short course to everything."*
Samuel Johnson, 1973 A.D.

"Never will I leave you; never will I forsake you."
Hebrews 13:5, NIV

A cold breeze ruffled the curtains at Marie's bedside. Stirring slightly she pulled the covers closer around her shoulders. A slight noise and movement roused her more. Yawning she opened her eyes and tried to focus on the clock on the night table. It looked like it said 3:00 a.m. The noise started to become more demanding and Marie looked to the foot of her bed. In the dim glow from her ever-present night-light she could make out the form of a person standing there. The noise was her dresser drawers and jewelry box being opened and rifled through. Briefly she hoped her dead husband had reappeared; then reality hit. The scream she heard in her ears sounded so far away she wasn't sure if she had even heard it.

The person wheeled and swore at her. Screams continued to come from what she finally realized was her own throat. She couldn't stop. Coming so close to her face that she could smell his foul breath, Marie's attacker gave her an evil grin and brought his fist down across her face. Mercifully, Marie lost consciousness and was spared further knowledge of his vicious and brutal assault.

When she stirred hours later there was a strange bell ringing over and over. Struggling to wake up she finally realized the phone was ringing. As if in a dream she reached out to answer it. A sharp pain made her gasp and become faint with the effort. The ringing stopped, and Marie drifted in and out of consciousness. Soon the ringing started again and she once again opened her eyes and began to reach for the telephone. She never reached the receiver before passing out again from a wave of pain.

On the other end of the phone, Karen was beginning to get concerned. Marie had promised to meet her for lunch and was nearly an hour late. Leaving a note with the hostess in case her mother should show up after all, Karen jumped into her car and sped over to Marie's home.

The first sight that met Karen's stunned gaze nearly caused her to vomit. Marie's car door was open, there was broken glass scattered about, and closer inspection proved the stereo had been stolen. Grabbing her cell phone Karen hastily dialed "911" as she ran toward the gaping door of the house. Nearly shouting into the phone she gave a clipped version of the scene: "My mother's house and car have been broken into. I need police immediately. Send an ambulance." Her mind raced way beyond her words. She retrieved Marie's address from one corner of her brain and sketched the blueprint of her house in another corner.

"What?" Something the emergency operator was saying brought her mind back to the moment. "No, I am not going to wait until the police arrive before I enter the house. My mother could be dying in there and I am a nurse. I can't wait." She snapped the phone shut. Then decided to call Bob and keep him on the line while she cautiously entered.

"Bob! Mom's been robbed! I'm going into her house to find her. Please come now. Stay on the phone with me in case someone is still inside. The police are coming." Karen gave him a thumbnail sketch of the situation and walked quietly into the house. It was a disaster. It seemed all the doors and windows were open. Broken glass, scattered dishes, drawers turned upside down. It was deathly quiet, and Karen was so frightened for her mother's safety she could scarcely breathe. Bob was telling her to wait for the police, so she didn't talk. She was not going to let anyone keep her from her mother.

Tiptoeing quietly toward her mother's bedroom she jumped

when a nearby door slammed. Then it banged open again and Karen realized the wind was just blowing through a broken window. She had never seen such a trashed house. It was like pure evil had been unleashed upon every part of it. At last she reached the closed door to Marie's room. Carefully she twisted the doorknob and opened the door just a crack. The mirror facing her showed there was no stranger hiding behind the door, so she opened it wider. A groan made her heart leap into her throat. Grabbing a nearby umbrella Karen threw open the door and rushed in, flailing her arms and umbrella all around to fight off any would-be attacker.

"Help." A faint voice she didn't recognize came from the other side of her mother's bed. "Help."

Not seeing anyone in the room, Karen ran over to the bed. "Oh, Mom!" she cried out. "Bob help me. My mother's dying!"

"Help." Marie struggled to make her voice heard. She raised one hand briefly, then let it flop back.

"Mommy, Mommy!" Karen was crying and screaming over and over. "Mommy, Mommy!"

The cell phone, still on, lay on the bed where she had flung it. Distant sirens were coming closer. Karen's nursing training began to gain control of the little girl Karen had briefly become. Rushing to her mother's side she started the assessment she could do in her sleep: Breathing, airway, pulse, shock. The thought crossed her mind that she herself was in shock, but it wasn't important.

At the front door voices were commanding, "Police!" The voices continued methodically until they reached Marie's bedroom. "Police! Put your hands up. Identify yourself."

Karen obediently stood, raised her blood-covered hands, and answered their questions. "Please, my mother is hurt. Please help her."

Another police officer escorted emergency medical personnel into the room. "Stand aside." One EMT efficiently repeated the same assessment steps Karen had just performed. The other began to put an IV drip line into a vein in her arm. Karen could only watch helplessly. Her mother was a pitiful sight, covered in blood and beginning to moan. The police officer first on the scene still wasn't sure if Karen was the perpetrator so he remained with his gun trained on her as the other officers swept the house for any intruder.

Bob, who had been on his way to the lumberyard when Karen's call came in, arrived in the middle of this scenario. He walked to the front door, careful not to disturb the chaos surrounding the car and entrance. "Hello," he called.

Immediately an officer appeared with weapon drawn. "Police! Identify yourself."

Bob raised and opened his hands to his side. "I'm Bob Johnson. This is my mother-in-law's home—Marie Golden. My wife, Karen, called me to come when she discovered the car and house had been broken into. I think she is with her mother now."

Another officer patted Bob down and motioned him outside. "I'm sorry, we cannot allow anyone in until the victim has been stabilized and evacuated."

"Is my wife, Karen Johnson, with her?" Bob had heard her terrified screams over the unattended cell phone. He had listened until he reached the driveway, then put his phone beside him on the seat—still on.

"I don't have that information. Please leave the premises until the police have finished their investigation." The officer was kind, but offered no help.

Bob walked quickly to his truck and drove down the street where he did a quick U-turn and parked on the opposite side of the street. There he watched the unfolding events. Picking up the cell phone he strained to hear any conversation that might be happening in Marie's room. The occasional moan or sob told him things weren't great inside, but the EMTs were silently doing their job. He could hear Karen softly talking in the background, giving them the required information about her mother's medical history. Then the front door opened and a gurney was pushed towards the waiting ambulance. He could see the lines of the IV and a portable EKG machine traipsing from Marie's body. An oxygen mask told him she was at least breathing.

Then his attention was turned to the cell phone. Apparently

Karen had picked up her phone and he could now hear the conversation between her and the police still inside. "Officer, I was waiting at the restaurant for my mother to meet me. When she was almost an hour late and didn't answer her phone I rushed over. You can call the restaurant—here is their card—I left a note at the front desk for Mom in case she came while I was gone. It has the time on it, too."

"Well, all right. We'll check it out and if that's true you may go. But don't leave the area; we still have no other leads." The officer's voice was stern.

"I won't be leaving the hospital until my mother is out of danger, sir." Karen tried hard to control the mounting frustration she was feeling. "Will you be checking for fingerprints?"

"Our officers are doing that right now, Ma'am. And we need your shoes to compare to any shoe prints we find." Then after a brief pause, "Your note from the restaurant has been verified. You are free to go."

Bob heard a hurried "Thank you," then his connection was cut off. Shortly Karen emerged from the house and headed for her car. Starting his engine, Bob inched down the street. Karen looked up as she stepped barefoot over the crime scene tape and waved her recognition, then motioned him to follow her. Together they turned down the street that led to the hospital.

24

THE TURNING POINT

"Into each life some rain must fall, some days must be dark and dreary."
Henry Wadsworth Longfellow, 1842 A.D

"The Lord is my helper, and I will not fear what man shall do to me."
Hebrews 13:6, NIV

Holding hands, Bob and Karen walked quickly from the parking lot at the hospital. She had found an old pair of gardening shoes in the trunk, but would have run barefoot across hot coals to see her mother. Entering the ER they exchanged a knowing glance, remembering the traumatic events that had unfolded there not that long ago. "It seems like it is happening all over again," Karen said while feeling faint from the blanket of sounds and smells that seemed to cover them.

Bob pulled her aside into a corner of the waiting room. "Karen, we have God now. He loves us and He loves your mother. Let's just say a little prayer for her." Then bowing his head Bob did something that had embarrassed him a few years ago when Marie had prayed at the museum; he prayed in public. "My Father in Heaven," he began, "We all need Your help. Marie has been tragically hurt and is fighting for her life. Please hold her in Your Arms and save her from further suffering. Give Karen and me strength and wisdom to help her, and help us not to be afraid. We ask in Jesus name. Amen." He gave Karen's hand a quick squeeze. "Now let's see what we can find out."

Karen let out a sigh and briskly strode along beside her husband toward the information desk.

"Thank you, Bob," she began. "I am so thankful we have God in our lives. He makes all the difference." Her voice radiating confidence she inquired of her mother's location and condition.

"I'm Karen Johnson. Can you please tell me where I can find my mother, Marie Golden, and what her condition is? I am a registered nurse and would like to see her chart."

"Certainly, Mrs. Johnson. She is in examining room 1A. You will need to check in at the ER desk to be allowed in to see her and to learn about her condition. Step right this way." The volunteer escorted them personally.

A familiar nurse stood poring over notes at the desk. "Lori! What are you doing here?" Karen was surprised to find their old friend working in the hospital.

"Oh, hi Karen, Bob. I just started working here last month. Got tired of private duty nursing—too uncertain. There's always a shortage of nurses in hospitals. What brings you here—are the children ill?" The last question brought a worried frown to Lori's attractive face.

"No, my mother was beaten up last night—they just brought her in by ambulance." Karen was craning her neck this way and that to try to catch a glimpse of her mother. "Can you help us get in to see her and find out how she is?"

"Of course! Oh, I'm so sorry. I had no idea that was your mother. She isn't my patient, but I'm sure I can arrange it." Lori scurried off with the Johnsons hurrying to keep up.

"Lori, could you get transferred to my mother's case? We—I—would feel so much better knowing she was being taken care of by someone she knows and trusts." Karen felt Bob's quick squeeze to her hand.

"If you really want me to, I would be honored. It wouldn't be any problem to transfer, I'm sure." Lori sounded pleased. "And thank you for your confidence in me. I can assure you she will be in my prayers constantly." Opening a curtain at last, Lori motioned the Johnsons to stand quietly in the background. She walked up to the attending nurse, said a few words, and took her place at the doctor's elbow. The other nurse nodded, then washed her hands, smiled briefly—sympatheti-cally—at the Johnsons, and left the room.

"Wow," Bob whispered into Karen's ear, "she really is effi-cient." Karen's smile told him all he needed to know.

The minutes dragged on with orders, dressings, stitches, and x-rays. Beeping monitors showed a slowly stabilizing heart, blood pres-sure, and oxygen rate. Karen knew what she was looking at and began to feel hopeful that her mother would live. One tiny tear escaped and trickled down her cheek. "Thank You, Jesus," she whispered under her breath.

Finally, much later that afternoon, the doctor stepped back and took a deep breath. Giving a few last minute instructions to Lori, he turned to leave. Seeing the Johnsons standing in a corner he walked up to them.

"I'm Dr. Smith. Are you family?"

Karen hastily spoke up "Yes, I'm her daughter, Karen Johnson, and this is my husband, Bob. Will she be OK?"

"I'm sorry to have ignored you so long, but it was touch and go for awhile and I had to keep focused. She has several fractures of her jaw and arm that may still need surgery. Either way she will have a long road to recovery with a lot of rehabilitation. There were numer-ous cuts that required stitches and there is much bruising—some of it internal. In her favor, she stabilized fairly quickly and her vitals are all at good levels now. So, yes, I think she will be OK—eventually." Dr. Smith rattled off the list with precision.

"Oh thank you, Doctor. I don't mind at all that you took good care of her and ignored us. I am a nurse also. Do you think we could take her home with us for the rehabilitation?" Karen asked.

"I foresee possibly a week in the hospital, then she should have full-time nursing care for a few more weeks and begin to do some rehabilitation during that time. Since you are a nurse I'm sure she would be much better off where she's loved and can feel safe, than in a long-term care center. Excuse me, that's my pager." And Dr. Smith hurried to respond.

Lori now motioned them closer to Marie's bed. "She has been

given sedatives to make her more comfortable so she won't be awake for awhile. I thought you'd like to join me and we can have prayer before the aide takes her to her room."

Karen was torn. She wanted to cradle her mother's broken body but it was painful to see her so bruised and bandaged. "I keep forgetting today that I'm a nurse. I'm just her daughter and it's so hard." Tears threatened to overflow.

"You should have seen the house." Karen spoke to both Bob and Lori. "I looked at it a little closer on my way out and it is destroyed. There is broken glass everywhere, furniture wrecked; everything is out of its place. I've never seen anything like it. Oh, Mama, I'm so sorry." She gently touched Marie's silver hair.

The three stood quietly holding hands around Marie's bed, then Lori prayed a touching prayer for Marie's complete healing, as well as for Bob, Karen, and the family to be supported through this ordeal. The aide arrived then, and Lori briefed him on a few things, then urged him to give her an extra soft ride.

"Thank you so much, Lori." Karen patted her arm. You were wonderful with her. I have one other question to ask that I can hardly bear to think about. Was—was she raped?"

"I'm sorry, Karen, but yes she was. The doctor said he had never seen such a brutal attack in his career. The beating as well makes this man a very dangerous criminal. The police have asked for a full report of any evidence found and will be putting out a warning through the media shortly."

Karen felt the room spinning, but she willed herself to focus on her mother's need. "God has spared her life and there is nothing more important than that. We will surround her with our love and God will heal her." The words gathered strength and sincerity as she spoke them.

"You are absolutely right, darling." Bob hugged Karen tightly. "She is a part of our family forever, as long as she wants." He smiled down at his wife. "We had better call the children and tell them something. James agreed to keep them occupied this afternoon, but that is quickly fading."

Lori excused herself to finish her charting. "I'll just be a few minutes, then I am going to be transferring to Marie's room. I'm a float nurse and able to take a special case full time when needed. I won't leave her side for the next few days. There is a recliner where I can catch some sleep when I need to." She smiled reassuringly. "Actually now would be the best time for you two to go home and prepare the children as well as rest up for some long days here. The doctors will keep Marie asleep for about twenty-four hours."

Bob and Karen consulted together. They had so many questions about the crime. Maybe they would go by the house and see if the police could let them pick up her Bible and glasses. Maybe they could find a clue as to who had done this. Maybe the police could tell them something. They hung around the desk while Lori finished her work, reluctant to leave.

"Karen, why don't you two come up to your mother's room with me and see her all tucked in?" Lori recognized the shock that still lingered with her friends.

Obediently they followed Lori to the elevators. A sudden wave of tiredness and sadness engulfed Karen such as she had seldom experienced. Leaning on the elevator wall she closed her eyes and prayed for strength. She had to be strong for her mother. "My mother has always been the pillar of strength, the comforter. Now she is going to need me, need us, to help her and I'm not sure I'm up to it." She spoke the last words to Bob.

"None of us is up to something this terrible, Karen. But God has promised to be with us and He will give us the strength as we need it." Bob's words were good, but his face was pale, too.

Lori led the way from the elevator to room 350A. "She will be in intensive care the first day or so until we are sure there are no surprises. The regular ICU crew will handle her care and I will be there just specifically to see that nothing goes wrong. I will double check everything and will be there if she wakes up."

They could only stay for five minutes while she was so fragile. "Mommy," Karen reverted to her childhood term of endearment, "I love you so much. You are my precious Mommy and I love you. I'm so sorry you are so hurt. I will be praying for you every minute." Tears dropped on the white blanket. "You come live with me now, Mommy. Bob and I, and the children want you to live with us. There are birds, and frogs, and deer all around us. You will love it. I can't wait until you come home with us. I love you."

Bob stood grimly beside his grieving wife. "Mom," he addressed Marie, "you are the best mother-in-law a guy could have. Karen's right, we are looking forward to you living with us. You hurry and get better, OK?" He cleared his throat and looked away. The nurse coming in gave them the "time's up" signal. "We have to go now, but Lori will be with you every minute and we will be back as soon as they let us."

Leaden feet carried them both to the elevator. Reaching the outside door they groaned when they realized they had two vehicles to drive the hour home.

"Why don't we leave the car here and just take your truck home tonight?" Karen pleaded. "That way even if the kids want to come see Nana tomorrow they can't because we won't have room. I can't bear for them to see her yet."

"I think that is a very good plan," Bob readily agreed. "Besides, it's not a good idea for either of us to be alone right now anyway."

25

ARRESTED

"More things are wrought by prayer than this world dreams of."
Alfred Lord Tennyson, 1859-85 A.D

"Is any one of you in trouble? He should pray."
James 5:13, NIV

Karen did a lot of praying to get through the night. Every time she closed her eyes she could see the terrible injuries to her mother's body. The children's reactions to the news replayed over and over in her mind, as well. She had wondered how much realism was necessary and good. In the end she had told them everything, deciding to enlist their help in praying for Nana. Their concern had been touching and instead of being frightened they actually rose to the occasion and showed how strong their trust in God had become.

The next morning was sunny and beautiful. The children had planned a surprise breakfast for Mom and Dad so Karen could get right in to see Nana. They had also made beautiful "Get Well" cards and even found a few stray flowers still blooming for a small bouquet. Karen was so pleased with their cooperation and thoughtfulness. Mark and Sara had grown closer—Karen couldn't remember their last squabble. It was nice.

Just as Bob finished drying the dishes the kids had washed, there was a knock at the door.

"Good morning friends, what do you say we move in today?" James asked his builder friend.

"I would say we have completed our job of getting the lodge in livable condition. So there is nothing to keep us from enjoying it,"

Bob agreed. Turning to Karen he added, "I'll go in with you another time to get the pickup. You stay with your mother as long as you like. Give her my love, and tell her I'm praying for her."

The rest of the day saw them moving things in and trying to make order out of chaos. Furniture, clothing, beds and bedding, tables, kitchen equipment and supplies, all found a place to reside. Most of the tarps were used to partition off "bedrooms" in the large new room added on. Some were used to cover the mossy roof in hopes of keeping the rain out. Then there were boxes of books. The Johnsons had books. But James had what amounted to a library. By nightfall, everyone was very tired and beds not used for months found familiar residents resting comfortably in them. Karen had decided to stay at the hospital with her mother.

By the third day after the assault, Marie was fully awake and aware of what had taken place. Oddly enough her first concern wasn't for herself, but for Karen, who hadn't left her side for more than a few minutes since she regained consciousness.

"Karen dear, don't look so worried. This old lady has seen quite a few bumps and bruises in her life. I just got a few more all at once this time!" Marie's attempt at a chuckle came out more like a grimace.

Karen smiled briefly. "I can't imagine how anyone could do what that man did to you. You're such a great person."

"I long ago gave up trying to make sense of evil. Bad things happen to good people all the time. It's because of sin, not because God has forgotten us. So I've decided I'm just not so special that I cannot suffer from time to time. God is still with me. He was with me during the attack. Mercifully, He let me pass out so I didn't have to experience the worst of it. He has promised not to allow more than we can bear. I will heal, Karen. I will heal." Marie spoke the last words firmly as though to reinforce the idea in her own mind.

"I'm so glad, Mom," Karen began, but tears soon took over. "I'm so glad," she sobbed, "that you are alive."

"Say, I never got to tell you my surprise at lunch!" Marie motioned Karen to bend closer. "The last few weeks I have been attending your church, you know. I have been talking to Pastor Ralph and Barbara . . . I have accepted Jesus as my Lord and I am going to be baptized in two weeks. I'm so happy!"

Karen was truly surprised. "Mom! I had no idea. I thought you weren't feeling well and just decided not to press the issue. How wonderful!" Then realizing her mother's physical injuries might pose a problem, "What are you going to do now?"

"I'm going to be baptized in two weeks. Lori has agreed to come out with me for awhile to help you with my physical therapy and, Lord willing, I will walk into the baptistery in two weeks." Marie was beaming. "I know I can't move a finger now without hurting, but God will help me, I'm sure."

"Well, I'm impressed. I was afraid this would affect your depression." Karen and her mom had always been open with each other. "How did you know we wanted you to come live with us?"

"Actually I thought it was a dream the other day, but apparently I heard what you and Bob were saying to me. It made me think, and I realized my depression started about the time I didn't get to see you and my precious grandchildren so often. So, I've decided it's a great idea and I'm coming to my new home just as soon as they spring me from here!" Marie was starting to wind down. "I'm really tired now. I think I'll rest."

"You rest, my Mother dear, take your rest." And Karen began to sing a lullaby her mother had sung to her as a little girl. Marie's face took on a peaceful appearance and she was soon asleep.

Lori came back from her break just then and Karen filled her in on her mother's plans. "I know, I know. Isn't your Mom doing great? I'm so impressed with her courage and faith. Actually, I am very much looking forward to spending a few weeks at your country retreat. She is such a dear."

"You know, I think I will go over to Mom's and try to rescue a few of her personal things. She'll need some clothes and things to make her feel it's her home, too." Karen was starting to feel upbeat for the first time in several days. "If she wakes up, please tell her I'll be back at suppertime."

Driving up to Marie's home, Karen was surprised to see the crime scene tape gone, everything cleaned up around the house, and the broken windows boarded over. There was a car in the driveway that she didn't recognize. At the doorway she cautiously called out "Hello, anyone here?"

A head popped out from around the kitchen door. "Oh, hi! I thought I heard someone. I hope you don't mind; I called Bob and he thought it would be OK." Barbara was talking as fast as her hands were cleaning. "When I heard what had happened—I visit at the hospital, you know—I just thought you folks had enough to handle without the clean-up here."

Karen was floored. "I am learning every day how wonderful it is to belong to the family of God," she finally said. "Thank you so very much. It is a job I have dreaded tackling, and here you have it almost completed. How can I ever repay you?"

"You just take good care of that sweet mother of yours and help her fulfill her wish to be baptized in a few weeks, if she can. That's all the payment I need." Barbara came over and gave Karen a hug. "This is good exercise for me." She turned to put away the cleaning supplies. "I was just getting ready to go home and clean up in time for a visit to the Bensons. You folks have certainly been letting your light shine since you came to know Jesus."

"Praise the Lord—for everything! For your help with my mother, and cleaning here today, and for the Bensons' decision to give their hearts to God. I can't remember what I used to do for fun before I became a Christian. I'm so much happier now." Karen sighed. "I wish I had known sooner how much God loves me."

"You know now and He has promised to restore the lost years. You will have forever to live in His courts and be loved. Remember, Jesus is coming soon!" Barbara finished with her favorite line and waved goodbye.

Karen thought how strange life had become. What used to be considered terrible events had become ways for God to bring blessings to her. There was no logic to it, but she didn't feel victimized anymore by her mother's attack. She felt loved by God; loved, forgiven—and forgiving. She picked up two suitcases full of her mother's clothing, some bedding, and mementos, and her dad's framed picture from the mantel. Giving the home a final glance, she locked the door, lifted her chin, and began singing "What a friend we have in Jesus."

It was hard to find a place to park at the hospital, so Karen was later getting back than she had planned. Riding up in the elevator, she hummed a song and reviewed the events of the day. As the doors opened on her floor, two uniformed police officers stepped on. She smiled at them and just as the doors were closing behind her, heard one say to the other, "That lady is lucky to be alive. I hope we find her assailant—we are so overworked."

"Hi, Mom. Oh, you have your supper tray. Can I help you with anything?"

Marie sighed. "Thank you, dear. Just set it here and help me move my arm onto the table. I'm going to try feeding myself this time."

"I just saw two policemen leaving. Did they visit you?" Karen thought she detected tears on her mother's face.

"Yes, they asked me to recount everything I could remember from that night. I'm afraid I wasn't much help. The man had a stocking cap pulled low on his forehead. But they assured me what I did remember would help." Marie paused. "I was just feeling a little sad for all the crime in our world. I have God to help me through this, but some people have no one and nothing to help them."

Karen deliberately changed the subject. "Guess who I discovered at your house this afternoon?"

"I can't imagine," Marie answered.

"Our Pastor's wife, Barbara! And, get this, she was cleaning your house when I arrived there to do some cleaning myself." Karen was beaming.

Marie was thoughtful a moment and began to shake her head. "I have to admit that no clergy has ever done that for me before. In fact no church member has done that for me before even when I attended regularly. I can't wait to be a part God's family."

After the visit with her mother, Karen made her way home.

Turning on the car radio at the top of the hour she listened to one grim story after another. Once again the stock market was down. Once again the unemployment numbers had worsened. Terrorism had struck in two more American cities. There seemed to be no solution for world and national problems. Karen shuddered with the realization that so many people were facing terrible problems with no one to pray for them.

As she turned off the freeway, Karen came to a stop behind other cars waiting for a traffic light to change. At the corner where the light was located she saw a lady holding a small child. From a distance she felt drawn to the woman and continued to observe her. Once the light changed, traffic moved forward giving her a much better look. Then just as she drove past the corner, the identity of the woman dawned on her. It was Denise Collier, John's wife. Quickly she turned into a nearby gasoline station and parked. Getting out of the car, she hurried toward the woman who was looking down at the child in her arms. "Denise?" she called above the noise of traffic.

Turning toward the voice, she saw Karen's smiling face but couldn't make the connection. "Yes," she said timidly.

"It's me, Karen Johnson."

"Oh, hi. I'm sorry I didn't recognize you," she apologized. "It's been a while."

"I know. It's been way too long." Then her eyes went to the child. "Is this your little girl?"

"Yes. This is Jennifer. She is my whole life right now."

Immediately, Karen sensed a story was begging to get out. An idea came to her. "Could you spend a few minutes with me at the restaurant just down the street? I really want to catch up on things in your life," she asked.

"Well, OK. For a few minutes." While answering, her eyes never left her daughter's face.

Once in the car Karen talked about her family and where they lived and how her children were doing home school. Then they were at the restaurant and promptly seated. "So tell me about yourself and your family," she asked.

There was a long pause in conversation. Denise continued to look down at her napkin and tableware. Then Karen noticed a tear bounce off her friend's blouse. Still nothing came from Denise's lips. "Denise, are you having trouble?"

"Yes," she responded. "But I am so ashamed. I don't want to tell you about it."

"Oh no. No. I'm your friend. You can trust me. I promise you. Maybe I can help in some way." Karen spoke quietly while reaching across the table and touching Denise's hand. Just then the waitress arrived to take their order. Karen took charge in an effort to avoid embarrassment to her friend. "We'll have two toasted cheese sandwiches, two herb teas, and applesauce for the little one," she said.

When the waitress left, Denise regained her composure. "All right, I may as well tell you," she grimaced. "Your husband was so nice to turn his business over to my husband. And for a while John was doing real well. Business was good and everyone liked his work. Then you and Bob came by and spoke with him about the Sabbath. You probably remember the conversation." Karen nodded but said nothing.

"Well, he and I had already signed the Sunday registration form," Denise went on. "But we talked about it after that on more than one occasion. We even studied the Bible to see if there was some way out for us. But our consciences would not let us alone. Finally, John went to the CCB in Salem and renounced his agreement to honor Sundays. Since then, things have gone bad for us."

Karen wasn't sure if she should be glad or sad for her friend. So she asked for clarification. "Wow, I'm awed by this decision. But I sense that your bad news has made your life difficult. Please share with me what has happened."

"Karen, this is so humiliating for me, I'm not sure I can say it. But I'll try." She took a deep breath and began. "A week after John went to the CCB we received a letter from them to cease and desist. John could no longer work as a licensed contractor. So he finished the job he was on and was planning to work for someone else when the police came and took him to jail for finishing the job. He is being held there until his trial next month. I have only seen him one time." Again the tears rolled down her cheeks.

Karen leaned forward in her seat and spoke quietly. "You are right. This is really bad news. I'm so sorry."

"That's not all." Denise seemed determined to get the whole story out. "Our house is being taken from us by the bank, so Jennifer and I moved in with my parents. That worked for a while. Then they made a big deal out of my decision not to go along with the Sunday registration. When I wouldn't give in, they made us leave. For the last two weeks we have been on the streets. It's really scary."

Karen's mouth opened but she seemed speechless for a moment. Then she found the words. "God has brought us together today so that you can have a home. You can live with us."

Denise brightened momentarily, then frowned. "We couldn't do that," she said.

"And why not?" Karen asked.

"Oh you know," Denise looked down. "You folks are white and we are, we are. . . . African-American."

"What? Do you really think that makes a difference to us? We consider you family. And I guarantee you there will be no family member of ours living on the streets as long as we have a leaf to put over our heads." Karen was emphatic.

After they had eaten, Karen loaded Denise and Jennifer into the car and went straight home. There the whole story was repeated for the family and James. All agreed that this was a providential meeting and their new guests were to become permanent residents with them as long as necessary. James, though, began to ponder what could be done for John in jail.

26

GOD WILL DELIVER

"Rather than love, than money, than fame, give me truth."
Henry David Thoreau, 1854 A.D.

"The King will reply, 'I tell you the truth, whatever you did for one of the
least of these brothers of mine, you did for me.'"
Matthew 25:40, NIV

Gather around everyone. I have some news which will interest you all." James motioned them toward the two worn couches and four chairs in the big unfinished room of the lodge.

"What's up James?" Bob questioned.

"God has been working, my friend," James said. "OK, looks like everyone is here. As you know, I went into town today to pick up a few things. While traveling along I began thinking of John in jail." He looked at Denise holding her daughter. "You know how it works when God has a plan for you—He just keeps impressing upon your mind what you should do. So, I swung by the jail and visited John."

Denise gasped. Suddenly she was engaged in this conversation. James addressed her. "Your husband sends his love to you and Jennifer. His faith in God is strong. And he is doing as well as can be expected for a Christian in jail. We had a good talk about his case. We prayed together and I left. Then I paid a visit to the courthouse. I must admit I was a little scared because I no longer have credentials to represent a client in court. But no one seemed to notice that fact." A big smile came over his face before he continued.

"Now for the really good news. God worked it out so that John's trial date is a week from today in Judge Steven Pierce's court." The small group was too stunned to speak for a moment.

Denise put her hand over her mouth until she could hold it in no longer. "Praise God!" she burst out. "And thank you, James, so very, very much."

The following day Marie was released from the hospital. Bob and Karen transported her directly to her new home. She took one look at her surroundings and fell in love with it. "This is the most beautiful area I've ever lived in," she exclaimed. Although her health was improving, there was a long way to go with much physical therapy. That is where Lori fit in so nicely. She was not only a nurse but was also trained as a physical therapist. After supper Lori also arrived to begin her part-time caregiving assignment in-residence.

Bob began to feel awkward about all their friends and family who were now living at the lodge. He decided to speak to James about it. "James," he said. "I feel like I owe you an explanation."

"For what?" James asked.

"Well, our guest list is growing way beyond anything we had anticipated. The last thing we wanted to do is to be a burden on you. So I just want to apologize and ask what we can do to make up for it?"

James laughed out loud. "Bob, you are closer to me than anyone else in the world. You have made this lodge come together. You are a constant inspiration to me; and not just you, but your whole family, and each person who has come to live here. God has arranged this so that we can be a help to each other, Bob. I have never been so happy in my whole life."

Early the following morning, before going to work at the hospital, Lori took a walk around the property. Upon returning she asked Karen about the hot spring she had seen.

"What hot spring?" Karen asked.

"It's just off the trail leading to the creek," she explained.

"Honestly, we have never seen it. But I certainly will go look at it today!" she exclaimed.

After breakfast Karen took Mark and Sara with her up the sloping trail toward the creek. There, just as Lori had said, was a lovely pool of water with gentle bubbles coming up and a small stream flowing down to the creek. "Go ahead," she told her kids. "Touch it and see how warm it is."

Quickly the two were down on their knees touching the water. "Wow, it's hot!" they said simultaneously.

Reaching into her pocket Karen pulled out a thermometer she had brought along just in case it might be needed. Dropping down to her knees she placed the end into the water. Then she looked at it. "One hundred four degrees," she announced.

Upon returning to the lodge, Karen excitedly told Bob and James about the new find on the property. "Maybe there is some way we can use this as part of Mom's therapy."

Bob and James wasted no time in taking the walk to see the hot spring. They were amazed at the sight. "God must have put it here," James asserted. "It certainly wasn't here when I got this property!" They immediately began to figure a way to make the pool accessible for Marie and anyone who needed a dip in the hot spring they labeled Lori's Spring. By the end of the day they had created a rough but very friendly and serviceable "hydrotherapy" hot tub.

When Lori returned from work, she was shown the newly enhanced hot spring and immediately made plans to transport Marie there for her first treatment. She had plenty of volunteers, including James. Slowly and carefully the recuperating Marie was lowered into the therapeutic water. All eyes were upon her to see if she could tolerate the hot temperature. A smile crept over her face as she sighed, "Mmm, this feels good."

After the therapy session was complete and Marie was transported back to her bed, James and Lori spent some time together getting acquainted. In time, they were seen reading from their Bibles, praying, and even laughing together. As the days slipped by, the attorney and the nurse became very close friends and it soon became obvious to the rest of the lodge residents that a romance was taking place in front of them. All were happy for their newfound relationship, especially Marie.

On the appointed day of John's trial, Karen volunteered to watch Jennifer so Denise could accompany James to the courthouse for John's trial. There was an emotional moment when John stepped into the room where his wife was waiting for him. After a few minutes John composed himself and sat down with James to go over the facts and strategy. James concluded his preparation with prayer that God would be in charge. Then looking up at his pro bono client, James asked, "John, do you still believe it is wrong for you to sign the Sunday pledge?"

"Yes, I do, and I always will," he stated without hesitation. James gave the thumbs up sign as he arose from his seat.

Court began in the usual manner with introductions and reading of the charges. The prosecuting attorney called his first witness, a clerk at the CCB office. After the swearing in she was asked if the accused had withdrawn his agreement with the state to abide by the Sunday Rest Act. She said that was the case. Then James stood and asked her if the accused had acted in any way other than as a gentleman when he had withdrawn his pledge.

"No, he was very nice," she answered. But James wasn't done with his questioning.

"Did he tell you why he had withdrawn his pledge?"

"Yes. He said that the pledge violated his conscience."

"Did he say why it violated his conscience?"

"Yes. He said Sunday was the false day of reverence to God, and Saturday was the true Sabbath that God had established."

"How do you recall so much of what Mr. Collier said?"

"Well. I have thought about it lots since that day. It kind of makes sense to me."

"Do you go to church on Sunday in compliance to the law?"

"Objection. The witness is not on trial here," the prosecution stated.

Judge Pierce reacted quickly. "Denied. The court would like to know if there is any bias here." Turning to the witness he said, "You may answer the question."

"Yes, I go to church on Sunday."

The prosecution had no other witnesses so the time was turned over to the defense. James had but one witness—John. After taking the oath John sat confidently in the witness seat as James began his questions.

"Mr. Collier, do you admit rescinding your pledge to keep the Sunday Registration Act?"

"Yes. I do."

"Do you admit to completing work for your customer, Thomas Jones, after receiving notice from the CCB that you were to quit conducting your construction business immediately?"

"Yes. I do."

"Why did you keep working?"

"Three reasons, really. First, my customer didn't think he would be able to find a replacement contractor within a reasonable period of time. So he asked me to complete the work. I did it to accommodate him and fulfill my original commitment to him. Second, I interpreted the letter from the CCB to mean when I had completed my current job. And third, I do not believe it constitutional for the government to force me to violate my own conscience."

James concluded his questions and the prosecutor was given a chance to question the accused. "Mr. Collier," he began. "What made you think that the cease and desist order from the CCB gave you the latitude to complete the job you were doing when you received the letter?"

"Thank you for asking that, sir," John began. "The letter stated that I should cease work immediately in accordance with CCB rules. When I looked up the appropriate section in the rules manual it stated that all jobs begun by a contractor must be completed before the contractor will be released from his responsibilities. In this way the public will be protected."

Immediately, the prosecutor began looking through his brief case. Suddenly he looked up and stated, "No further questions, Your Honor."

Judge Pierce then asked, "Does the defense have any other witnesses?"

"No, your Honor," James replied.

In an unusual style, Judge Pierce addressed the court without a recess. "In the interest of time," he announced, "I am ready to announce my verdict without a recess." James and John stood with eyes fixed on the judge. Then the announcement was made. "I find the accused, John Collier, to be not guilty of this infraction." Then looking directly at John, he said, "You are free to go."

It was over. The two months incarceration was now history. There were hugs all around. Then as James, Denise, and John were exiting the courtroom the bailiff tapped James on the shoulder. "Sir, Judge Pierce would like to speak to you."

"Of course," he replied. He showed Denise and John to a bench outside the courtroom and followed the bailiff to the judge's chambers. Once James was inside, the bailiff left. Judge Steven Pierce and James shook hands and reminisced for a few minutes. Then the judge turned serious.

"James, you remember the evening we spent together trapped by that terrible storm." James nodded. "Well, I have never forgotten some of the things you said that evening. In fact I have been studying some things from the Bible as a result of what you said. Now I'm on the verge of making a big change, one that will greatly affect my future. But first, I would very much appreciate your input. Could you find some time to spend with me concerning this?"

"Certainly, Judge Pierce," James replied. "I know a quiet little restaurant in Oregon City named Millie's. Would that work for you tomorrow at six o'clock?" Judge Pierce knew of the place and agreed to meet James there.

When James arrived back at the lodge with Denise and John everybody was out under the front porch to meet them. It was like a long overdue school reunion. When the complete account of what had happened was told, James suggested they all join hands and give thanks to God for John's deliverance. All agreed that God had made it all happen. They bowed their heads in a prayer of thanksgiving.

At the restaurant the next day Judge Pierce surprised James with a tale of his adventure through Bible truths. He claimed that his expanded interest in Bible truths was a result of the experience he had the night of the big storm when he was at Bob and Karen's house. "By the way," he asked, "How is that family?"

"Couldn't be better, Your Honor," James was succinct, but then added, "If we have time, I'll tell you all about them later."

"Good, I want to hear all about them. Now if you don't mind, since we are not at work, I would prefer you call me Steve. And in this case I am really asking you for advice."

James smiled. "Sure, Steve. I hope I can be of help to you."

"OK then. Here is the dilemma I am facing. My research has led me to the belief that God has a special day on which He has agreed to meet with mankind. If we put away our business and pleasure pursuits on that day, He will pour out a blessing on us such as we could only imagine otherwise. That part is the theory. Here is the practical part. The special day God has for us is Saturday. Well now, that presents certain problems for us today doesn't it?"

James was nodding, barely able to restrain himself. "Yes and no," he said. "I'll explain later. But first go ahead with your thought."

Judge Pierce continued, "As you are more than aware, the law of the land is to pledge allegiance to Sunday as a day of recreation and worship to honor God. But just like your client yesterday I now believe it is unconstitutional and goes against the love and law of God. Do you think I would be crazy to rescind my commitment?"

By this time James was not able to mask his joy any longer. He shook Steve's hand and complimented him on making the right decision. He told his own story of Sabbath fellowship with God and the immeasurable blessings of the Lord. Then he related the story of how God had provided a country place for him and his new extended family to live. It was getting late when they finally agreed to meet regularly for Bible studies. As they were parting, Judge Steven Pierce made his commitment out loud. "Tomorrow I will resign my job as judge and rescind my Sunday registration."

James could hardly hold it in till he arrived back at the lodge. The adults still awake were anxious to learn what had been on the judge's mind. James was happy to recall all the details. Then he summarized, "Getting John set free was the blessing of the Lord. Having a sitting judge take his stand for God and the Sabbath is an all out miracle."

Following John's release from jail, he and Denise settled into the family-style life at the lodge. John felt blessed for his own release, but was in prayer often for those Christians still sitting in jail that had lost their trials or appeals. He had been a thorough Bible student and shared the love of God while in jail, yet he had many questions about God still unresolved. Denise was still catching up, but doing so rapidly. Neither of them had been baptized. So when they learned that a baptism was going to take place at the church where the Johnsons attended, they wanted to be included and take their public stand for God.

Also in the weeks ahead, Steven Pierce proved to be a man of his word. As proof of his commitment to accept the sacrifice of Jesus on his behalf, he was baptized along with Marie and the Colliers. Pastor Ralph and Barbara both participated joyfully in the ceremony. The little church seemed to be filled with a Holy Presence as first Marie, then Judge Pierce, and finally John and Denise were laid under the waters then raised, as the Bible says, "into newness of life." Lori attended the service along with James and shared in the joy of the extended family. She had been been a member of another denomination for many years and had lived the life of a devout Christian. Yet on this day, watching these friends take this step toward God, she sensed something deeper and more important than she had ever known.

The next two weeks saw some subtle changes taking place in world affairs. All of the NATO members implemented Sunday legislation that limited commerce on Sundays. Other nations in Africa, Asia, and South America adopted similar resolutions. Some church leaders were pushing this trend worldwide, and their message was obviously being taken seriously.

Lori was reading a weekly news magazine she had brought home from the hospital, when an article caught her attention. The title of the article was "World Wide Sunday Mania." The staff writer, author of the article, documented all the Sunday legislation in the world up to that time, giving crime, world unrest, and devastating national disasters as the motivating reasons for such legislation. This appeared to be true even in countries with large Muslim populations. Then the author cited statistics indicating that all the problems that nations were trying to solve were actually getting worse despite such legislation. The article likened this scenario to a giant vortex.

Lori was thoughtful as she laid down the magazine. Looking at her watch she jumped up as the realization hit that she was late for Marie's hydrotherapy. With a cheerful apology Lori transferred Marie to the walking wheelchair and headed for the door. "James, do you want to help me with Marie today?" The shy smile she gave him was an instant encouragement.

"Happy to!" He took over the handles and began helping Marie up the small incline. "It is such a beautiful day today." They all had a good laugh as they slogged through the rain-dampened countryside to the hot spring.

At the spring Marie was lowered carefully into the therapeutic water. A tarp had been arranged over the area to keep her head from getting too wet and chilled. Standing by in its shelter, James and Lori began chatting about the weather. Pausing for a moment, Lori sighed. Speaking to no one in particular, she started to discuss the article she had just read.

"You know, all my life I have been taught that Sunday is the Sabbath and I have honestly tried to keep it sacred for communion with God. But talking with Marie, living with you folk—and this article I just read—I'm seeing something different. I can see from the Bible that God has never changed or authorized the change of His Law. He hasn't changed the Sabbath from the seventh day Saturday to the first day Sunday. He surely wouldn't force people to keep Sabbath, anyway." Here a tear trickled from the corner of her eye. "I think it's important to follow the Bible. I've been keeping the wrong day! Can God forgive me?"

James took her hand in his. "Lori, God is in the business of forgiving people. In fact, He says in Acts 17:30 that the times of this ignorance He winks at. You have accepted His sacrifice for you and you are willing to follow Him when you learn more from His Word. Surely there is great joy in heaven as God hears your testimony right now."

"Well, there is great joy in my own heart right now," Lori commented. "I am going to resign at the hospital tomorrow and rescind my registration. I can't continue to work there after the medical profession finally caved in to the demands of not treating those without registration cards."

Marie, having heard Lori's comments, lifted her hands toward heaven in a spontaneous gesture of praise. "Hallelujah! We have been praying for you," she said. "God has answered our prayers. Lori, I know from experience that your time spent with God will be even more special." Marie winced as she lowered her arms back under the water.

27

THE MARK

"I warn everyone who hears the words of the prophecy of
this book: If anyone adds anything to them, God will add to
him the plagues described in this book."
Revelation 22:18, NIV

It was Saturday evening just before sundown when the extended family met for sundown worship. This had become a much-anticipated routine for the dwellers of the lodge. There was singing, praying, studying, and sharing, all of which added up to a high experience for everyone. On this particular occasion sharing time held some surprises. First, James made an announcement. "Today Lori and I were talking as we walked up the hill to the rocky pinnacle. We each had come to the conclusion that our lives are so much more fulfilled since we have become better acquainted. One thought led to another until we decided to combine our lives into one."

For a second no one spoke. Then Bob tried for clarity. "Does this mean—you two—"

"Yes! We are going to be married." James was jubilant.

Everyone was excited for them, and hugs were the order of the hour. Asked when the wedding would take place Lori said, "within the next couple of weeks. We still haven't asked Pastor Ralph yet."

When the excitement of this announcement had begun to diminish, Marie began to speak. "There are some things I want to tell you all," she began. One by one she looked at the individuals in the room and told what she perceived as their strong points. Everyone was feeling good when the thrust of her message changed.

"Now, I have some news for you all that may not seem so

happy." This was definitely an attention getter. "I am getting old, and am not in good health. You all have done so much for me that I'll never be able to thank you enough, especially Lori and my dear daughter, Karen. I believe tough times are ahead, too tough for a person in my condition. So, if the Lord should see fit to let me rest in the grave until He returns, I am just fine with that decision."

There was silence in the room. Then Karen got up and went to her mother. Putting her arms around her, she kissed her gently on the cheek and shed a few tears. "Mother, you have been such an inspiration to me, and to all of us here. I cannot know the mind God in this matter, but I can say that I would miss you a great deal if you were gone. I hope that is not going to be the case, but if it is God's will, I know we will all meet you on the resurrection day."

Later in the evening there was talk among the group regarding the significance of what Marie had said. Several read Bible scriptures that seemed to support what Marie had said about tough times near the close of earth's history. "Maybe God has revealed this to her," someone said. No one could deny that possibility. At bedtime Lori and Karen put Marie to bed as usual, with Karen putting special care into the ritual. Then she kissed her mother and turned out the light, still wondering what the future held for the woman who had so long nurtured her.

The next day Mark and Sara seemed inseparable from Nana. Mark went out of his way to bring special treats, drinks of fresh spring water, and even found a few early wildflowers to brighten her day. Marie gave him a "manly" hug each time he got close enough and whispered her thanks and an "I love you" into his ear. Mark would blush and rush to another errand.

Sara mostly sat beside her talking and listening to Nana's soft and happy voice. "Nana," Sara ventured, "I hope you don't die. I would miss you too much."

"Sweet child, I'm not going anywhere on purpose. I just want to be prepared for whatever God has in mind for me. I'm not afraid and I don't want you to be afraid, either." Marie hugged her granddaughter close. "We have both been through a lot of trials and have had a lot of time to talk with each other. You have been such delight to me. I'm so happy that you love Jesus, too, and I know we will live right beside each other in heaven."

"I know, Nana. But, right after you were hurt by that bad man, I was scared for a little while that something would happen to me again. Then you were so sure that God was with you even when you were hurt that it made me stop being afraid. I can't wait to be in heaven with you. I love you." Sara gave her Nana such a big hug she nearly toppled her out of her chair.

Marie laughed, "I love you, too, Sara. I love you, and God loves you best!"

Daylight was just breaking a few days later when Karen heard a knock on her bedroom door. Slipping out of bed and putting on a bathrobe she opened the door. It was Lori. Motioning for her to follow, Lori moved toward Marie's room just a few steps away. As soon as she entered the bedroom where Marie slept, Karen knew. Her mother had died peacefully in her sleep.

That day was busy for Karen and Bob making arrangements for a funeral and burial at the little country cemetery nearby. They notified her friends, picked out a simple casket, and selected pallbearers. Flowers would have to come from the woods. The arrangements took all the rest of Marie's meager savings. She had lost her home when the government seized all unregistered assets, though she had withdrawn all her cash from the bank just days before the deadline and had buried it in a jar on the property. The tiny country mortuary didn't seem too concerned with their cash payment and explanation that they didn't have a registration card.

Although these tasks are not considered pleasant under normal circumstances, Karen commented to her husband that it was a lot easier this time than when her father had passed away. She attributed this to her faith in God and her belief in the soon coming of Jesus when her mother would be resurrected.

On Friday the funeral took place at the church Marie had just joined. The sanctuary was nearly full of family and friends, as well as church members. Many people stood up and told a story of how Marie had blessed their lives. Pastor Ralph and Barbara gave the eulogy and a short talk about how Marie would be resting until the resurrection that surely wasn't very far off in the future. He offered her life as a testimony to the power of God to heal, and invited any who needed healing and hope to accept His love.

Later the family lingered by the casket at the cemetery. Karen told stories about how it was to grow up with Marie as mother. There was a sense of joy in the sadness, which could not be articulated or defined. As Barbara pointed out, this was not a goodbye, but rather a goodnight.

Eight days later, following the church service, James and Lori were united in holy matrimony. It was a joyous event, simple and spiritual, with the couple stating their pledge to be faithful to each other and to God. The reception was a church potluck where everyone was able to get better acquainted with the new couple. Steven Pierce was in attendance and publicly told of James' influence in his own decision to take a stand for the Sabbath. Then he prayed a prayer of dedication for the newly married couple.

Within a few weeks, changes in communities all around the country became more noticeable. There was a heightened sense of frustration in people that manifested itself in out-of-control behavior. If a neighbor offended another neighbor, he retaliated violently. Families became increasingly fractured and belligerent. There was a sense of chaos everywhere and the news reports that trickled in to them noted it also in many other countries around the world.

At the same time, Sabbath keepers everywhere began to withdraw from public life and ceased their thrust to evangelize the world around them. James first noted this to the other extended family members one evening at the supper table.

"Something's changed," he began. "I think the great controversy between God and Satan is about over. The evidence points to this as a unique time in the history of the world. Jesus leaves the heavenly sanctuary in preparation for His triumphal return to this earth where He will redeem us for all eternity. Does everybody here know what I'm talking about?"

Denise raised her hand and with a shy grimace said, "That's something I'm not familiar with."

James heard several others voice, "Me, either." So he suggested they study this subject from the Bible. Within a short time the table was cleared and Bibles were produced in anticipation of the study.

"To begin with," James said, "let me just say that this subject can get very technical. But it's my goal to make it simple for all our benefit. First let us ask God to open our eyes to His truth right now. "Our Father, we are dependent upon you for understanding the words of scripture. We ask for help as we discuss this important topic. In Jesus name, amen." Looking up from his prayer James saw the faces of people he loved and respected. He determined to hold nothing back.

"Let's turn to Revelation 22:12." When all had found the text he asked Bob to read it.

"Behold, I am coming soon! My reward is with me, and I will give to everyone according to what he has done." Bob looked up.

"It's obvious from this statement of Jesus," James began, "that when He comes he has already looked at the record of everyone's life. He knows who is safe to save.

"One of the special days God instructed the Israelites to observe was the Day of Atonement. We find this in Leviticus, chapter 16." The group read the chapter, verse by verse, around the circle. Then James spoke again. "Let's see if we can summarize this. Throughout the year the sins of God's people were symbolically transferred to the tabernacle through animal sacrifices. These pointed forward to the blood of Jesus that would cover the sins of repentant sinners.

"Once a year, on the Day of Atonement, the most holy place in the tabernacle was symbolically cleansed. This represents the final blotting out of our sins. God was trying to teach people how serious the sin problem is and how it will ultimately be dealt with. Remember, these ceremonies were really a visual aid to help us understand what takes place in heaven. Therefore, the real Day of Atonement is God looking at the records of every individual who has ever claimed Jesus as his Savior.

"Now please turn to Daniel 8:14 and I'll ask Karen to read the text from her New King James Version."

Karen found the text and waited for the others, then she read, "And he said to me, 'For two thousand three hundred days; then the sanctuary shall be cleansed.'"

"As we have studied before," James reminded them, "this is a prophecy from God. And we know from Numbers 14:34 that a day in prophecy equals a literal year. So 2,300 days in prophetic time is 2,300 years. Previously, we also learned that Daniel's prophecies all had a starting point at the year when the decree was given for the Jews to re-build Jerusalem. That year, history tells us, was 457 B.C. When you do the math, you find that the cleansing of the Heavenly sanctuary—or as we now also know it, the Day of Atonement—began in 1844. God has been looking at the record of our lives. When we have been sorry for our sins and asked for His forgiveness, He has been faithful to write 'Forgiven' on that record. So when looking at these records, God has been able to declare this person to be safe to save. He or she is now saved by the blood of Jesus."

James took a big breath, then he elaborated. "All these years God has been doing His part to save mankind. There comes a time when all that will be saved, are saved. God is not willing that anyone should be lost, but that all should repent and be saved. Yet people are given freedom of choice and God honors their decision.

"The evidence is, that mankind's probation is now finished. God has pronounced the stunning announcement found in Revelation 22:11, 'Let him who does wrong continue to do wrong; let him who is vile continue to be vile; let him who does right continue to do right; and let him who is holy continue to be holy.' The Holy Spirit has been withdrawn from the people of the earth, but not from the people of God."

There was a solemn silence in the room. The enormity of these events weighed on the minds of all sitting around the big table. Mixed emotions and uncertainty were the ingredients of the beginning of the end. Bob and Karen decided to go for a walk together.

"Bob," Karen began hesitantly, "when James read that verse

about it being too late to change your minds, or to repent and be forgiven and turn to God . . ." Her voice trailed off.

"I know, Karen. I was just thinking about the same things. I've been such a sinner in my life. I've shaken my fist in God's face. How can I be sure He has truly forgiven me and that I will be saved? I couldn't bear to be separated from Him for eternity." Bob's voice cracked.

"Honey, I know I won't be able to go through everything that the Bible says is coming on the world. I can't do it without God. Can we pray together? Maybe God will give us extra strength." Karen looked pleadingly into Bob's eyes.

"We sure are going to need something extra," Bob agreed. "We soon won't have any earthly way of feeding our family and all those people at the lodge." And together they knelt in the soft earth beside Lori's Hot Spring and poured out their concerns and supplications to God. They stayed for a long time, then. Talking, holding each other. Praying again. Remembering Bible verses that comforted them.

"Jesus said He would never leave us nor forsake us," Bob finally concluded. We have no choice but to trust Him." He gave Karen a hand up. "Let's go back and talk with Mark and Sara. They are too young to understand what is about to happen."

The following morning Bob turned on the pickup radio to hear the public broadcasting station news while he worked around the yard. The reception was poor, and the voice was scratchy but he could still hear that this day's news was big and not a little frightening for Sabbath keepers. The anchor began, "In the nation's capital this morning, the President went before Congress asking for tough measures against people who refuse to abide by the comprehensive Sunday legislation already in effect. In his speech he quoted statistics generated from state and federal sources that somewhere over two million people have refused to sign allegiance to the law as mandated. Following the President's speech, Congress heard from Cardinal Woodman, a ranking Roman Catholic leader in the U.S., and Reverend Martin, the popular charismatic Protestant reformer. Both clergymen held to the position that current national problems of the severely declining economy, rampant crime and violence, and worldwide unrest and war are a direct result of citizens refusing to abide by the law of God. Like the President, they both urged tougher consequences for those who refuse to submit to God in this matter.

"Now we are going to Robert Beckley, standing by outside the Supreme Court Building, where a spokesman for the ACLU is being interviewed. Let's listen in."

"It has always been our position that the current Sunday law requiring registration is a violation of freedom of religion rights. The additional emphasis now being proposed by the President does not change anything. Next question."

"Why hasn't the ACLU tested the current law in court?"

"We would have done it before now had it been possible. Due to the huge backlog of cases in federal courts and the difficulty in getting Supreme Court attention, it has not been a reasonable course of action up to this time. We will be monitoring this daily and surveying our options."

Bob turned off the radio and went inside the lodge. James looked up from his study as Bob entered the room. "Good morning, Bob. What is the good news?" he asked in a cheerful voice.

Bob was up to the challenge. "The good news is that God is in control of our lives. The bad news is that the President is asking Congress to pass an addition to the Sunday law which will prevent Sabbath keepers from buying or selling unless they sign the Sunday pledge."

"How do you know that?" James asked.

"I just heard it on the news. It sounds like a sure thing to me." Bob seemed resigned.

"Here we are at Revelation 13:16 & 17, Bob. We knew it would happen some day." James paused a moment and stared into space, then spoke again. "It's just hard to believe we are truly there, isn't it?"

"Yes. Yes, it is. It's kind of like Satan is tightening down the screws on us, one turn at a time." Bob was having a hard time getting his mind around the fast moving spiritual warfare affecting his life.

By the end of the week the President's modification to the Sunday law had passed through Congress. The new measure would go into effect in forty-five days. Hearing this, the residents of the lodge decided to pool what little money they had and purchase items they were sure to need in the weeks and months ahead. Everyone made a list, then pared it down. There seemed to be a sense of dependence on God for the necessities of life.

The sun shone hot on Friday that week. Residents of the lodge were busy with laundry, food preparation, and gardening. No one spoke of the difficulties they were sure to face because of their faith in the word of God. Yet all felt more than the heat of the day. There was the undeniable heat of society trying to force them to conform. After supper, the mood was somber. Bob and Karen decided to take a walk. The moment they stepped outside, they heard a sound coming from up the trail that led to the hot springs.

"What is that?" asked Karen.

"Sounds like singing." Bob answered while still straining to hear. "Let's go up the trail and find out who it is."

As they walked, the sound of singing grew louder. A rich baritone voice was reaching out, as it were, to the heavens with a message from the heart:

"Where you there when they crucified my Lord?
Where you there when they crucified my lord?
O! Sometimes it causes me to tremble, tremble, tremble.
Were you there when they crucified my Lord?"

As they came in sight of the hot spring, Bob and Karen were arrested by the sight and sound before them. On an outcropping of rock high above the lodge, Denise and Jennifer listened while husband and father, John, sang out his feelings for all the world to hear. It seemed a sacred moment. Bob and Karen sat down on a rock just off the trail and listened. Within a few minutes Mark and Sara joined them. The song had changed but not the message or the emotional level.

"I want Jesus to walk with me.
I want Jesus to walk with me.
All along my pilgrim journey,
I want Jesus to walk with me."

174

Bob felt his courage growing and his trust in God expanding. He felt like singing, and that is exactly what he did.

"In my trials, Lord, walk with me.
In my trials, Lord, walk with me.
When the shades of life are falling,
I want Jesus to walk with me."

Before long his entire family was singing along. Then they saw James and Lori coming up the trail singing along—it was now a choir. Together they all joined the Colliers in singing to the glory of God. And what a fitting tribute it was as the Sabbath hours began.

28

CAST OUT

"Then I heard a loud voice from the temple saying to the seven angels,
'Go, pour out the seven bowels of God's wrath on the earth.'"
Revelation 16:1, NIV

The next morning the whole group piled into vehicles and headed for church. Everyone expressed the desire to be in the company of other Sabbath keepers to gain strength. Arriving a bit early, they were perplexed to see a number of people standing outside, reading a sign posted on the door. Standing on either side were Pastor Ralph and Barbara.

Pastor Ralph turned toward the gathering crowd. His face was a mixture of puzzlement, joy, and caution. "Precious church family, this is the time that saints of all ages have looked forward to with great longing. It cannot be long now until our Lord comes back to rescue His children." His voice cracked here. "This is it! We have been closed down for not complying with Sunday legislation. This property has been seized by the state and we are to leave the premises immediately."

There was a moment of silence, then one by one the individual members began quietly to say "Amen. Praise God." Someone began to sing "God be with you 'til we meet again." The group joined in swelling the chorus "Til we meet, 'til we meet, 'til we meet at Jesus feet." They were holding hands and many tears were falling: tears of sadness over those missing from their fellowship and tears of joy for the future.

Barbara raised her hands in blessing them, and began to pray for the little group. The earnestness and sincerity in her voice conveyed the close relationship she enjoyed with her Savior. She prayed for God to surround each individual and family with His Holy Spirit and with multitudes of heavenly angels. Recognizing the seriousness of the events unfolding, she prayed for strength to face the trials and peace amidst the coming convulsions of planet earth in its death throes.

There were many hearty and lingering hugs. Here and there someone was heard to reminisce about a special moment in the church. Bob and Karen's family were talking with amazement about having just been baptized here and now never being able to return. James and Lori held each other close. Steven Pierce was holding little Jennifer Collier while her father watched the scene in amazement and her mother cried silently.

"We just became acquainted with you all," John began. "If it hadn't been for the encouragement of Bob and Karen, well, I know we wouldn't be here. Thank you, Bob, for sharing Jesus' love with me." Denise added her appreciation for Bob and Karen and for James taking them in when they were homeless and desperate. They both gave glory to God for His perfect timing and great love.

Similar thanks and praises were heard around the circle. Worship may have been forbidden in the church, but it continued, perhaps even more pure than before, right on the steps. Soon discussion turned to those members still living in town, closely surrounded by hostile neighbors. Their good friend and former judge, Steven Pierce was one of them.

Taking a quick poll of his lodge-mates James extended the invitation to any that needed a haven to come share their country home. He suggested that if there were RV's or even tents they could help families maintain a bit of privacy while still eating and bathing in the lodge. "Forty acres of God's land will shelter quite a few people," he added. He gave simple directions and again assured everyone they were all welcome.

They were just getting ready to leave when a car came careening and honking down the street. A man, vaguely familiar, thrust his head out the open window and yelled obscenities at them. "You're gonna get what you deserve now!" he shouted. "Go on, get out, you self-righteous law breakers. I told you you'd get thrown out." He passed by James, "And I know where ya'all live, lawyer-boy." He leered at Lori. "Let's see if all yer fancy learnin' saves yer hide now."

James gasped as he recognized the former church member and trusted friend. His face turned ashen as he realized this man had turned his back on God and now had betrayed them—even threatened their safety. It was a sad ending to their impromptu worship service.

Returning to the country property the extended lodge family could see no reason to waste a perfectly good Sabbath so they improvised a spiritual service of their own. There was singing, Bible study, and prayer—lots of prayer. For the first time in their young lives Mark and Sara led out in the services. They were thrilled to take part, and the role they played inspired the others.

The weeks that followed went slowly, while counting down for the new Sunday measure to go into effect. Then, with two days left, a battered pickup drove in and stopped next to the Johnsons' trailer. All eyes watched as a man and woman exited from each side of the truck. In that instant, the lodge residents knew that part of their church family, Sue and Roberto Gonzales, had come to live on the property with them.

James was the first to welcome them with a big hug. Soon the others joined in the welcome. Right away they all speculated where the best place might be for them to stay. James offered them his and Lori's bedroom, but they adamantly refused. Karen suggested they stay in their trailer. Then Bob suggested that the decision really belonged to the Gonzales family. This kind of treatment—this freedom of choice—was something they were not used to experiencing. They smiled appreciatively and soon shyly asked if it would be OK to stay in the trailer.

At lunch time the new family joined the others around the table, simply set with the few vegetables available from the little garden. After awhile, Sue began to feel safe enough to share with the others what had led to their need for a move. "We were living in my parents' apartment building in the city. The other residents were getting more and more angry with us. Anything that went wrong they blamed on us. Then Roberto lost his job because we are Sabbath keepers. He was robbed on the way home from the bank with his last paycheck." Sue looked at her husband.

Roberto picked up the story. "We came here because Pastor Ralph told us it is OK." He spoke with a Spanish accent. "On the way, there is no gas in our pickup, but we have no money. Still we kept moving. God made a miracle so the pickup kept going." He took his wife's hand and smiled at her.

"Praise God," was heard around the room. Here was concrete evidence that the Lord was still in the miracle business.

"One more thing we want you all to know about us," Sue was quick to point out. "I am five months pregnant."

All the women were excited for Sue and looked forward to the big day when she would give birth to her firstborn. Bob remembered the words of Jesus from Matthew 24:19, "How dreadful it will be in those days for pregnant women and nursing mothers." Even so, he smiled in recognition of her joy.

After supper was cleaned up someone was heard to ask, "Is there a name for this place?"

James picked up on that immediately. "No, we've never thought about that," he said. "But this would be a good time to name it."

One by one names were mentioned and discussed until someone suggested Elijah's Hide-away. The name really clicked with the group, and it was immediately so named.

The following day was the last before the new Sunday ruling went into effect. The Sabbath keepers living at Elijah's Hide-away made use of their freedom to purchase without showing a Sunday registration card at the checkout counter. All empty fuel containers were filled with gasoline. Karen purchased dried beans, fruit, and several bags of grain and rice with their pooled funds. It wasn't much for so many.

She had done business at this store for years. No one asked for a Sunday registration card. But there were signs everywhere stating that the cards would be required before purchases could be made on the following day. A woman waiting next to Karen seemed angry about the requirement to present another card in the future. "I was raised as a Sabbath keeper," She confided to Karen. "But when this whole Sunday thing came up I saw it was going to be necessary for me to change. So I did. But, I'm really not happy about it."

"I'm sorry for you," Karen smiled. Then she added, "I wish you well." Later, on her way home Karen pondered the fate of this woman and thought to herself, "How sad for her that she compromised her relationship with God for some need to get along in this world."

The next day dawned beautifully with no clue as to the significance of what had just taken place. This was the first day of the new Sunday registration ruling requiring a card before any purchase could be made. The microchip in the card identified the person who had registered. This information went to a state computer that allowed or denied the transaction to proceed. There was a wave of other countries following the example of the United States. Their similar actions were set to take effect anywhere from a week to several weeks in the future.

By suppertime the residents at Elijah's Hide-away were curious to know how the new system was working. After starting up the generator they plugged in an old radio to listen to the news. Sure enough, the reports were full of data and interviews from locations all over the nation—all dealing with the new card system. In the end people didn't like it, but were willing to go along for the good of the nation. Then near the end of the news, a report was briefly given about people who had suddenly come down with an unknown boil condition. Doctors who had seen the boils said they had never seen anything quite like it before. Tests were in progress to determine the cause of the condition, but it could be days before they would know for sure. Until then, patients were being hospitalized and put on high doses of state of the art antibiotics. "The good news," stated the reporter, "is that, so far, only people in Los Angeles and San Francisco are affected."

James turned off the radio and spoke quietly to the group. "This may be the start of the first plague of Revelation 16," he announced.

"Do you realize the significance of this?" The tone of his voice was chilling. No one stirred in the silence that followed.

Then Mark asked, "How long will the plagues last?"

"Good question," James responded. "I've tried to figure that out. But so far, I have not found the answer in scriptures. However, you all may want to search for the answer on your own. Even if you don't find the answer to that question, you will find answers to a whole lot of other questions."

The next day they checked the news again. Many more people were coming down with the mysterious boils. This time it was seen throughout the nation. The CDC was frantically looking into the cause of the unusual condition that manifested itself in large red boils as well as a good deal of pain. Over the next week the problem became even more widespread.

At the workplace, absenteeism started to become a problem for employers. Many companies began to take on temporary help to fill in the vacancies caused as more and more employees became ill. As productivity and sales began to decline, the economy spiraled further out of control. When the outbreak of boils became a worldwide problem, the World Health Organization issued a rare worldwide health alert. Country after country was hit hard—apparently soon after they passed some sort of Sunday law restricting the rights of dissenters. It took some time for that fact to be noticed. But when it did there was a knee-jerk reaction blaming Sabbath keepers for the scourge of boils around the world.

At Elijah's Hide-away, the families were starting to feel the pinch. The food had to be rationed, but they were committed and went about their duties with a song or a prayer on their lips. For a time it seemed no one was going to challenge the group of Sabbath keepers living on this forty acres of remote property. Then that changed.

It was Saturday morning at eleven o'clock. The residents of Elijah's Hide-away were enjoying a Bible study and prayer meeting. Since they could no longer go to church on Sabbath, they had services of their own at home. Suddenly there was a knock at the door. It was surprising because no one had heard a car in the driveway and for months there had been no visitors. James stood and walked to the door. Opening it, he looked into the faces of two men who were not in the best of moods.

The older of the two spoke first. "Who are you people any-way?"

James was quick to respond. "We are just your average hard working American citizens. How can we help you?"

The younger man was poorly dressed and appeared to have red spots about his neck. He was not going to waste time getting down to the real issue. "We believe there are Sabbath people at this place. Where are they?"

"Sabbath people?" James asked. Then he added, "Why would you want them?"

"They are the ones causing my boils," the young man spat out the words.

"You don't say! How is it that they are giving you these boils?" James questioned.

"That is what the authorities are telling us. That's all I know."

James moved out of the doorway onto the porch where the men stood. "You know—what did you say your name is?"

"Joe Bundy"

"OK, Joe Bundy. It might be a good idea to question the authorities for data supporting this kind of accusation, don't you think?"

"Well, maybe. How should I know anyway?"

"Look at the facts, Joe. You probably don't have any contact with the Sabbath people. Yet some would have you believe these people caused your boils. Does that make sense?"

"Well, maybe not. All I know is that I'm real tired of them." Joe seemed a little calmer now.

"I hope you find help for your condition real soon." James said as the two men turned to leave.

Back inside James told the others, "I saw a revolver in the young man's jacket. Considering his state of mind when I opened the door, I believe he had bad intentions. Thank God we were spared any harm." They all knelt in thankful prayer, and pled with God to protect them.

The following morning a modest sedan arrived at Elijah's Hide-away. It came into the driveway, then backed into a vacant spot between two trees. By this time the people living here were alert to any vehicle coming on the property, so many eyes watched with interest. Soon a man opened the door and stepped out. It was Steven Pierce.

There was an instant sigh of relief and everyone gathered around to welcome him. "What brings you to Elijah's Hide-away, Judge Pierce?" James asked.

"First off, I am not Judge Pierce anymore," he said with a smile. "Thank God I am now Steven Pierce, sinner who has been saved by the grace of God. Secondly, I wanted to see all the good people at this place which you call Elijah's Hide-away. Finally, I have a request for you all to consider." Then he waited for some reaction from the group.

"Go ahead, tell us your request. We're pretty easygoing," someone said.

"All right then," Steven began again. "I have been under tremendous pressure from my neighbors over my Sabbath keeping—for weeks now. Then last night, an old friend from the police department came by and tipped me off that a vigilante group was on its way to take out their frustrations on me. So it seemed like a good time for me to take an extended vacation. I just grabbed my tent and a few clothes and left. There was a large band of tough-looking men coming up the sidewalk as I pulled out, but they didn't seem to see me. I watched them in my rearview mirror, pounding on my doors and windows. They were carrying baseball bats. Now here is my question to you all. May I live here on this property with the rest of you?"

The group pondered their friend's close call. Then James extended his hand. "Can a duck float on water?" he asked with a chuckle. "What do you say everyone?"

"Yes, yes, yes," came the replies.

The former judge looked at all the smiling faces in front of him. He had seen many of them in his courtroom and by some unknown force was able to make the right decision—for them and for himself. Now he could only give thanks to God for working in such great and marvelous ways.

29

A PLAGUE OF BLOOD

"...And surely I am with you always, to the very end of the age."
Matthew 28:20, NIV

We start our news report this evening with, by far, the most spectacular sight the world has witnessed in the memory of the living. On ocean shores throughout the world people awoke to a new and most unusual sight. Instead of looking out over the usual white waves of the sea, what they witnessed was a sea of blood. It looked red, it smelled different, and in the end it really was blood. But this can't be, you might say. Well, let's take you to New York's Mt Sinai Hospital medical lab, where Peter Jones is with Dr. Susan Banes."

"Thank you, Tom. First, Dr. Banes, please tell us what you discovered when you tested the fluid taken from the ocean today."

"It is apparently ocean water with the addition of hemoglobin and other components at similar levels to human blood."

"How did these components get into the oceans, Dr. Banes?"

"Peter, this is something for which we have no explanation."

"There you have it, Tom. Although we don't have an explanation for it, we do know it is real blood."

"Reports have come in from every continent on the globe witnessing this same phenomena. And naturally there is great concern for industries that rely on the ocean for their living. By late afternoon, innumerable carcasses of the ocean's occupants were beginning to pile up on beaches everywhere. As to a plausible explanation for how the ocean could suddenly turn to blood, we can only speculate. Some religious leaders held news conferences this afternoon and offered this spin on it: God is punishing us for allowing some people to desecrate the day He has set up as the day of rest."

Bob turned off the radio. He had read Revelation 16 many times in the last few weeks. Every time, this event appeared as the second plague. Stepping out of his pickup, which was fully loaded with firewood, he walked to the lodge.

"Good morning, everyone." There was a big and friendly response. Then he broke the story to them. "I just heard on the news that the sea has turned to blood." That is all he needed to say. Everyone knew the significance.

This condition of the sea lasted for only a short time. People around the world breathed a sigh of relief, but it was short-lived. Suddenly rivers turned to blood. First one river then another would turn red. This lasted long enough to cause serious problems to municipal water treatment facilities. In many places people would turn on their water facet to find red liquid streaming out. Home water filters were inadequate to solve the problem. Previously bottled water, pop, and canned foods were sold out of stores in a few minutes. People were afraid to eat out.

While this was going on, the suffering from the plague of boils continued for many people. CDC scientists had managed to isolate the bacteria that caused the condition and were able to develop a drug that was effective in curing it. However, it was very expensive, which meant that only the wealthy or those with the right kind of medical insurance were able to get it.

At Elijah's Hide-away, life was changing week by week. Whereas, for a while several had cell phones that continued to work, soon the fact that these people didn't have Sunday registration cards came to the attention of cell phone companies. Then the cell phones went dead. At this point communication with friends and family was limited to mail, if stamps were on hand, or in person. As long as a vehicle still had a valid license plate, it could be driven—if there

185

was gas. However, insurance companies had dropped customers who failed to produce evidence of a Sunday registration card. This made travel very risky.

Then there was the matter of food and other personal supplies. After a few months most provisions were gone. Strict conservation became a necessary part of everyday living. Offsetting these issues a bit was the garden near the lodge. Roberto was in his element while working his craft in that plot of ground. Vegetables produced enough to supplement the scanty meals. Everyone marveled at the beauty and quality of the produce. Then, as winter came, everyone expected the garden to die out or freeze. Yet, first Thanksgiving, then Christmas came and went and the garden continued to send up new shoots here and there. There seemed to always be just enough to keep them from starving. By this time the whole group knew that God was at work for them there. It was a humbling consideration.

One day a family drove into the driveway looking for a friend's house. James walked over and spoke with the people. After a short conversation the man was about to leave when he noticed the garden. "Wow," he said, "is that a real garden?"

James didn't dodge the question. "Sure is. My friend has a real green thumb."

"But I've never seen a garden around here growing in the winter," he said gawking at the beautiful sight. "Mind if I have a look?"

"No. There's no time for that. We're late!" nagged the woman next to him.

James was thankful for the woman's diversion. It was not that he didn't want to be cordial or social. He just didn't want word to get around that special things were happening on this property. The more people who might come to see, the greater the chance that trouble might erupt.

Shortly after this, Sue's time had come. Then the lodge was transformed into a maternity ward. Here, the women were in total control. The men became gofers, cooks, cleaners, and all around supporters. Within twelve hours, nurse Lori brought the new girl baby into the world. The baby took her first breath and cried the cry of a healthy infant. The lodge rang with cheers at the welcome sound. Once Roberto held his newborn daughter in his hands, he didn't want to let her go. In fact, very soon the new baby—named Carlena—became a favorite of everyone, including Mark and Sara. There was no lack of help in taking care of this baby, and everyone shared just a bit more of their food rations so Sue would have enough milk to feed her.

A month later another major event took place throughout the world. Beginning at the international dateline, as the sun came up it began to penetrate the earth's atmosphere as never before. Tremendous heat was generated on the earth. Wherever there was no cloud cover, people wilted under the sun's rays. Heat strokes were common, resulting in massive overloads in hospital emergency rooms. Hundreds of thousands died. Day after day this condition went on. There was no place on earth where the effect of the sun was not felt.

The damage caused by the increased solar activity had a severe effect on the world economy. This plague just added to the economic downturn of the first three plagues in a domino effect. The President of the United States was urged by his counselors to further toughen the Sunday law. The United Nations Security Council began to consider new and unusual concepts that had been off-limits to them before. Whereas in the past, religious solutions to world problems were avoided, now they were openly considered. Psychics were brought in to explain why these terrible plagues were happening. Uniformly, they placed the blame on Sabbath keepers.

The residents of Elijah's Hide-away were still able to follow these world events by means of occasional radio news reports. Since they were not suffering any effects of the plagues, they were curious as to how other Sabbath keepers were faring. This prompted Bob and Karen to travel the twenty miles to the residence of Pastor Ralph and Barbara in the daylight hours. It was an unnerving venture.

Before leaving Bob checked everything on the family van to be sure it was road-worthy. He noted that the license plate was valid for one more month. He put five containers of water in the back, just in case they might be needed for some reason along the way. After kissing their children goodbye, Bob and Karen climbed in and headed down the driveway. It was a warm sunny day and they were enjoying the ride. Then Karen noticed something. "I don't see the usual signs of spring. Where are the flowers and the green grass?" she asked. "Even the evergreen trees are brown and shedding their needles."

Bob looked around as he drove and then agreed. "You're right. Do you suppose the hot sun has affected nature?"

Then they started to notice the look on people's faces. It seemed everyone looked angry, or sad, or gloomy. They started to search for a smile on anyone's face, but it was in vain. The astonishing reality started to sink in—there was no peace for those who had chosen to reject God.

As they merged onto the freeway they saw cars abandoned along the edge of the road. Not only abandoned, but stripped. Vandals had obviously taken anything of perceived value and left the barest shell to rust in the weather. "Look at that!" Bob spotted it first, "There's someone breaking a window in that car!"

Karen gasped and her hand flew to her mouth. "Oh, no! There's someone inside and . . ." But before she could finish her sentence they saw the glint of steel and, just as they drove by, heard a sharp explosion. "Bob, someone was just shot! Oh, what can we do?"

Bob raised his foot from the gas pedal and started to brake. It was an automatic response for him to try to right any wrong. Looking in his rearview mirror he saw the sudden flash of red lights. "Oh, good! There's a police car. Surely they will be taken care of now." But even as he continued to glance back he could see the exchange of gunfire and wasn't so sure what might happen.

"Oh, Bob! Please go back and let's try to help whoever is in the car." Karen had seen several people in the vehicle as they drove by.

They were already slowing, so Bob pulled over to the shoulder. Other cars whizzed past as if nothing unusual was happening. Watching for a few minutes, they decided there was no more activity and cautiously exited the van. "Hello? Hello!" Bob hoped the gunman wasn't going to answer. There was no answer, no movement. They quickly crossed the several hundred feet remaining and recoiled in horror at the scene before them. Lying in pools of blood were the gun-man and the two police officers.

Karen quickly took the vital signs of all three, the assailant and two officers, and declared them dead. Their wounds were too severe to even attempt CPR. Turning her attention to the car, she watched in amazement as Bob was helping a shaken family out of the doors and away from the bloody scene. They all appeared to be unhurt.

"Karen," Bob spoke quickly, "take these folks to the van while I see if I can report this incident on the police car's radio."

Twin girls about four years of age turned wide eyes toward Karen as they clung to their parents' hands. Karen's heart immediately went out to them and she urged them to follow her quickly to their car. She didn't like the looks that passers-by were beginning to give them. Getting the family settled into the back seats, she saw Bob jogging toward them. He gestured for her to get into the van. Her heart rose up in her throat at the look on his face. It wasn't quite fear, but concern etched itself onto his normally peaceful face.

Slamming his door, Bob signaled and swiftly merged into the traffic. "The police said to stay put, since we witnessed the incident, and they would be there in five minutes. I didn't think it would be helpful or prudent for us to stay." His explanation brought murmurs from all the adults.

"I'm sorry—in all this haste, I've quite forgotten my manners." Karen directed her comments toward the back seat. "We are Bob and Karen Johnson. Uh, we live out in the country and were just on a drive to visit friends."

The couple in the backseat held their daughters closely. "We are Anni and Nucomb, and these are our daughters Hali and Hani." The husband and father hesitated, then ventured a question. "Why did you stop to help us? You could have been killed."

Bob and Karen searched each other's eyes. The right answer to the wrong person could place them in even greater peril. Bob nodded. "We are Christians and Jesus taught us to help those in need," Karen answered simply.

"You are Christians?" Anni's voice sang out. "We are Christians! We were on our way to, well, I'm not sure where." Her voice trailed off. "We ran out of gas and didn't know what to do next."

"Dear," her husband cautioned her quietly, then turned to Bob and Karen. "Where did you folks say you were going? Maybe we could ask you to kindly buy us a container of gas and we could pay you back."

Bob was stumped. If he told them he didn't have the Sunday registration card, he risked his family's welfare. Then a thought struck him. Maybe they didn't have a card, either! "That's one solution," he replied. "But, wouldn't it be much better if we took you to our pastor's home, where we were just going, and you could call your emergency roadside service?"

"We do not have a roadside service, but if you will just let us off at the corner when you get to your destination, I am sure we can catch a bus." Nucomb seemed as noncommittal as Bob.

The rest of the trip was taken in silence. Both families appeared lost in their own thoughts about this strange encounter and Bob silently prayed for everyone's safety.

"We're here." Bob pulled into the driveway of a modest home in a rather upscale neighborhood. "Wow! Look at the devastation of these homes." Then looking at their pastor's home he added, "Pastor Ralph and Barbara's home is a beautiful oasis in this desert of dryness."

"Pastor Ralph? Barbara?" Anni's voice was hopeful. "They live here? You know them?"

"Yes," Karen began, "He is our pastor."

"Oh, praise God!" Anni could no longer be contained. "They brought us to Jesus just a few days before these awful plagues began. We know them—he is our pastor, too!"

At that moment the door of the house flew open and the first smiling face of their trip greeted them. Barbara came out to the car and asked if she could be of service. Then recognizing Bob and Karen, she held out her arms.

"Welcome! Come in and rest; it is so good to see you." She bent to peek into the back. "Oh! I thought Mark and Sara would be with you and here you have my dear friends, the Lee's!" Her voice registered a happy confusion. "Where did you all meet?"

Noticing a car driving slowly by, its occupants pointing first to the brown neighborhood, then to the green around her home, the pastor quickly led the visitors indoors. "We wanted to stay in our home, ministering to our neighbors as long as we could." Her voice broke. "We have given them cool, clear water to drink, have bandaged their sores and wept over their losses. It breaks my heart. Now they are beginning to wonder why we have escaped these plagues and are becoming bold and menacing. We may have to leave soon." She gestured for them to be seated and went to find her husband.

Now that all the uncertainty was cleared up, the two families quickly exchanged information. One thought that had been bothering Bob, he now felt free to express. "Why isn't anyone injured? I know we saw and heard gunshots into your car while we were driving by." He looked to Nucomb for the answer.

"It was a miracle, Bob." Nucomb smiled broadly. "The bullets just dropped from the end of the gun barrel as if they had hit a barrier. The gunman cursed and fired again and again, but until he turned his gun toward the police officers, they did not meet their destination." He pulled his children and wife closer to him. "God delivered us with a mighty miracle. Delivered us." His eyes filled with thankful tears.

Pastor Ralph and Barbara had entered as he was giving his testimony and were full of questions about the incident. Bob began to realize that he and Karen had been a part of God's plan from the moment they awakened that morning with the desire to visit their pastors. It was a joyful realization.

30

COMPLY OR DIE

"He who testifies to these things says, 'Yes, I am coming soon.'"
Revelation 22:20, NIV

It was a very relieved and surprised family that welcomed Bob and Karen home at the end of that trip. Not only were they home later than had been expected; they also had the Lee family and Pastor Ralph and Barbara Smith with them. The pastor and his wife had decided to join Elijah's Hide-away. Making introductions all around, Bob asked the obvious question: "Now where shall we put everyone for the night?"

Steven Pierce spoke right up. "The Lee family is more than welcome to use my tent. I've been dying to do some camping up the hills a bit farther. I'll just throw my sleeping bag on the ground under God's stars. It isn't fancy, but it will keep the rain off. Mostly. Welcome to your new home." He winked at the twins peeking out from behind their mother's skirt. "I won't take 'no' for an answer, either." He chuckled as the Lees tried to object. The twins were bouncing up and down in anticipation of "going camping."

"My mother's room is empty, too." Karen spoke to her pastors. "I know she would love you to use her room."

James chimed in, "Absolutely. You must accept our offer. God has blessed us with so much—we want to share with you."

A chorus of "thank you" was heard from the Lee's and Smith's. Lori also welcomed their new guests and invited them to sit down at the rustic table. They were willing to share their last crumbs, if necessary.

The children were just beginning to clear the dishes when there was a "beep, beep" heard from the driveway. Rushing to the doors and windows they were all surprised to see a car and an RV pulling in. James was the first out the door.

"Hello, may I help you?" James squinted against the setting sun trying to identify the visitors.

"James! We found you at last." The familiar deep voice boomed out. "Come on, Eva, we're at the right place." A tall, slender woman alighted from the car.

"Why, Larry and Eva Jenkins! Welcome to you both." James recognized the faces of the people he had met in a restaurant many months before. "Who are these children? I don't remember them being at your home when we had Bible studies." He sounded confused as two more of the car's occupants hopped out.

"James, meet my daughter Cathy and my son Jason. They were living with my ex-husband, but when things got tough and they wouldn't steal for him he beat them up and threw them out on the street. They have lived with us ever since and accepted Jesus as their Savior just before the plagues began." Eva beamed with joy.

By now the whole group had tumbled out of the lodge and there were many introductions, greetings, and hugs. The occupants of the RV soon climbed out and stretched weary muscles. In the ensuing moments, Tom and Ilene Benson were introduced to those they hadn't already met. Then the questions began.

Bob and Ilene told a harrowing story of people crowding into their home to eat their food, drink their clean water, and stay cool. So rude had the guests become, that they were forced to walk away from their own home. They camped in the RV until they had been kicked out of the campground.

It seemed everyone had a story of trials and persecutions to relate. "How glad I am, Ilene added, that I know God. I don't know how we would have survived without Him.

"We know what brought you folks out here, but how did you

ever find each other?" Bob puzzled. He knew the two families hadn't met before.

Larry began. "James told us he had this place—even gave me a map once. 'Course I lost it," he laughed. "But I knew the general directions. When the government confiscated our place, we voted to take James up on his offer that if we ever needed help to come on out." He paused. "This RV was wandering the roads around here and I decided to follow it—just in case." Larry anxiously looked around at the multitude of faces surrounding them. "I hope we won't be over-burdening you here."

"No, there is always room for one more, as they say. God has blessed and we are happy to share what He gives us." James, looking around at the group and their smiling faces, nodded to Larry. There are still some couches in the living room. We'll all crowd together a bit more.

"Or you can stay with us in the trailer." Roberto offered.

"We have an extra bed in the RV," the Bensons added.

"Well, OK. And thank you all so much, we will be happy to stay—somewhere!" Relief flooded Larry's face as he spoke.

"Hooray!" Sara chimed in. "Cathy, do you want to come see the hot spring?" She looked happy to have someone close to her age to play with. Everyone laughed

Bob and Karen were so glad to see their former neighbor friends, the Bensons. Bob quickly helped them pick out a suitable parking place in the fast-gathering shadows. Tom spoke quietly, "Bob, if you hadn't piqued my interest with that book about the Bible—well, I think I would be a lost man, right now. I don't know how I can ever thank you enough. What if I hadn't decided to sell my trailer?" He shook Bob's hand and gave him a bear hug. Bob was speechless for a change.

Lori had joined her husband and now extended an invitation to all the newcomers to join in evening worship. She and Karen proceeded to prepare a light snack for the newest members of their group. Then, as it had been a long day for all, beds were quickly made, the few suitcases unpacked, and preparations made for a restful night's sleep.

As Bob and Karen snuggled into their warm bed they smiled lovingly at each other. "Karen, you can't imagine how thankful I am that I offered that book to Tom Benson. It's like a golden chain—one person learns truth, shares it with another and that one with still another. Who knows what surprises will be waiting for us in heaven? Here there are folks still coming that we didn't know had accepted Jesus—and all from some little contact we had made. Think of all the good that has come from Sara almost getting kidnapped!" They quietly contemplated that statement as they offered their prayers to God and slipped into the undisturbed sleep of the innocent.

A few more weeks slipped by relatively uninterrupted. Great portions of each day were spent studying the Bible and sharing with those who were new to being Christians. Whether they were around the table, working in the garden or kitchen, or sweeping the unfinished floors, young and old alike seemed hungry for more of the Word of God. The hot spring and surrounding rocky heights had become a gathering place for song, and all the new voices added richness and dimension to the old familiar melodies. The newest members of the group started to feel refreshed from their harrowing ordeals in the city. The blessing and peace of God rested upon each one and upon their property.

One day, James spotted Steven Pierce jogging down the trail toward the lodge. "Hi, Judge! Good to see you. How's the camping going? You don't show up very often for provisions. Are you getting enough to eat?" James' questions tumbled out on top of each other.

"Plenty, thanks." The former judge chuckled at his warm welcome. "I've been enjoying my quiet time with God—learning a lot as I read my Bible and just explore nature each day. You have a beautiful piece of land here. Trouble is I've noticed a few neighbors also beginning to realize just how beautiful this land is." Judge Pierce became sober. "I was hiking around the southeast edge of the property just at dusk yesterday and overheard a couple of men talking about hunting. At first I thought they were deer hunters, but then one of them mentioned the deadline coming up when they would have 'open season on those Sabbathkeepers ruining our land,' as they said. I quietly retraced my steps and have spent the night in prayer. I know God will take care of us, but I just can't help thinking, sometimes—what if I haven't confessed some cherished sin? Will I bring dishonor to His name? Will I fail Him?"

James began to encourage his old mentor and friend with one verse of scripture after another. "One of my favorite scriptures, Luke 12:32 is 'Fear not little flock, for it is your Father's good pleasure to give you the kingdom.' Then there is 1 John 1:9, 'If we confess our sins, He is faithful and just and will forgive us our sins and purify us from all unrighteousness.' Those verses tell me that God isn't going to leave any stone unturned to save us. Just the fact that you are searching, but haven't found any unconfessed sin tells me it is more likely Satan trying to discourage you. Come fellowship with our families today and soak up some of God's love from this great group."

One by one, throughout the day, the extended family welcomed Steven into their conversations. They shared the great and small miracles that God had performed for them. They sang together, searched their hearts together, prayed together, worked together, and ate together. At bedtime, James invited Steven to sleep on the sofa for the night and he accepted.

"Thank you, James, and all my friends"—he gestured toward the group as they were lingering—"thank you for helping to restore my faith in Jesus as my Savior. There is nothing I can do, but He has done it all, and I rest in that security. I must keep my eyes on His power, not my weakness. Praise God!"

Toward morning there was quite a rustling heard from the garden area. Peeking from windows and around tent-flaps, the Elijah's Hide-away residents were astonished and concerned to see about a dozen people harvesting and destroying the little garden and surrounding vegetation. They could see, in the new light of the dawn, several men standing guard with rifles slung over their shoulders. No one moved or gave any indication to the marauders that they had been observed, though many silent prayers ascended for the protection of God's angels. Then after completely stripping the garden, and throwing trash and beer bottles all over, the invaders trooped down the driveway, loaded into waiting vehicles and left.

Quietly, the occupants of the RV, tent, and trailer slipped into the lodge. Though alone now, there was still a blanket of shock covering them. "What are we going to do for food, Mommy?" Sara was the first to voice the second concern on everyone's mind.

Sue clutched her new baby closer.

"Honey, God has said our bread and water will be sure." Karen's answer showed she had learned a lot in the months they'd lived at the lodge. "We know where our water is, and we will pray for God to send us our bread, OK?" She reassuringly stroked her daughter's head.

Mark grinned—this was an adventure for him. "Maybe the ravens will feed us just like they did Elijah!" He spoke hopefully.

"Maybe so, son, maybe so." Bob answered thoughtfully. "This is different for me; I'm used to being the bread winner of the family." His face showed the battle inside.

There was a spontaneous gathering of all the residents into a large circle. They joined hands and knelt on the cool floor. For a while there was silence. "Our Father which art in heaven," Pastor Ralph began the old familiar prayer. "Hallowed be thy name."

Others joined in; "Thy kingdom come. Thy will be done in earth, as it is in heaven." Even the children were repeating the familiar prayer of Jesus. "Give us this day our daily bread." Everyone said these words, pausing as new meaning struck them. "And forgive us our debts, as we forgive our debtors. And lead us not into temptation, but deliver us from evil: for thine is the kingdom, and the power, and the glory, for ever. A-men."

Reluctant to leave the Presence of God, someone began to sing "Praise God from Whom all blessings flow, praise Him all creatures here below, praise Him above, ye heavenly host, praise Father, Son and Holy Ghost, Amen." The beautiful soprano strains of the "Doxology" died away. Still they remained on their knees. First one prayed, then another. They had nothing and no way to provide for their daily bread. They struggled and wept. It was a holy time. The light of the morning sun began to stream into the windows.

"It's all right, Mom." Sara looked up at Karen. "God will send us some bread." Her sweet voice sounded like an angel. Her eyes turned expectantly toward the table, clean and bare, save for a small bouquet of wildflowers.

Karen hugged her daughter closer. "I'm sure He will do what He sees is best, honey," she answered.

But Sara was sure God would give them bread. Now. She sprang to her feet and ran over to the table. Not seeing any bread there, she went into the tiny kitchen.

Lori hastened to soften the blow she felt sure Sara would feel when she saw how bare the kitchen supplies really were.

"What's this?" Sara asked her.

Karen followed her gaze. "The flour container is full!" She sniffed and tasted the powdery substance. "Fine, whole wheat flour. And look, there is oil in the jar." They had been out of flour and oil to bake bread for a number of weeks. Now the containers were full. "We can bake bread!" Karen was enthusiastic. "A miracle." She ran back into the dining room. "A miracle—flour and oil."

"Just like Elijah and the widow!" Mark said ecstatically. "Just like that."

Pastor Ralph asked for everyone's attention. "I believe we are starting into a new phase of our walk with God. We are going to have to depend upon Him entirely for our very existence. But He will be faithful to us." All eyes turned to him in an effort to grasp the meaning of his words. Slowly they returned their gaze to the flour and oil, sparkling in a shaft of sunlight.

They contemplated for a while about the best way to bake their bread since the generator was out of gas. Someone went outside, just to make sure, but it was still empty. Just as they had decided to gather some sticks and bake flatbread over coals in the fireplace, the door opened. Steven and Roberto walked in with hands full of blackberries—out of season. For the second time that morning they were shown the mercy of God. Kneeling again, they thanked God for providing food for the day. None doubted at this moment that God loved and accepted them.

Children ran to look for dry sticks and branches. The men all followed Steven and Roberto to the berry patch they had found close to the spring. Hastily stirring up some dough, Sue expertly patted it into thin rounds ready to bake. Soon a fire had been properly prepared and she slapped the dough onto the sizzling griddle. Never had baking bread smelled so wonderful. The men came back with their containers full of berries and sniffed appreciatively at the delicious fragrance.

Gathering around the table, each person shared what this special meal meant to them. Holding it in their hands, they looked at the food God had sent them—food from heaven—borne by angel hands. It was nearly too much to absorb. Hunger pangs soon overcame awe for the four-year-old Lee twins and little Jennifer. Biting into the juicy blackberries, they chorused together, "Yummy, these are good!"

31

THE WRATH OF GOD

"The tyrant will soon be gone. The day of your liberation is near."
President George W. Bush, March 17, 2003 A.D.

The adults were more subdued as they took their first bites of "angel's food" as they were calling it. The sense of God's presence filling the room was overwhelming to Bob. He felt strengthened and encouraged as never before. Even while God was keeping their garden growing, he still had a sense of their own work in the end product. This showed him more clearly his true dependence upon God. Looking at the faces of those around him, he saw the tears in their eyes and knew they were moved also. It was a sacred communion.The ladies decided to bake up a few days supply of flat bread while they had the fire going. The men checked the garden and cleaned up the trash strewn about the yard. Bob ambled over to his pickup to get a tool and stuck the key in the ignition. Turning it, he flipped the radio switch on and dialed to his old favorite news station. "While scientists and meteorologists haven't yet figured out the cause of the unearthly darkness, they remain optimistic that it will soon lift. The coming of Jesus Christ to the Congress and the UN in general assembly has greatly encouraged leaders of all countries. His counsel, guiding them in the changes God is demanding, has brought unity of purpose to the nations of the world." The voice of the anchorman paused, then continued; "In breaking news, the President's Five Star Commission has just issued a final deadline for all people to sign the Sunday rest day registration. Forty-five days from today, at 12:00 midnight, anyone found not in compliance with this order will be put to death. The House of Representatives and the Senate both voted unanimously to accept this recommendation and the President has signed it into law. Religious leaders hailed this action as a great step toward world peace. 'There is no place,' the President said, 'for anyone harboring subversive and evil motives calculated to bring down our great nation.' The UN Security Council, also, endorsed this legislation unanimously."

The newsman paused again in his reading. His voice was flat and unemotional. Bob wondered aloud how someone could possibly be saying such things and not seem affected by them. He listened as the speaker continued, "The Oscar Award nominations were announced today." Bob switched the radio off.

Jumping out of the cab, he strode purposefully toward the men. "Hey, guys, could we talk away from the kids for a few minutes?" Bob spoke quietly.

Tom Benson nodded and answered, "Come on over to our RV. The boys want to head up to the spring, anyway."

Tom led the way as Pastor Ralph, Bob, James, Roberto, Larry, Steven, John and Nucomb followed silently. Crowding around the tiny living area of Tom's RV, they all looked expectantly at Bob. "I just listened to a news broadcast," Bob began. "First the guy said something about some unearthly darkness that had everyone stumped. Then he said Jesus Christ had appeared to the Congress and UN assembly with new directions from God. Now there is a new law to enforce a final deadline for the Sunday rest day registration. It goes into effect at midnight tonight and the clock ticks down for forty-five days. Then at midnight on the last day anyone not in compliance with the law will be put to death. Can you believe all that?" Bob asked. No one moved.

Pastor Ralph cleared his throat. "It sounds like the fifth plague has happened and the sixth, Armageddon, is at our door. Matthew 24 tells us false Christs will appear with signs and miracles, designed to deceive. I think we should gather everyone together and study this out in detail from Revelation. This will affect everyone, including the children." He spoke with deliberate calmness.

After discussing the details a bit more, the men adjourned and carried their thoughts out the door. Some wandered through the decimated garden area. Some headed to the berry bushes. Some went into the lodge to see if the ladies needed help. All were somber and thoughtful. There was no longer a sense of adventure to their little hide-away.

The mid-afternoon meal arrived, and with it a repeat of the sense of God's closeness and care for them. Roberto, ever the gardener, had checked all the garden space and found some carrots and greens missed by the morning's marauders. Nestled close to the freshly baked bread, it seemed a meal fit for kings. There was a renewed vigor and courage even as they ate the food provided by God's hand. As they were finishing, Pastor Ralph suggested an afternoon Bible study.

"I'd like that," Mark spoke up. "I want to know what you guys were talking about at the Bensons' this morning. Is something wrong?"

Bob patted his son's shoulder, "No, Mark, everything is right. We just learned some news that tells us where we are in this world's history. We want to study it from Revelation. So, how about helping me clear the table and let's get started, OK?"

There was a brief flurry of cleaning and tidying. Gathering Bibles, paper and pens, the group made themselves comfortable around the living and dining area. Sue rocked comfortably, nursing baby Carlena, whose tiny hands reached for her mother's face. It was a serene picture.

Picking up his Bible, Pastor Ralph looked for a long moment at his wife: "Barbara, I just want to let you know how much I have appreciated being your husband. We have loved each other many years and I can't think of anything I'd rather do than walk into the kingdom with you." Looking around at the extended family surrounding them, he added, "It has been such a blessing being among you all these past weeks. You have fed my soul over and over through your words of encouragement, your eagerness to learn from the Bible, and your prayers. Thank you."

His spontaneous testimony prompted others to share their joy in each other and in the Lord. Several people mentioned how harmoniously the household had worked together. The talk gradually turned toward Revelation and the events taking place in the world.

Pastor Ralph offered a short prayer, began to read, then stopped. "Let's read these texts in unison, starting with chapter sixteen, verse one," he suggested. Shortly he began again. 'Then I heard a loud voice from the temple saying to the seven angels, "Go, pour out the seven bowls of God's wrath on the earth."' The Pastor stopped speaking for a moment and just listened to the strong voices around him reading the word of God.

They continued: "The fifth angel poured out his bowl on the throne of the beast, and his kingdom was plunged into darkness. Men gnawed their tongues in agony and cursed the God of heaven because of their pains and their sores, but they refused to repent of what they had done." On they read through verses 12, 13, and 14, learning about the battle of Armageddon. Verse 17 began: "The seventh angel poured out his bowl into the air, and out of the temple came a loud voice from the throne, saying, 'It is done!' Then there came flashes of lightning, rumblings, peals of thunder and a severe earthquake. No earthquake like it has ever occurred since man has been on earth, so tremendous was the quake. The great city split into three parts, and the cities of the nations collapsed. God remembered Babylon the Great and gave her the cup filled with the wine of the fury of His wrath. Every island fled away and the mountains could not be found. From the sky huge hailstones of about a hundred pounds each fell upon men. And they cursed God on account of the plague of hail, because the plague was so terrible."

No one spoke as they reached the end of the chapter. Sara broke the silence; "Mama, it's so sad." The depth of her understanding showed on her face. "Why do so many people hate God, when He is so good to us all?" Her question hung in the air.

Karen spoke softly to her daughter, "Honey, there is no good answer to that. If there was a good reason, then sin wouldn't be sin. There is no good reason for hate and sin, but God doesn't force us to love Him. I guess that's the reason—some people don't want to be happy and loved by God. It is sad."

"Is God really so mad at people who don't love Him?" Mark asked bluntly.

Barbara responded this time; "God hates sin because it has hurt so many of his children and caused the death of His Son, Mark. But he doesn't hate sinners. It's just that sin is all wrapped up inside the sinner and when God destroys sin, the sinner holding onto sin is destroyed, too." Barbara caught the glint of tears in the boy's eyes.

Bob now repeated the newscast he had heard earlier. When he was done, everyone looked through Revelation 16 again to see exactly what had happened and what was next. It seemed incredible to them that they were living in the fulfillment of these very prophecies. They decided to read through to the end of Revelation and were greatly comforted by the beautiful word pictures of heaven and the new earth. They were just finishing verse 20 of the last chapter, "Amen. Come, Lord Jesus," when a knock was heard at the door.

James opened the door, "Good afternoon, friends," he said. "What brings you up our way?"

The men at the door stepped back for a moment, seeming confused. Then rallying, they moved forward, brandishing rifles. "Just a little hunting practice," one sneered. "Getting ready to move into our new home here." He poked his head around the corner. "Hmm, looks mighty nice. Look at those berries on the table—where'd you get them? All the berry bushes are dead. There's nothin' at the stores anymore." He said the last words almost as an afterthought, pushing his way past James.

Lori hurriedly took a bowl of berries and several pieces of flatbread to the door and offered some to all the men on the porch. Taken aback, the men awkwardly helped themselves, mumbled something and retreated to their car.

Closing the door, and locking it, James and Lori held each other closely. Looking at the surprised faces around them, James had a suggestion. "I think we should consider moving on up into the woods," he said. "It doesn't appear we will be safe here much longer."

A big discussion broke out, with all the pros and cons laid out in the open. In the end, it was decided that when God stopped supplying their food at the lodge, they would take that as a sign that it was no longer safe to stay there. In the meantime, each family would take a crude map and hike around the countryside each day, trying to find suitable shelter for the day it would be needed. After a session of prayer and praise, the group adjourned.

Sue and Roberto approached James. "James, do you suppose our family could go with you and Lori?" Roberto asked. "It's so hard with a new baby, and I know Sue would feel more comfortable with a nurse close by."

"Of course," James and Lori spoke in unison. "We can all go in small groups to aid those with younger children," James added. "We need each other's prayers, too. Maybe we'll find a place that will accommodate all of us." He smiled at the relieved looks on the Gonzales' faces.

Days went by with no further disturbance from the outside world. When Bob tried to catch the news in his truck again, he discovered wires had been cut and ripped out under the hood. Checking the other vehicles in the area, he found they had all been sabotaged. Someone definitely had them in their crosshairs. The group reassessed their plans, earnestly entreated the Lord, and decided to wait for the Lord's clear leading.

One morning, there was an exceptional sunrise. Arising early, Bob and Karen enjoyed the brilliant colors, then walked into the kitchen to begin breakfast. Going to the deck where the flour and oil were stored, they found a surprise. The jars were empty. Karen's heart leaped into her throat. A strange combination of shock and joy swept over her. She looked up at Bob. "This is it. This is really the end!" There was wonder and awe in her voice as she choked out the words, "Jesus is coming!"

"We'd better wake everyone up and leave. There is no food for breakfast, and I take that to mean we should leave now," Bob said.

They hastened to knock on doors in the lodge. "Wake up folks, the time has come. We need to leave now." Heading out to the families living outside, they repeated their warning. Steven Pierce had moved back close to his tent, since his encounter with hostile neighbors a few months before. He had covered his bed with a leafy bower for shelter. Bob stood trying to figure out how to knock on the branches, when he saw Steven out behind it, reading from his Bible.

"It was a beautiful sunrise, wasn't it?" Bob suggested.

"Good morning—yes it was." Steven replied. "What brings you out so early?"

"Today is the day. There was no flour or oil this morning. I have already notified the other residents that it's time to leave." Bob said. Their eyes held the questions impossible to answer.

32

NO TURNING BACK

*"Pray that your flight will not take place in winter or on the
Sabbath. For then there will be great distress, unequaled from the
beginning of the world until now—and never to be equaled again...
but for the sake of the elect those days will be shortened."*
Matthew 24:20-22, NIV

Within minutes everyone was gathered in the living area,
dressed and carrying Bibles, flashlights, and water bottles.
Without looking back, they began, single file, on their final trip to
the mountains. As they hiked along, the morning mist rose up around
them, and the filtered sunlight made it glow like gold. Someone began
to sing: "I have decided to follow Jesus." Others joined in. "I have
decided to follow Jesus, I have decided to follow Jesus—no turning
back, no turning back." The songs of the birds joined their voices and
the blended chorus wafted on the breeze. Distant sounds of gunshots
told them Elijah's Hide-away was in their past.

After a few more minutes they softly began the second verse.
'The world behind me, the cross before me, the world behind me, the
cross before me, the world behind me, the cross before me—no turning back, no turning back."

"Mama, I think it should say the crown before me—we're almost to heaven." Sara spoke the words with confidence. So she started
the verse again and once more their voices rang fearlessly upon the
air.

Soon they came to a junction in the trail. "This is where we get
off," James said. "Come this way—Eva, can I carry Carlena over the
rocks?" Roberto had his hands full with their water bottles and Bibles.

"God bless you, my friends. We will see you in the morning." James and Lori waved their farewell.

By twos, and by small groups, the remaining families dispersed to crude shelters in rocks and caves they had found in the preceding days. There would be nothing to sustain them, except the grace of God. Still there was heard no murmur or complaint. Only praises to God for their care.

As Bob and Karen led Mark and Sara to their shelter, they came upon some ripe blueberries. "Hey, look at this!" Bob said. "Breakfast is served, kids." He laughed with relief as he put the first handful of the juicy berries into his mouth. "I'm constantly amazed at how God is seeing to our needs," he added.

"I'm sure each of our friends is finding their breakfast just about now, too." Karen said. "I will hardly know what to do with my time if I'm not fixing breakfast for a crowd. I've enjoyed so much our friendships at the lodge. God has taught me so much from His Word through our studies together. I can't wait to see them again, in heaven."

The days and nights were spent with basic survival. The weather was mostly cool at night. Some nights they slept fitfully, huddled together on the pine-bough beds to keep warm. Other nights the cold kept them all awake and they spent the time agonizing in prayer, searching their hearts, clinging to the promises of God to deliver them. The frequent sounds of coyotes howling sent shivers up their backs. Occasionally they heard the scream of a nearby cougar and were reminded of the Devil going around as a roaring lion.

During the days, they found a few blueberries to eat, here and there, but they were hungry and thirsty most of the time.

One night Sara confided, with tears, "Mama, I'm so hungry I can't sleep."

"I know, baby." Karen replied. Her heart ached for the suffering her children were experiencing. "Let's pray and ask God to send us something special in the morning, OK?" Karen held the thin body of her child closer and in her mind vowed she would never let go of God's hand again. Sin was done for her. She had seen too much pain and suffering and for the first time Karen understood a little of how

God must feel, watching His children suffer for thousands of years. For the first time she understood how He could even think of sending His Son to rescue them from the evil Satan had brought upon the world. Sobbing, she breathed her prayer of understanding and complete surrender into Sara's soft hair. She lost track of time and space, just communing with her Heavenly Father, leaving herself and her family totally in God's care. At length she noted the even breathing of her daughter and thanked God for giving Sara respite from her pain for a few hours. Karen also found respite in the arms of God that night.

As the light of another day began to touch the ground mist, Karen noticed something falling around them. Almost like snow, although it didn't seem that cold. Becoming more and more curious, she watched as it began to gather and pile up. Sara stirred then and awoke with a soft whimper.

"Mama did God send us something special this morning?" Her childish faith never wavered.

"Well, let's just get up and see, honey." It began to dawn on Karen that the falling flakes might be the answer to her prayer.

Together they stared out at a world, desolated in many ways, but now covered all around them with something small and white like snow. It covered all the bushes like frosted sugar and was sparkling and beautiful in the rising sunlight.

The two looked at each other with big grins. Sara reached out, and picking up a pinch of flakes, popped them into her mouth. "Bread!" She shouted gleefully. "Bread, bread, bread!"

Her dance of joy awakened Bob and Mark. They looked around in confusion. Mark was the first to understand what was happening. He jumped up and took the handful of flakes his sister was offering him. Eagerly he tasted the substance. "I think it tastes like honey—just like in the Bible." He asserted.

Bob joined his wife and looked questioningly down at her tear-stained face. "What's happened?" he inquired.

"I finally understand, Bob. I finally understand how much God loves me." Karen hadn't even tried the "manna" as the children were calling it. She seemed satisfied with the spiritual bread God had filled her with during the night. She smiled at her husband as he took her in his arms.

They all gathered the "manna" in whatever containers they could find or make from large leaves. They were able to fill their stomachs for the first time in many days, and it felt good. They felt strength renewed, and hope and courage revived.

For several weeks they were able to gather "manna" and satisfy the hunger of their bodies and souls. Every bite they ate seemed to draw them closer to God and they spent much time in Bible study and prayer. Most days they hiked around, close by, just to keep physically fit.

One evening just before dusk, they heard voices coming up the hill. Curious—hoping James and Lori or some of the others were coming to visit—they wandered down the trail. Coming around a corner they came face to face with several armed men.

"Well, looky there," the lead man snorted. "I think we have our first deer of the season."

Bob gathered his family close to him. "We welcome you, friends," he spoke quietly. "Won't you join us in our camp and rest awhile?" He was courteous.

"Nah, we'll just build camp right over here and wait for midnight. Wouldn't want the judgment of God to fall on us, you know," the man spoke again.

The Johnsons watched as the men set camp and hung up a lantern. Someone brought out a small radio and pumped it up as loud as it would go. The discordant music was hard for Karen to listen to. She thought about how far her family had come since the day Sara had almost been kidnapped. Once, she enjoyed just this kind of music. Now, her mind was far above the crude and vulgar thoughts expressed in the lyrics. She felt so sorry for these poor men. Lost, without God and without hope. And they didn't even care.

Taking his family back to their shelter, Bob got out his Bible and a flashlight. "I have kind of lost track of time up here," he began. He looked at each face in the dim light. "I love you all so much. I am so glad you have all chosen to love God and let Him change your hearts.

So glad we are together here in this simple shelter, waiting for Jesus to take us home." Here he paused and bowed his head a moment. Then looking up he continued, "Time was, the sight of those guns would have scared me to death. Now I just look above them and see God taking care of me—of us.

"James taught me a Bible verse some time ago, I think it's in Timothy, "God has not given us the spirit of fear, but of power and of love and of a sound mind." It's taken me a long time to let go of the fear a father carries for the safety of his children." Here he paused and looked for a long moment at Sara. "But God has finally taught me that He is with each one of us in every situation that happens to us. He never forsakes us, and He won't forsake us now. Let's repeat our favorite chapter together. They began reciting Psalm 91. "He who dwells in the shelter of the Most High will rest in the shadow of the Almighty. I will say of the Lord, 'He is my refuge and my fortress, my God, in whom I trust.'" Bob's voice rang out, even drowning out the raucous scene below them. On and on they quoted, looking up to the heavens as if they could read the words there. Bob lifted his hands as he reached the end of the chapter. There was no fear in his voice. There was no fear on his face. Lying down to rest, he committed their lives to God once again and fell into a peaceful sleep.

33

THE DELIVERANCE

*"He said to me: 'It is done. I am the Alpha and the
Omega, the Beginning and the End.'"*
Revelation 21:6, NIV

It seemed but a few moments later, when a loud noise awakened them. They crawled out of their shelter and stood in the light of the full moon. The men in the camp below had heard the noise, too, and suddenly all was quiet. A news bulletin broke into the music: "We interrupt this broadcast with breaking news. An earthquake of at least 9.9 magnitude—off the charts— has just been reported on the continent of Europe. It seems to be traveling in a wave, westward, through Italy, France, England, and every country surrounding. Satellite images show the ground swelling, even moving the ocean. Just a moment: New information shows a meteor shower beginning to rain down upon a major portion of the earth." The reporter's voice was rising, beginning to sound stressed. "This just in: Hail stones a hundred pounds apiece are starting to fall in the wake of the earthquake. Oh no—no!" Static in the receiver prevented any further transmission.

Above them the moon first turned blood red, then nearly disappeared in the shower of falling stars. The earthquake reached their mountain and began to shake violently, tossing huge boulders around like toys. Trees swayed and crashed to the ground. The terrified men below were cursing and shaking their fists at the heavens. When hailstones the size of basketballs began to fall, they ran, calling for the rocks and mountains to fall on them and hide them from the face of God.

Thrown to their knees by the violent upheaval, the Johnsons gazed into the turbulent heavens. Karen wept, quoting Revelation 6:17 (KJV), "the great day of His wrath is come, and who shall be able to stand?"

Suddenly, the heavens parted and a brilliant light illuminated the earth like the sun at noonday. Above the noise of the elements a voice like thunder was heard saying: "My grace is sufficient for you." The voice seemed to roll through the earth. The little family forgot everything around them. There was only one focus. One thought. Jesus was coming and His grace included them.

Hardly sensing the passing of time, they waited. They had no need of food or water. Soon they saw in the east a small cloud—different than any they had ever seen. As it drew nearer, it began to change. It grew brighter and a distant sound was heard. Like a trumpet call, loud, true, and piercing, it grew until it filled every corner—like transcendent light. There was a tremendous explosion like the earth shattering, breaking, giving up its inmost secrets.

They were transfixed, not with the devastation and death all around them, but with the scene unfolding in the heavens above them. Karen looked at the faces of her beloved family, not now pinched with hunger or concern, but reflecting the joy she herself felt welling up. All fear, all worry, all sadness was gone, all pain forgotten. There was only purest joy, and love, and peace. Her eyes returned to the growing brightness. Never could she have conceived of the beauty she was now seeing and experiencing.

Only one face now drew her eyes—the face of the Son of God, the face of Mercy, the face of the One who had forgiven her sins. More brilliant than the noonday sun, He seemed to be looking directly into her soul. She felt His gaze into every cell. Her heart answering His gaze went out to meet Him—communed with Him through resplendent energy. She felt the very structure of her being coming alive, changing, waking up.

As the cloud began to blend with their surroundings, the forms of beings—splendid in form and majesty—began to emerge beside them. The first audible words from her guardian angel seemed familiar. Karen had heard that voice in her mind many times, pointing her to the better path. Now she looked with open amazement into the eyes of her guardian. Felt the arms of love embrace her. Listened to the joyous singing over her. Looking around she saw Sara, transformed and radiant.

"Mama, Mama!" Sara cried, her eyes shining; "My angel! Arella—who helped me at school when I was hurt—she's my angel!" Sara was hugging the magnificent being with the flaming red hair.

Karen looked at Bob and was aware of the tremendous love and gratitude she felt for him. He had led their family faithfully. He had been strong, humble, and willing to follow God at all costs. She was aware of how much she owed him for being a faithful shepherd for their little flock. Now he was swept up in the embrace of the angel who had guided his footsteps from a Godless life into fullness of joy.

Mark was trying to take in the whole scene at once. Karen could almost see his budding scientific mind already expanding with the power and majesty around and within him. His angel had one arm around his shoulders and was pointing to Jesus. The look of love and happiness on Mark's face brought tears of joy to her eyes.

There was a moment when Karen looked about her and noticed they were all far above the cold, heaving earth. For the briefest second Karen was aware of the darkness surrounding it. It seemed to suck in all the glory from Jesus, but return nothing of it back. Almost like it wasn't even there.

Turning her attention back to the future, she saw their friends from Elijah's Hide-away, welcoming their own angels. With joy, she watched them receive into their arms loved ones long separated by death. Received her own beloved mother into her arms, now young and beautiful.

Her family gathered close, embraced in the wonder and mystery of the ages—that God so loved them that He gave His only Son to bring them into eternal joy. They sang and shouted with ten thousand times ten thousands of angels and the countless number of the redeemed—their eyes never far from the face of Him who had become their all-in-all.

34

ETERNITY AND BEYOND

(While the preceding chapters are fictional, the following is not fiction,
but excerpts from the book "The Great Controversy" pp 657-678.

At the coming of Christ the wicked are blotted from the face of the whole earth—consumed with the spirit of His mouth and destroyed by the brightness of His glory. Christ takes His people to the City of God, and the earth is emptied of its inhabitants.

"Behold, the Lord maketh the earth empty, and maketh it waste, and turneth it upside down and scattereth abroad the inhabitants thereof. The land shall be utterly emptied, and utterly spoiled: for the Lord hath spoken this word. Because they have transgressed the laws, changed the ordinance, broken the everlasting covenant. Therefore hath the curse devoured the earth, and they that dwell therein are desolate: therefore the inhabitants of the earth are burned." (Isaiah 24:1, 3, 5, 6.)

The whole earth appears like a desolate wilderness. The ruins of cities and villages destroyed by the earthquake, uprooted trees, ragged rocks thrown out by the sea or torn out of the earth itself, are scattered over its surface, while vast caverns mark the spot where the mountains have been rent from their foundations.

Now the event takes place foreshadowed in the last solemn service of the Day of Atonement. When the ministration in the holy of holies had been completed, and the sins of Israel had been removed from the sanctuary by virtue of the blood of the sin offering, then the scapegoat was presented alive before the Lord; and in the presence of the congregation the high priest confessed over him "all the iniquities of the children of Israel, and all their transgressions in all their sins, putting them upon the head of the goat." (Leviticus 16:21.) In like manner when the work of atonement in the heavenly sanctuary has been completed, then in the presence of God and heavenly angels and the host of the redeemed the sins of God's people will be placed upon Satan; he will be declared guilty of all the evil which he has caused them to commit. And as the scapegoat was sent away into a land not inhabited, so Satan will be banished to the desolate earth, an uninhabited and dreary wilderness.

The revelator foretells the banishment of Satan and the condition of chaos and desolation to which the earth is to be reduced, and he declared that this condition will exist for a thousand years. After presenting the scenes of the Lord's second coming and the destruction of the wicked the prophecy continues: "I saw an angel come down from heaven, having the key of the bottomless pit and a great chain in his hand. And he laid hold on the dragon, that old serpent, which is the devil, and Satan, and bound him a thousand years, and cast him into the bottomless pit, and shut him up, and set a seal upon him, that he should deceive the nations no more, till the thousand years should be fulfilled: and after that he must be loosed a little season." (Revelation 20:1-3.) . . .

For six thousand years, Satan's work of rebellion has "made the earth to tremble." He has "made the world as a wilderness, and destroyed the cities thereof." And he "opened not the house of his prisoners." For six thousand years his prison house has received God's people, and he would have held them captive forever; but Christ has broken his bonds and set the prisoners free. (Isaiah 14:16, 17.) . . .

At the close of the thousand years, Christ again returns to the earth. He is accompanied by the host of the redeemed and attended by a retinue of angels. As He descends in terrific majesty He bids the wicked dead arise to receive their doom. They come forth, a mighty host, numberless as the sands of the sea. What a contrast to those who were raised at the first resurrection! The righteous were clothed with

216

immortal youth and beauty. The wicked bear the traces of disease and death.

Every eye in that vast multitude is turned to behold the glory of the Son of God. With one voice the wicked hosts exclaim: "Blessed is He that cometh in the name of the Lord!" It is not love to Jesus that inspires this utterance. The force of truth urges the words from unwilling lips. As the wicked went into their graves, so they come forth with the same enmity to Christ and the same spirit of rebellion. They are to have no new probation in which to remedy the defects of their past lives. Nothing would be gained by this. A lifetime of transgression has not softened their hearts. A second probation, were it given them, would be occupied as was the first in evading the requirements of God and exciting rebellion against Him.

Christ descends upon the Mount of Olives, where, after His resurrection, He ascended, and where angels repeated the promise of His return. Says the prophet: "The Lord my God shall come, and all the saints with Thee. And His feet shall stand in that day upon the Mount of Olives, which is before Jerusalem on the east, and the Mount of Olives shall cleave in the midst thereof...and there shall be a very great valley. And the Lord shall be king over all the earth: in that day shall there be one Lord, and His name one." (Zechariah 14:5, 4, 9.) As the New Jerusalem, in its dazzling splendor, comes down out of heaven, it rests upon the place purified and made ready to receive it, and Christ, with His people and the angels, enters the Holy City.

Now Satan prepares for a last mighty struggle for the supremacy. . . . He will marshal all the armies of the lost under his banner and through them endeavor to execute his plans. The wicked are Satan's captives. In rejecting Christ they have accepted the rule of the rebel leader. They are ready to receive his suggestions and to do his bidding. Yet, true to his early cunning, he does not acknowledge himself to be Satan. He claims to be the prince who is the rightful owner of the world and whose inheritance has been unlawfully wrested from him. He represents himself to his deluded subjects as a redeemer, assuring them that his power has brought them forth from their graves and that he is about to rescue them from the most cruel tyranny. The presence

217

of Christ having been removed, Satan works wonders to support his claims. He makes the weak strong and inspires all with his own spirit and energy. He proposes to lead them against the camp of the saints and to take possession of the City of God. With fiendish exultation he points to the unnumbered millions who have been raised from the dead and declares that as their leader he is well able to overthrow the city and regain his throne and his kingdom. . . .

Satan consults with his angels and then with these kings and conquerors and mighty men. They look upon the strength and numbers on their side, and declare that the army within the city is small in comparison with theirs, and that it can be overcome. They lay their plans to take possession of the riches and glory of the New Jerusalem. All immediately begin to prepare for battle. Skillful artisans construct implements of war. Military leaders, famed for their success, marshal the throngs of warlike men into companies and divisions.

At last the order to advance is given, and the countless host moves on—an army such as was never summoned by earthly conquerors, such as the combined forces of all ages since war began on earth could never equal. Satan, the mightiest of warriors, leads the van, and his angels unite their forces for their final struggle. Kings and warriors are in his train, and the multitudes follow in vast companies, each under its appointed leader. With military precision the serried ranks advance over the earth's broken and uneven surface to the City of God. By command of Jesus, the gates of the New Jerusalem are closed, and the armies of Satan surround the city and make ready for the onset.

Now Christ again appears to the view of His enemies. Far above the city, upon a foundation of burnished gold, is a throne, high and lifted up. . . . In the presence of the assembled inhabitants of earth and heaven the final coronation of the Son of God takes place. And now, invested with supreme majesty and power, the King of kings pronounces sentence upon the rebels against His government and executes justice upon those who have transgressed His law and oppressed His people. Says the prophet of God: "I saw a great white throne, and Him that sat on it, from whose face the earth and the heaven fled away;

and there was found no place for them. And I saw the dead, small and great, stand before God; and the books were opened: and another book was opened, which is the book of life: and the dead were judged out of those things which were written in the books, according to their works." (Revelation 20:11, 12.)

As soon as the books of record are opened, and the eye of Jesus looks upon the wicked, they are conscious of every sin which they have ever committed. They see just where their feet diverged from the path of purity and holiness, just how far pride and rebellion have carried them in the violation of the law of God. The seductive temptations which they encouraged by indulgence in sin, the blessings perverted, the messengers of God despised, the warnings rejected, the waves of mercy beaten back by the stubborn, unrepentant heart—all appear as if written in letters of fire.

Above the throne is revealed the cross; and like a panoramic view appear the scenes of Adam's temptation and fall, and the successive steps in the great plan of redemption. The Saviour's lowly birth; His early life of simplicity and obedience; His baptism in Jordan; the fast and temptation in the wilderness; His public ministry, unfolding to men heaven's most precious blessings; the days crowded with deeds of love and mercy; the nights of prayer and watching in the solitude of the mountains; the plottings of envy, hate, and malice which repaid His benefits; the awful, mysterious agony in Gethsemane beneath the crushing weight of the sins of the whole world; His betrayal into the hands of the murderous mob; the fearful events of that night of horror—the unresisting prisoner, forsaken buy His best-loved disciples, rudely hurried through the streets of Jerusalem; the Son of God exultingly displayed before Annas, arraigned in the high priest's palace, in the judgment hall of Pilate, before the cowardly and cruel Herod, mocked insulted, tortured, and condemned to die—all are vividly portrayed.

And now before the swaying multitude are revealed the final scenes—the patient Sufferer treading the path to Calvary; the Prince of heaven hanging upon the cross; the haughty priests and the jeering rabble deriding His expiring agony; the supernatural darkness; the heaving earth, the rent rocks, the open graves, marking the moment when the world's Redeemer yielded up His life.

The awful spectacle appears just as it was. Satan, his angels, and his subjects have no power to turn from the picture of their own work. Each actor recalls the part which he performed. . . .

The whole wicked world stands arraigned at the bar of God on the charge of high treason against the government of heaven. They have none to plead their cause; they are without excuse; and the sentence of eternal death is pronounced against them.

It is now evident to all that the wages of sin is not noble independence and eternal life, but slavery, ruin, and death. The wicked see what they have forfeited by their life of rebellion. The far more exceeding and eternal weight of glory was despised when offered them; but how desirable it now appears.

"All this," cries the lost soul, "I might have had; but I chose to put these things far from me. Oh strange infatuation! I have exchanged peace, happiness, and honor for wretchedness, infamy, and despair." All see that their exclusion from heaven is just. By their lives they have declared. "We will not have this Man (Jesus) to reign over us."

As if entranced, the wicked have looked upon the coronation of the Son of God. They see in His hands the tables of the divine law, the statutes which they have despised and transgressed. They witness the outburst of wonder, rapture, and adoration from the saved. . . .

Satan seems paralyzed as he beholds the glory and majesty of Christ. . . . The aim of the great rebel has ever been to justify himself and to prove the divine government responsible for the rebellion. . . . Satan sees that his voluntary rebellion has unfitted him for heaven. He has trained his powers to war against God; the purity, peace, and harmony of heaven would be to him supreme torture. His accusations against the mercy and justice of God are now silenced. The reproach which he has endeavored to cast upon Jehovah rests wholly upon himself. And now Satan bows down and confesses the justice of his sentence. . . .

Notwithstanding that Satan has been constrained to acknowledge God's justice and to bow to the supremacy of Christ, his character remains unchanged. The spirit of rebellion, like a mighty torrent, again bursts forth. Filled with frenzy, he determines not to yield the great controversy. The time has come for a last desperate struggle against the King of heaven. He rushes into the midst of his subjects and endeavors to inspire them with his own fury and arouse them to instant battle. But of all the countless millions whom he has allured into rebellion, there are none now to acknowledge his supremacy. His power is at an end. The wicked are filled with the same hatred of God that inspires Satan; but they see that their case is hopeless, that they cannot prevail against Jehovah. Their rage is kindled against Satan and those who have been his agents in deception, and with the fury of demons they turn upon them.

Saith the Lord: "Because thou hast set thine heart as the heart of God; behold, therefore I will bring strangers upon thee, the terrible of the nations; and they shall draw their swords against the beauty of thy wisdom, and they shall defile thy brightness. They shall bring thee down to the pit. I will destroy thee, O covering cherub, from the midst of the stones of fire. . . . I will cast thee to the ground, I will lay thee before kings, that they may behold thee. . . . I will bring thee to ashes upon the earth in the sight of all them that behold thee. . . . Thou shalt be a terror, and never shalt thou be any more." (Ezekiel 28:6-8, 16-19.) . . .

. . . "Upon the wicked He shall rain quick burning coals, fire and brimstone and an horrible tempest: this shall be the portion of their cup." (Psalm 11:6 margin.) Fire comes down from God out of heaven. The earth is broken up. The weapons concealed in its depths are drawn forth. Devouring flames burst from every yawning chasm. The very rocks are on fire. The day has come that shall burn as an oven. The elements melt with fervent heat, the earth also, and the works that are therein are burned up. (Malachi 4:1; 2 Peter 3:10.) The earth's surface seems one molten mass—a vast, seething lake of fire. It is the time of the judgment and perdition of ungodly men—"the day of the Lord's vengeance, and the year of recompenses for the controversy of Zion." (Isaiah 34:8.) . . .

. . . All are punished "according to their deeds." The sins of the righteous having been transferred to Satan, he is made to suffer not only for his own rebellion, but for all the sins which he has caused God's people to commit. His punishment is to be far greater than that of those whom he has deceived. After all have perished who fell by his deceptions, he is still to live and suffer on. In the cleansing flames the wicked are at last destroyed, root and branch—Satan the root, his followers the branches. The full penalty of the law has been visited; the demands of justice have been met; and heaven and earth, beholding, declare the righteousness of Jehovah. . . .

While the earth was wrapped in the fire of destruction, the righteous abode safely in the Holy City. Upon those that had part in the first resurrection, the second death has no power. While God is to the wicked a consuming fire, He is to His people both a sun and a shield. (Revelation 20:6, Psalm 84:11.)

"I saw a new heaven and a new earth: for the first heaven and the first earth were passed away." (Revelation 21:1.) The fire that consumes the wicked purifies the earth. Every trace of the curse is swept away. No eternally burning hell will keep before the ransomed the fearful consequences of sin.

One reminder alone remains: Our Redeemer will ever bear the marks of His crucifixion. Upon His wounded head, upon His side, His hands, and feet, are the only traces of the cruel work that sin has wrought. . . .

The earth originally given to man as his kingdom, betrayed by him into the hands of Satan, and so long held by the mighty foe, has been brought back by the great plan of redemption. All that was lost by sin has been restored. . . . God's original purpose in the creation of the earth is fulfilled as it is made the eternal abode of the redeemed. "The righteous shall inherit the land, and dwell therein forever." (Psalm 37:29.) . . .

A fear of making the future inheritance seem too material has led many to spiritualize away the very truths which lead us to look upon it as our home. Christ assured His disciples that He went to prepare mansions for them in the Father's house. . . .

. . . "The tree of life yields its fruit every month, and the leaves

222

of the tree are for the service of the nations. There are every-flowing streams, clear as crystal, and beside them waving trees cast their shadows upon the paths prepared for the ransomed of the Lord. There the wide-spreading plains swell into hills of beauty, and the mountains of God rear their lofty summits. On those peaceful plains, beside those living streams, God's people, so long pilgrims and wanderers, shall find a home. . . .

Pain cannot exist in the atmosphere of heaven. There will be no more tears, no funeral trains, no badges of mourning. "There shall be no more death, neither sorrow, nor crying. . . . for the former things are passed away. The inhabitant shall not say, I am sick: the people that dwell therein shall be forgiven their iniquity. (Revelation 21:4, Isaiah 33:24.) . . .

In the City of God "there shall be no night." None will need or desire repose. There will be no weariness in doing the will of God and offering praise to His name. We shall ever feel the freshness of the morning and shall ever be far from its close. "And they need no candle, neither light of the sun; for the Lord God giveth them light." (Revelation 22:5.) . . .

There, immortal minds will contemplate with never-failing delight the wonders of creative power, the mysteries of redeeming love. There will be no cruel, deceiving foe to tempt to forgetfulness of God. Every faculty will be developed, every capacity increased. The acquirement of knowledge will not weary the mind or exhaust the energies. There the grandest enterprises may be carried forward, the loftiest aspirations reached, the highest ambitions realized; and still there will arise new heights to surmount, new wonders to admire, new truths to comprehend, fresh objects to call forth the powers of mind and soul and body.

All the treasures of the universe will be open to the study of God's redeemed. Unfettered by mortality, they wing their tireless flight to worlds afar—worlds that thrilled with sorrow at the spectacle of human woe and rang with songs of gladness at the tidings of a ransomed soul. With unutterable delight the children of earth enter into the joy and the wisdom of unfallen beings. They share the treasures of knowledge and understanding gained through ages upon ages in contemplation of God's handiwork. . . .

And the years of eternity, as they roll, will bring richer and still more glorious revelations of God and of Christ. As knowledge is progressive, so will love, reverence, and happiness increase. The more men learn of God, the greater will be their admiration of His character. As Jesus opens before them the riches of redemption and the amazing achievements in the great controversy with Satan, the hearts of the ransomed thrill with more fervent devotion . . . and ten thousand times ten thousand and thousands of thousands of voices unite to swell the mighty chorus of praise.

"And every creature which is in heaven, and on the earth, and under the earth, and such as are in the sea, and all that are in them, heard I saying, Blessing, and honor, and glory, and power, be unto Him that sitteth upon the throne, and unto the Lamb for ever and ever." (Revelation 5:13.)

The great controversy is ended. Sin and sinners are no more. The entire universe is clean. One pulse of harmony and gladness beats through the vast creation. From Him who created all, flow life and light and gladness, throughout the realms of illimitable space. From the minutest atom to the greatest world, all things, animate and inanimate, in their unshadowed beauty and perfect joy, declare that God is love.